Short Stories

TIM TROTT

Tim Trott Publishing

Contents

Prologue

Good fiction, like a good lie, requires an element of truth.
Tim Trott

Chapter One

Static

WKPX overnight disc jockey Brian Reed was coming to the end of his show.

"Playing the oldies for you on a Thursday morning here on WKPX radio. Coming up at the top of the hour, Talk of Maple Ridge with Dave Daniels."

Reed pressed the key for the computer to sequence the scheduled commercials before returning to the automated music program.

He glanced at the clock. Taking the headphones off and laying them next to the control panel, he got up and walked to the window, expecting to see Daniels' car in the parking lot. There was enough daylight that he could see Dave's car wasn't there.

The staff phone numbers were listed on a bulletin board by the studio door. Brian repeated the number listed beside Dave's name to himself as he returned to the "air chair". He reached for the studio phone and dialed the number.

Getting no answer, he called the station manager. After several rings, Greg Owens picked up the call. Greg was not what you would call an early riser.

"Good morning. This is Brian."

Greg coughed and cleared his throat as he answered.

"Hey, Brian. What's up? Is there a problem?"

"Yeah, we have a problem! The Talk of Maple Ridge starts in three minutes and David Daniels hasn't shown up. What now?"

"If he's not there, I guess you'll have to fill in. That's not like Dave, though. Did you call his cell phone?"

"Of course I called his number. It went straight to voicemail. I didn't bother to leave a message. Hey, gotta go. The automation is about to come back to me."

The on-the-air light lit up as Brian flipped on the mic.

"That winds up my show, but I'll be filling in for Dave Daniels for the Talk of Maple Ridge, right after the national news at the top of the hour."

He punched the button on the control console and pushed up the volume slider as the network sounder began the network newscast.

Brian watched the minutes ticking by on the studio clock until the end of the news. He switched back to the automation for the show opener for Talk of Maple Ridge. As the recording faded, Brian opened the talk show.

"Good morning, Maple Ridge. I'm Brian Reed, still here. Looks like Dave Daniels is a little late today, so I'll be filling in. Let's see what you want to talk about today. Hello, caller, what's on your mind?"

"Hi, this is Margaret Riley. I'm one of Dave's favorite callers. Where is Dave?"

"He might be stuck in traffic somewhere. I'm sure he'll be in any minute. Is there something you want to talk about today?"

Margaret didn't, so Brian went on to the next caller, and the next, and the next, along with five commercial breaks from the automation system. By then, it was noon and time for the local news. From the other side of the control room window, the newsman signaled he was ready.

"Well, that will do it for the Talk of Maple Ridge. I'm sure Dave Daniels will be back for tomorrow's show. Right now, it's time for the local news. Here's Phil Grant."

Brian switched to the newsroom and took off his headphones.

At that moment, the light on the request line phone lit up. He turned down the control room speakers.

"Sorry, no more requests," he answered, without waiting to hear the caller. "Call me back tomorrow morning."

He was about to hang up when he heard a gruff voice on the other end.

"Bet you wonder where Dave Daniels is, don't you."

"Who is this?" Brian was annoyed. "If this is a joke, it's not funny."

The caller spoke louder this time.

"If you want to see Dave Daniels again you better listen. We want fifty thousand. Get it ready and wait for my call with instructions this time tomorrow."

The caller hung up.

Stunned, Brian looked up to see the newsman's frantic gestures. Greg waved back and switched to the automation for the syndicated music broadcast. He leaned back in his chair and ran his fingers through his hair, smoothing out where the headphones had been for the last twelve hours.

The newsman poked his head through the studio door.

"Where's Dave?" Phil asked.

"Some guy just called." Greg stared at the newsman in shock. "Said he wants fifty thousand dollars if we want to get him back. I thought it was a crank call."

"Did you call the police?" Phil looked worried. He and Dave had been with the station for ten years.

"Not yet. That should be the station manager's decision."

"Did you check where the call came from?"

Brian stretched to see the display. "It says 'not available.' How can that be?"

"Anybody can block the display with star-sixty-seven. I don't think that was a crank call. Don't wait for Greg. You need to call 9-1-1."

After Brian finished telling the police about the threatening call, he left the control room and went to find the station manager.

Brian knocked on the office door.

"Yeah," came the reply.

"Hey, Brian, Dave never showed up?" Noting the expression on Brian's face, Greg stiffened. "What's wrong?" he asked.

"Somebody called demanding fifty-thousand dollars. I think Dave's been kidnapped."

"Did you tell the police? It should be pretty easy to trace the call."

Brian had to explain. "No number. The display said 'not reported'. Phil says it's easy to block out a number."

Greg's mood turned somber. "Does Marty know about this? He and Dave have been friends since high school."

The station sales manager (and only salesperson) was Marty Coleman. The sales manager's desk was in an open area next to the receptionist. Greg was hoping to find Marty at his desk, but he wasn't there. Brian figured he was seeing an advertising client.

Looking out the door at the front office, Brian noticed two officers talking to Susan Mills, the receptionist. Susan pointed toward Greg's office and the officers headed that way.

Greg stood behind his desk as the officers entered. Brian followed them in.

One officer pulled out a notepad while the other showed Greg his badge and ID.

"We understand one of your staff may have been kidnapped, is that correct?"

"Our talk show host, Dave Daniels didn't show up for work today. Then somebody called demanding a ransom."

Greg gestured toward Brian. "Our early morning DJ took the call. I'll let him tell you about it."

"What time did the call come in?" the officer with the notepad asked.

"We just went to news when the call came in on the music request line. It must have been just a few minutes after noon. And before you ask, the number was not on the display."

"What did the caller sound like? Young, old, male, female?"

Brian thought for a moment. "It was a gruff voice, definitely male. I think it could have been somebody trying to sound older than they were."

"What did the caller say that made you think it was a kidnapping?" asked the officer with the notepad.

"He said if we want to see our friend again, we better have fifty thousand ready."

"Did they say how they wanted the money delivered," the second officer asked.

"He said he would call back with instructions."

Greg interrupted. "We're a small operation. I'll talk to the station owner, Myron Wells, but I see how he could come up with that kind of cash."

"We'll need to talk to your staff," the police officer with the note pad said.

"Not everybody is here at the station. The sales manager is out meeting with clients and the engineers at the transmitter run the automation by remote until Brian gets in at midnight." Greg gestured at Brian as he spoke.

Turning to Brian, the officer asked, "Did the caller say when they would be calling back?"

"He said he would call back at the same time tomorrow."

The two officers glanced at each other as if communicating a secret message.

"Let the caller think you have the money and find out how they want to make the exchange."

The officer handed Greg a card. "When your sales manager gets back ask him to call this number."

With that, the officers left the station.

Greg turned to Brian. "I'll come in and handle Dave's show. I don't know what I'm going to say, but I want to be here to take that call from the kidnapper. And where the heck is Marty?"

As if in response, Marty Coleman walked into Greg's office.

"I hope you made a big sale, because we need to come up with a lot of money."

"What are you talking about?" Marty asked.

"In case you haven't heard, Dave's been kidnapped.

Just after noon the next day, Greg was in the control room when a call came in on the request line. He turned down the monitor speakers and glanced at the display: "not reported"

He picked up the phone.

"This is WKPX."

The gruff voice responded, "Who is this? Do you have the money?"

Greg noticed the newsman watching through the soundproof window from the newsroom.

"This is Greg Owens. I'm the station manager. How do you want your money delivered and when will you release David Daniels?"

"Here is what you do: you create a digital wallet on BitSafe and deposit the money there. Then wait for a message to the station's email that will have a transfer code. Send the money to that code. When we see the money, we will release the hostage. Do you understand my instructions?"

"I understand," Greg answered."

"Remember, no police," the caller emphasized.

As Greg hung up the phone, he turned to see one of the police officers just inside the studio door.

The officer keyed the radio microphone clipped to his uniform and turned his head to speak.

"Got it?" he asked.

"Roger," came the reply.

"We got an emergency court order to trace the calls to that line," the officer explained. "We got a hit."

"I thought they blocked the caller ID!"

"It still shows up at the phone company. It won't take long to track it down.

"Even if it's a burner phone?"

"We assumed it would be. Even a burner phone has an IMEI code and the call has to go through a cell tower. Triangulating on the tower, we should know the caller's location very shortly. We can confirm the phone from the IMEI."

"What good does that do?" Greg complained to the officer. "We don't have the fifty thousand!"

"We think the kidnapper is operating alone. When we track down the suspect, most likely the hostage will be nearby."

By now, Marty Coleman had joined the group in the crowded control room studio.

"What's going on?" he asked.

"The police think they can find where the kidnapper is hiding," Greg volunteered.

The police officer stiffened. "We don't know that for sure, yet."

Coleman abruptly left the studio and went to his car.

"What the hell do you think you're doing?" he demanded of the person on the other end of his phone call. "We agreed on ten thousand."

"It's all under control," came the reply.

"No, it's not. You got greedy and sloppy, and by now the police probably know where you are."

Just then, there was a knock on the car window. Greg turned to see a police officer with his gun drawn. He dropped the phone and raised his hands as the officer opened the door.

At the same moment, across town, a SWAT team broke down the door of an apartment, burst inside, and arrested the kidnapper. They also found David Daniels (real name, Charles Hinton), unharmed, hiding in a bedroom.

Later, the evening TV news revealed the entire story.

"Earlier today, police rescued kidnapped WKPX talk host and radio personality, David Daniels. They reportedly used an emergency wiretap to trace the kidnapper's call. However, upon his rescue, Daniels was immediately arrested. The arrests include the station sales manager, Marty Coleman. According to police, Coleman confessed to concocting the kidnapping scheme with Daniels to make headlines for the radio station. They convinced twenty-three-year-old Dylan Hayes to act as the kidnapper. All three are currently free on bond."

The next morning, there was a new commercial running on the air at WKTX.

"WKPX is currently looking for an experienced talk radio announcer and a sales manager. Contact the station manager, Greg Owens, online at the station website at WKPX Radio dot com."

***

Chapter Two

Mind Reader

"**R**obbery in progress: Signal eleven: silent alarm, twelve thirty-eight Emerald, cross street Maple."

The radio call came in as Frank Hayes and his partner, Bradley Smith, were on a routine patrol. Frank recognized the location, only a few blocks away. Reaching for the microphone, he let the dispatcher know he was responding.

They pulled to a stop across the street from a jewelry store. The area was a mix of high-end boutiques and run-down tenements.

"10-97: Officers on scene."

Frank and Bradley arrived and quietly approached from across the street with guns drawn.

Suddenly, the heavy commercial glass door of the jewelry store opened, and two masked figures rushed out. One carried a dark bag, the other spotted the officers and opened fire.

Frank instinctively ducked as a bullet struck a metal pole just inches away from his head.

Smith returned fire. The shooter fell backward, his gun flying from his hand as he fell, motionless, to the ground. The other criminal dropped the bag and raised his hands.

Officer Smith turned to look for Frank.

Frank wiped blood from the side of his head where shrapnel from the metal pole had struck him. At that moment, he fell to the ground, unconscious.

Frank awoke in the hospital to the sounds of medical monitors and equipment. The room was a blend of sterile pastels, and the air was thick with antiseptic scents.

But as Frank tried to focus, he realized with growing unease that the thoughts flooding his mind weren't just his own.

"The doctor should be in pretty soon. Only two more hours until the shift change and I can go home. Did I see him move? He's awake!"

Frank wondered, *is she talking to me? Why don't I hear her voice?*

Frank lay there, overwhelmed by the cacophony of unspoken thoughts, trying to make sense of this strange and unsettling new ability.

"Hello. Good morning. Good to see you awake," the nurse spoke aloud. "How do you feel?"

"Hi. I'm feeling kind of dizzy," Frank replied. His voice was raspy at first as his hand reached to touch the bandages on his head.

"The doctor should be in to see you soon. Can I get you anything? Are you thirsty?"

"Water would be good. I'm really thirsty."

"Your chart says to give you ice chips when you wake up. I'll go get that for you. Is there anything else?"

"Yeah," Frank answered, "What day is it?"

"Tuesday. I'll go get your ice chips now."

"Here I was expecting a dull morning, " the nurse thought as she left the room.

There it was again. Frank was having trouble adjusting to the noise in his head. How could he hear what the nurse was thinking, if that's what it was?

A moment later, the doctor came in, looked at Frank's chart, and glanced at the monitors. Frank could hear the doctor's thoughts.

Heart rate looks good, respiration and O-2 look good. Glasgow Coma Scale is almost back to normal. ICP is OK. Let's see what he feels like.

Then the doctor spoke. "Well, I see you're awake!" He smiled. "We were starting to wonder."

"I told the nurse I'm a little dizzy. And thirsty."

"That's totally normal, after what you've been through. The nurse is getting ice chips for you. It appears you suffered a TBI, or Traumatic Brain

Injury. From what your partner told us, a bullet shattered a light pole above you, and debris hit your head during the incident."

"I need to call my wife. Where's my phone?"

"We've already notified your wife and the department," the doctor assured him.

Frank worried about how his wife was dealing with the stress of the situation.

"Your phone should be here in your room. I'll ask the duty nurse about that."

When the nurse returned with a paper cup of ice chips, the wet coolness felt good on Frank's chapped lips.

"The doctor said you could get me my phone."

I hope he doesn't start calling people at this hour, the nurse thought.

"I don't plan on calling anybody until it gets a little later in the day," Frank said.

The nurse gave him a startled look, but shrugged it off.

Around regular people, it was all fun and games, but he would need to be more cautious on the job. Reading minds could get him into trouble. He realized his new ability seemed to have a limited range. Otherwise, he would be hearing the thoughts of everybody in the building. For that, he was grateful.

Frank became more aware of a throbbing in his head.

"Can you give me something for this headache? It seems to be getting worse."

"That's the opioid tapering off. Let me get you some acetaminophen," the nurse replied.

She produced a paper cup with water, along with two tablets. After taking the pills, Frank laid back and closed his eyes.

The nurse tapped him on the shoulder and handed him his cell phone. He noticed there was still some charge left. Glancing at the screen, there was a missed call from his wife. He touched the screen to return the call.

"Hey, Frankie! You finally woke up. You really had me worried. How are you feeling?"

"I think I'm fine, other than a nasty headache," Frank answered. "Oh, Nancy, when you come to the hospital, can you remember to bring a phone charger? The battery is almost gone and I'm afraid it will shut off."

She replied, "No problem."

Just then, he saw a familiar face. Detective Ron Reynolds from his special operations squad.

Frank picked up on Ron's thoughts. *He sure looks like shit, but at least he's alive.*

"Hey, buddy, it's about time." Ron touched Frank's shoulder as he grasped a handshake.

"How did the raid turn out. I seem to have left the party early."

"Oh, we finished the job for you: one in custody and one in the morgue. I guess we can call that a win."

"The doctor hasn't said, but I probably won't be back on duty for a while."

"I guess we can keep covering for you until you get back," Ron said with a smile. "I'll let Chief Riggs and everybody else know you're all right."

Ron shook Frank's hand again before leaving.

A short time later, Frank's wife arrived. Nancy's face lit up with relief as she almost ran to Frank's bedside.

"How are you, I mean how are you really?"

"I'm pretty good. A little weak, maybe, but otherwise I'm good," Frank answered.

Meanwhile, Nancy's thoughts were running wild.

I can't imagine what it would have been like if Frank didn't make it. I sure wish he could find another job.

"I saw Ron. Have you heard from anybody else in the department?" she asked.

"I've only been awake for a few hours. I was surprised to see Ron so soon. They'll have to get along without me for a while."

"Are you sure you want to go back to that job?"

Why can't he have a regular job where people aren't shooting at him? Nancy was thinking.

"It's what I know. Besides, we're a team. I can't let them down."

What about me? Nancy thought.

Frank smiled and held Nancy's hand. "You're my team, too."

Two weeks later, Frank was ready to check out of the hospital. His doctor again warned him against strenuous or stressful activities for the next few months.

Within a week, Frank was already going stir crazy at home. TV was boring, and he soon ran out of small tasks to occupy his mind. The occasional sound of a passing siren triggered his instinctive response, only to bring him back to the reality of his present isolation.

He had to go back to work.

Respecting the doctor's warning about his recovery, Chief David Riggs assigned Frank to desk duties—an arrangement that felt more like a punishment than a return to his normal life.

The familiar scent of fresh coffee greeted him as he arrived at the station to the sounds of phones and printers. Somehow, the symphony of chaos was like music.

On Frank's first day back on the job, it seemed like everyone in the department stopped by the office to welcome him. He couldn't decide if he missed the action more than he hated the thought of paperwork and being stuck behind a desk. His office was an open space, but to Frank, it felt like a cage.

Later in the morning, Frank's boss came to the office.

Frank heard Riggs thinking, *Frank's the oldest guy on the squad. Maybe he needs to finish out his career where he's not a target.*

Out loud, Riggs was saying, "You know, we could always use a good training officer. You could teach the new cops how to stay out of trouble."

"Like dodging bullets?" Frank joked, while thinking, *"Is he trying to put me out to pasture?"*

"I think the recruits could learn a lot from you. It would sure put a lot less stress on Nancy. It's something to think about." Riggs raised his index finger to add emphasis to the point as he left the office.

Chief Riggs again stopped by the office where Frank was working a few weeks later.

"I bet you are tired of being stuck behind that desk all day," Riggs said as he beckoned. "Come on, I need your help with an interrogation."

Frank was eager to escape the paperwork jungle. They stopped at Chief Rigg's office to review the case.

"Here's the situation," Chief Riggs explained. "The suspect is James Cochran. We're pretty sure he was the one who attempted to rob the Sam's Mini-Mart. The would-be robber panicked and ran when the clerk pulled out a gun. Unfortunately, the surveillance video didn't get much. What we got was a description of the getaway car from the store clerk. Cochran was caught running a red light three blocks away, driving a car that matched the description of the vehicle used in the attempted robbery. That gave us probable cause for an arrest. But we still need to tie him to the attempted robbery. Got it?"

Frank nodded, and they headed to the interrogation room. As they entered, the suspect was nervously drumming his fingers on the table.

"Mr. Cochran," Chief Riggs said, "this is detective Frank Hayes. He's going to be assisting me in the interview. Have you been advised of your Miranda rights? Do you want to tell us your story?"

Cochran nodded confirmation.

"Why are you keeping me here? All I did was run a red light. That's my story."

"We're detaining you because your vehicle matched the description of a car used in the attempted robbery at Sam's Mini-Mart just minutes earlier."

"You're wasting your time. I didn't have nothing to do with no robbery."

"What did you do with the weapon? We didn't find one in your vehicle," Frank asked.

Cochran was silent. Frank picked up on Cochran's thoughts.

"They've got nothing. Otherwise they wouldn't be talking to me."

"Can you explain why you ran the red light that got you pulled over, three blocks from the store?" the chief asked.

"I was in a hurry. I had someplace I had to be," Cochran answered.

"We've got a video that places you at the convenience store," Frank said.

Cochran squirmed in his chair and glanced off to one side.

They're bluffing, he thought.

"It wasn't me. I was coming from downtown. I had some things to do."

"What kind of things would that be?" Riggs asked.

"None of your business, that's for sure," Cochran replied with defiance. Meanwhile, he was thinking, *If they had anything, I wouldn't be sitting here.*

"Here's what we have on you." almost exactly quoting the suspect's thoughts, "The store clerk is ready to testify it was you that made the attempted robbery," Frank told him.

Chief Riggs turned to Frank, his eyebrows raised in a curious stare.

Cochran looked shocked. *I had a mask. There's no way he could recognize me,* he thought. Finally, he said, "I want a lawyer,"

With that, the interview was over.

Frank mentally gasped. Had he slipped up? Reading minds was clearly a violation of the Fourth and Fifth Amendments. If someone discovered his ability, they could throw out the case and he would lose his job.

"Are you ready to get back in the action?" Chief Riggs asked the next morning, as Frank was settling into another day of shuffling papers and filing reports.

"What do you have in mind?" Frank asked.

"Nothing complicated. Anderson needs to serve a warrant. He wants you to ride along as backup."

"Sure. It will be nice to see daylight for a change."

It was late afternoon when Frank and Bob Anderson pulled up at the address on the warrant. The building was a rundown duplex just inside the city limits. The overgrown lawn and peeling paint stood in stark contrast to the surrounding neighborhood.

As Frank and Bob got out of the car and approached the house, a pungent odor struck them.

"Do you smell that?" Frank asked.

"Smells like ether," Bob answered. He looked at Frank. His eyes narrowing. "I'm thinking Meth lab."

"Exactly," Frank replied.

Just then, a deafening explosion rocked the air. The garage door flew outward, just missing Anderson by inches. Frank was not as fortunate. The heavy metal door struck him and knocked him to the ground.

As Frank hit the ground, his world spun as the acrid smell of burning chemicals filled the air.

Frank's world went dark.

Once again, Frank awoke to find himself in a hospital bed, once again surrounded by pastel colors and antiseptic smells. He opened his eyes to see the face of a nurse standing over him. The room was strangely quiet. He reached up to his head, relieved there were no bandages this time.

"How are you feeling?" the nurse asked.

"What happened?" Frank asked.

The nurse smiled. "Don't you remember? They brought you in for observation. They said you have mild concussion when you got hit in the head by a garage door."

Why was it so quiet? Frank thought.

While his own thoughts were racing, he realized what he was not hearing was the nurse's thoughts.

All the time could invade other people's thoughts, he had a fear of slipping up, of revealing his secret.

But all that was gone, and Frank felt relieved. Maybe losing his ability to read minds was a good thing.

"I guess I need to be more careful," he admitted to the nurse with a smile.

Just then, he saw a familiar face.

"You trying to get out of work again?" Chief Riggs joked.

"No, sir!" Frank replied firmly. "It's too damn quiet around here."

Have you wondered what it would be like if you could read minds? Would it be a blessing or a curse to know what people are thinking? How would you feel if others knew what you were thinking? Would they use your thoughts against you? What if you had to wrestle with the morality of knowing other people's thoughts? Or the legal repercussions?

That's something Frank Hayes no longer had to worry about.

***

Chapter Three

Alien Update

A *secretive guest on a YouTube channel hints at a galactic revelation.*

Episode #211:

"Hello. I'm Alan Green, and welcome to Alien Update. This is the channel where we bring you news about UFO reports, alien abductions, and other topics relating to the alien presence. If this is your first visit, be sure to click the subscribe button."

Alan Green was a man in his early fifties with salt-and-pepper hair, meticulously trimmed by his wife, who had a former career as a hairdresser. His standard broadcast wardrobe was casual but tidy, often featuring polo shirts. Sitting behind the desk, it didn't matter if he wore jeans or pajamas. His voice gave hints of his time as a news reporter for a local radio station.

The video "studio" was, in reality, a spare bedroom, modified for the purpose. A thick carpet deadened echoes from the floor while blackout shades and heavy curtains covered the windows. A ring light stood on one side of the desk with a camera mounted just above a computer screen. On the wall, in the camera view, was a sky mural.

Out of view of the camera was a laptop where the video producer could control the stream. Alan's son took on the producer role—partly because he knew what he was doing, but mostly because he was around to do it. In his early 20s, Jason Green was still living at home.

To the livestream audience, Alan urged, "Be sure to click *Subscribe* if this is your first time visiting us, and check the little bell to be notified when we drop the next update. If you're watching during the live session, we are monitoring your comments."

"On today's program, we have a very special guest. I can't tell you who it is, because I don't know. All I can tell you is, this may be the news we've been waiting decades to hear. But I'll let our guest explain."

Addressing the remote guest, Alan asked, "Are you there?"

"Yes, I'm here," came the reply in a disguised voice. The video screen displayed a dark outline of a figure.

"As you can tell, our guest's voice is being altered with an electronic filter for security," the host noted as he continued.

"First, tell our viewers why you contacted the Alien Update channel."

"Of course. I work in a very classified part of the government. I became aware of an event that the government is refusing to disclose. Not only our government, but other governments are also hiding what we know what is coming."

The host interrupted. "How did you come by this information?"

"I can't tell you that, but I can assure you it is accurate. There will be no avoiding the truth this time." the secret guest replied.

"I assume you must have top secret clearance?"

"I have clearance *above* top secret. My special security level is known as Majestic."

"I thought the security levels only went to Top Secret?"

"There are several security levels beyond even what the President is allowed to know."

"I see. We all saw David Grusch and the others in congressional hearings over the last couple of years. Bob Lazar told us about Area 51 thirty years ago. That's all old news. So what else is there?"

"The government is never going to admit that they have been lying to us for decades. That's why full disclosure will have to come from them, and by 'them' I mean the aliens. What I can tell you now is that an event is coming. That's all I can say."

"You said event. What is the event? When is it coming?"

There was no response. The host glanced at his son, who was shaking his head.

"My producer says the guest is gone. Well, I guess we won't have the answers today. Maybe we can get the guest back to tell us more. Meanwhile, let's look at your comments."

"*@SpaceDebunker* wants to know how a government whistleblower contacted the channel. An email or phone call would leave a trace that the government could track down."

"Our *CipherChat* address is listed on the Alien Update website. The app has end-to-end encryption for all messages, calls, and media shared between users. It doesn't require a phone number or email to register and it has a self-destruct timer."

"Here's another comment. *@UFOWatcher* asks when the secret caller will be back. Well, we don't know. I guess when or if he contacts us again."

"According to Galaxy Skeptic, the whole thing is a hoax. Well, it might be. We just have to wait and see what happens. The mystery caller hinted at an 'event'. Did that mean the aliens will come out in the open? We can only guess."

"Well, until our next program, be sure to click subscribe and like. This is Alan Green, saying *always keep your eyes on the skies.*"

Jason nodded and said, "We're out" as he switched off the video feed.

He then glanced at the computer screen.

"Check your social media feeds. We're being flooded. Some look like news media. How are we going to handle all this?"

Alan leaned back in his chair and rubbed his hands through his hair.

"I think the smart thing to do is to use Ai to generate a news release, post it on the website, and refer everyone there. We don't really have any answers so we can't really deal with questions. They're just going to ask who this guy is, and we couldn't tell them that even if we knew, which we don't."

Jason volunteered. "I'll get to work on the news release. We should probably let the social media go for now."

Episode #212:
"Hello, again and welcome to another Alien Update. Everybody's still talking about last week's guest. The views were more than double what we normally get. There were tons of comments. Some of you said you thought

the guest was a total hoax. Some even blamed me and said I was just trying to get a lot of views. Other commenters were anxious to know what else we could find out, and what the *'event'* could be."

"Unfortunately, we have not heard from our government whistleblower since our last update, but we have another guest today, who perhaps can address the questions we're all asking."

"We welcome to the show: Dr. Rick Navarro. I understand you were once with military intelligence."

Navarro appeared on screen from what appeared to be a corporate office wearing a suit and tie.

"That's correct, but I left after twenty years."

"So now you're retired and you spend your time investigating UFO reports, is that right? Your background sounds a lot like Luis Elizondo."

"I know and respect Luis, but that's all I can say," the caller responded.

"You said you heard our update last week. Can you tell us what you thought about our guest's claim that it's all about to be out in the open?"

"Certainly. I have to say, I found the claim intriguing but highly improbable. The idea that extraterrestrial beings would suddenly reveal themselves defies all the patterns and behaviors for decades."

"How so?" Alan asked.

Navarro responded, "First, if these beings have indeed made arrangements with the major world governments, as many of us believe, they would not risk breaching those agreements. There's too much at risk on both sides. Such an act could lead to chaos, not just among our citizens but potentially within their own ranks. It's in their interest to maintain the status quo, just as they have always done."

"That's an interesting point. You said first. What else?"

"Second, the infrastructure required for a mass revelation is immense. We're talking about a coordinated global effort, which would be impossible to hide from our intelligence networks. To date, I've seen no credible evidence of such preparations. Third, we've always held that the risk of cultural and societal destabilization is enormous. If they truly have our best interests in mind, as many theorize, they would avoid actions that could lead to widespread panic and disorder."

Alan considered the answer. "Now that you say it, that makes sense. So, do you think the whistleblower could have been misinformed or perhaps even part of a disinformation campaign?"

"It's possible. Disinformation is a powerful tool. It wouldn't be the first time it has been used to muddy the waters around this topic. If you remember, they said Roswell was a weather balloon with crash dummies, as if that made any sense, but a lot of people still believe that, even today."

"So, in your opinion, we're not going to see an alien revelation anytime soon?"

"I believe that any significant disclosure, if it ever does happen, will be carefully managed and controlled, involving both humans and extraterrestrials. Sudden, unilateral action from the aliens is highly unlikely."

"Thank you, Dr. Navarro. Well, what do you think? Let us know in the comments. Be sure to join us again next week. I'm Alan Green and this has been your Alien Update. And remember to *keep your eyes on the skies.*"

"Are you still there?" Green asked after the feed had stopped.

"Yes, Alan."

"You don't think our whistleblower is for real?"

"I didn't say that. I just think he's been intentionally fed false information for the usual reasons. Let's put it this way, wherever they say the aliens will land, I won't be camping out for the event."

Jason posted comments reflecting the reaction from viewers. The comments appeared as scrolling text at the bottom of the viewer's screen as Alan closed out the broadcast..

@DebunkIt posted "I've listened to every episode and it's all just circumstantial evidence. No actual proof. This is classic conspiracy theory territory. #NoProof".

@EarthBound commented, "I'll believe it when I see it. Until then, it's just another wild story. Entertaining, but not convincing. #ShowMeProof"

Episode #213

"Hello, and welcome to Alien Update. I'm Alan Green. Well, everybody's still talking about our mystery guest last time. The views are still growing, and there were tons more comments on the channel after the live program ended."

Alan continued, "Unfortunately, we have not heard from our government whistleblower, but we do have a guest today who could provide some insight."

The view switched to a split screen showing the host and a remote guest.

"Alex Morgan, welcome to the show. Some of our viewers will recognize you because you host your own channel, *'The Coverup.'* But you say you disagree with our guest last week. Do you think we could see a real *'take me to your leader'* event?"

"That's right, and thanks for having me on the show."

"Alex, you watched last week's update. What do you make of the whistleblower's claim that it's all about to be out in the open?"

"Honestly, I think there's a lot of merit to the idea. The things I'm hearing all point to a revelation."

"So, you believe the whistleblower could be right?"

"If you've noticed, we've been seeing more and more reported UFO sightings and they're more and more credible. The pictures are better and the reports are more reasonable. I mean, not just here, but in places like South America and even Russia. These aren't just random people with shaky camera images, we're talking about credible witnesses, like police officers, as well as both civilian and military pilots."

"That's true, the credible sightings have definitely increased. They're hard to ignore."

"Your whistleblower isn't alone, either. I've been hearing leaks that could be intended to prepare the public for something. The Pentagon's acknowledgment of UAPs and the formation of task forces to investigate them were the first steps, I think, that hint at a broader agenda."

"You think the government is ready to let us in on the secret?"

"Precisely. It's a methodical approach to avoid mass hysteria. By gradually releasing information, they're conditioning the public to an extraterrestrial presence. This whistleblower could be just the latest step in that process."

"What about the argument that the infrastructure for a mass revelation is too immense to hide?"

"That's a valid concern, but remember, we live in an age of unprecedented secrecy and technological capability. It's entirely possible that the necessary preparations have already been made under the cover of black budget projects and compartmentalized operations. We've seen glimpses of this with the rapid advancement in aerospace technology and unexplained projects over the years."

"Interesting point. And how would you address the risk of societal destabilization?"

"That's a big one, but we've seen people adapt to massive changes before. Think about the impact of the internet or global pandemics. As humans, we do adapt. If the revelation is managed properly, it can lead to a new era of understanding and cooperation, both among ourselves and with these extraterrestrial beings."

"So, you genuinely believe the whistleblower's claim holds water?"

"I do. The patterns, the evidence, and the broader context all align too well to be dismissed. I think we're on the cusp of a historic moment, and we should be preparing ourselves for the possibilities. I've heard things from my own contacts say this could be the real thing."

"Thank you, Alex. I'm sure our viewers will find your arguments interesting to consider."

Before the show ended, Alan checked through the comments.

@StarGazer123 posted; "I've been following this channel since day one. The interviews are so compelling! I'm convinced we're not alone in the universe. #AliensAreHere"

@UFOBeliever92 said "This is the moment we've all been waiting for! Finally, the truth is coming out."

"Keep those comments coming in," he said. "Well, that's this weeks program. I'll be back again next week with another Alien Update show. See you then. And remember, *to keep your eyes on the skies.*"

Episode #214:

"Here we are with another Alien Update," the host began. "Everybody's still talking about last week's guest. The views were more than double what we normally get. There were tons of comments. Some of you said you thought the guest was a total hoax. Some of you even blamed me and said I was just trying to get a lot of views. Others in the comments were anxious about what else we could find, and what the 'event' could be."

"Unfortunately, we have still not heard from our government whistleblower since our last update, but today we have another guest who might provide some answers."

The screen changed to show a second video box.

"Dr. Michael Anderson, welcome to the show." To the audience, Green said, "Dr. Anderson is an astrophysicist from the University of California, Berkeley. Thanks for joining us today."

"Thank you for inviting me."

"Dr. Anderson, you've heard the recent claims about an imminent alien revelation. What's your take on this?"

"Well, I'm a firm believer in the principle famously stated by Carl Sagan: 'extraordinary claims require extraordinary evidence.' As of now, we have no such extraordinary evidence to support the existence of extraterrestrial life, let alone any impending revelation."

"Can you explain why you think the evidence we've seen so far isn't enough?"

"Certainly. The vast majority of evidence for UFOs and extraterrestrials comes from anecdotal accounts and ambiguous footage. While some of these accounts are indeed intriguing, they don't meet the rigorous standards of scientific proof. In science, we rely on repeatable, verifiable evidence, and so far, none of the claims about alien encounters have been substantiated in this way."

"What about the recent declassifications and government interest in UAPs? Doesn't that lend some credibility to the claims?"

"It does show that there are phenomena we can't yet explain, but unexplained doesn't mean extraterrestrial. The universe is vast and complex, and there are many natural and human-made phenomena that can account for what people are seeing. We need to remain cautious and not jump to conclusions without concrete evidence."

"Some argue that the government is slowly disclosing information to prepare us for a big reveal. What do you think about that?"

"I think it's important to differentiate between transparency and sensationalism. The government's interest in UAPs is more about national security and understanding potential threats, rather than preparing us for an alien revelation. If there were solid evidence of extraterrestrial life, it would be the most significant scientific discovery in history, and it would be shared openly with the global scientific community."

"Do you think it's possible that this information is being kept secret because of its sensitive nature?"

"Anything is possible, but it's highly unlikely. Science thrives on collaboration and peer review. Keeping such a monumental discovery secret would go against the very principles of scientific inquiry. Furthermore, the idea that every scientist and government in the world is part of a grand conspiracy is implausible."

"So, in your view, the claims of an imminent alien revelation are unfounded?"

"Yes. Until we have extraordinary evidence to support these extraordinary claims, we should remain skeptical. It's vital to approach this topic with a critical mind and not let sensationalism override scientific integrity."

"Thank you, Dr. Anderson. Your perspective is invaluable, and I believe our listeners will appreciate your emphasis on evidence and scientific rigor.

The comments started as soon as the video stream began.

"Let's scan some comments, " Alan said.

"*@GalacticFan* commented: The interview with the astrophysicist was mind-blowing. He made some really good points about why this could be real. #ScienceMeetsMystery"

"*@NebulaNerd* posed an interesting question: What do aliens eat?"

"*@AlienAdvocate* responded to that by saying undersea aliens would have no problem finding food. Well, that's one answer. "

Alan checked his phone and found a new message on *CipherChat*. It was from the whistleblower.

"Maybe we will have some answers in our next update, "Alan concluded. "Until then, remember to *keep your eyes on the skies.*"

Episode #215

"This is Alien Update, number 215, and our whistleblower has returned, hopefully with more to tell us. Welcome back."

"Thank you. I do have crucial information that the public needs to hear."

"Alright, what can you tell us?"

"I can tell you the date, time, and location of the arrival. It will happen on the north lawn of the United Nations building, in New York. An alien spaceship will appear on Thursday morning."

"That's incredibly specific. Why the United Nations?"

"The UN has been secretly aware of aliens existence for decades, evidenced by the fact there is a United Nations Office for Outer Space Affairs."

Alan glanced at the comments, now rushing by in a torrent too fast to read.

"I guess that is where we should end the program for today. Thanks to our special guest and thanks for you for watching. This is *Alien Update*, and I'm Alan Green reminding you *to keep your eyes on the skies.*"

After the show ended, the negative comments kept piling in. With that, the livestream stopped. The word was spreading, but not everybody was ready to be convinced. Among them were two that summarized the general reaction:

@RealistRandy asked, "Aliens showing up at the UN? Not buying it. Sounds like a Hollywood script to me. #TooGoodToBeTrue"

@RationalThinker had a similar response, posting, "Really? Aliens landing at the UN? This is just sensationalism at its finest. Let's focus on real issues instead of fairy tales.

A few of the comments were less skeptical. For example, @AliensAreReal posted, "We knew it would happen."

The answer was not long in coming.

Three days later, a disc-shaped alien craft, perhaps 20 meters across, silently descended through the clouds over the UN building. It hovered briefly before coming to rest where police had cordoned off the north lawn. What appeared to be military helicopters hovered above, as if as a shield. There were no other aircraft to be seen anywhere in the sky, likely the result of an FAA flight restriction.

Emerging from the UN building, the Director of UNOOSA, the Nations Office for Outer Space Affairs[1] , approached the spacecraft. The alien descended from a stairway opening beneath the spaceship. The alien

---

1. Note: UNOOSA is a real thing: https://www.unoosa.org, but it is not about alien contact... as far as we know.

appeared in a military-looking uniform in shades of dark gray and black, with a gold emblem on the chest. Its body had a humanoid shape, but with features that clearly set it apart. Its head was smooth and elongated, with a gray-blue color. Large, black, almond-shaped eyes dominated the face. The director met the alien, and together they proceeded to the assembly chamber.

The members of the assembly sat in silent anticipation as the alien stood at the speaker's podium.

What would the alien tell the world? Would the alien provide answers to questions that have lingered for centuries? What event or activity could have motivated the aliens to reveal their existence to the world? How would that appearance affect the world and its continual conflicts?

How do you think the story will end?

***

Chapter Four

Kingdom of Fools

The storm clouds drifted away on that special day. It was the occasion of the king's glorious coronation. And what a stupendous event it was! The town square of Absonantville was filled with colorful bunting and children lined the street, waving little flags with big smiles on their little faces.

Of course, there was a parade!

A team of four white horses led a brigade of marching cadets from the military academy, their polished hooves splashing through the puddles from the overnight rain.

The king emerged from a special tent erected for the occasion, waving to the crowd. The grand square echoed with the triumphant sound of trumpets heralding the momentous event.

King Gilbert Bertram strutted to take his place on the platform, his eyes gleaming as he basked in the glory of his adoring subjects.

The crowd hushed in anticipation as the new king stood at the podium to speak.

"Today, I become your rightful ruler! And I *AM* your ruler, of course; that is as it should be because I am the only one who knows how to be your king. There has never been a king like me." King Bertram stretched out his arms as if they were wings.

The king's smile all but devoured his face with self-satisfaction as he turned to each side, expecting a reaction. The crowd remained silent, perhaps wondering if he would say more, but when he didn't, they erupted into cheers and applause.

Well, most did, anyway. Of course, there were doubters, arms crossed and unimpressed. Nonetheless, they remained quiet, recognizing the wisdom of avoiding open disloyalty. That was one thing this new king had made it clear he could not countenance.

Assembled behind the king, of course, were his loyal courtiers, such as they were. They had once comprised the city council, but now the king made all the decisions. There they were, clad in their finest three-piece suits, their faces expressing unquestioned loyalty to their pompous leader, even if they didn't comprehend most of his promises and policies. They clearly understood one thing well, and that was the intoxicating allure of power and prestige. On this day, they were soaking in as much of that as they could.

To some in the crowd, the scene might have brought to mind the words of the character in a 1932 movie: "I don't know where I'm going, but I'm on my way!" If you don't remember that line, it was clear before your time.

The celebration ended as chaotically as it had begun, and everybody went back to whatever they had been doing. The king retired to the golden throne in his dining room. It would have to do, as no castles were currently available on the local market.

Gilbert Bertram did not come to be king in the customary way. There was no long lineage of kings. No, this had come to be king as the result of an election, an election for mayor, to be exact. On winning the election, Mr. Bertranm decided there was no further need for elections and he declared himself king. Oddly, there were no objections raised. Either the citizens didn't notice or they didn't care.

That was just part of his genius.

Of course, the king was a genius. If anyone had any doubt, they needed only to ask, and he would eagerly explain the reasons. One had only to look at his many genius inventions, inventions that only he could have imagined.

Many of the inventions had yet to take shape because of some minor technical obstacles yet to be overcome. For example, there was the problem of providing power for the windshield wipers for sunglasses or the stability issue with the *waterproof umbrella*, designed to capture the rain rather than letting it go to waste by spilling over the sides and splashing on the pavement. That was an updated version of the earlier *invisible umbrella*. Then, there was the glue developed so that it would not stick to fingers. Unfortunately, it wouldn't stick to anything else, either; another detail that still needed to be worked out. But the obvious genius was that the king had thought of them before anyone else. That's what makes a genius, as he would explain.

In his first week, the new king was ready to unveil his most recent invention: the self-driving bicycle.

Sadly, there were no television cameras on hand to record the momentous event. The town was too small to attract attention from the national media. Still, the reporter for the local weekly shopping paper was there. The Weekly Squirrel shopping news, recently renamed Squirrel News. The report later appeared on the front page, next to the weekly recipe from Aunt Mable.

And so, at last, there it stood, the bicycle with a clunky control mechanism mounted where the front fork met the bike frame, with wires running back to a battery pack under the seat. There was no need for handlebars since the computer controlled the steering. The unfortunate person selected for the demonstration stood at attention next to the two-wheeled horror, ready to begin the test demonstration.

With a nod from the king, the demonstration began.

The rider climbed aboard the machine and grasped the center rail to hold on. He pressed the large red button, and the bicycle lurched ahead. The terrified rider clung on as it swerved around the square, zigzagging between market stalls, and sending startled vendors scrambling for safety. Soon, the front wheel snagged a cobblestone paver, causing the machine to crash into a park bench, and launching the unfortunate test rider into a Ligustrum hedge.

Some muffled chuckles could be heard, but nobody risked laughing out loud.

Soon, emergency personnel aided the injured cyclist, and someone carted off the bicycle with its crumpled wheel. Everyone went about their business, including the king, who hurried off to consult his staff on resolving the "minor" design flaws in the automated bicycle.

Word of the great self-driven bicycle debacle was bound to spread. That was to be only the first in a series of disasters. Soon, the discussion spread to Bertrand's own media platform, "The Social." We can't say if there was any truth to the rumors of other inventions, including a square wheel and a waterproof teapot. One, posting under the anonymous name "K" and claiming to be inside the king's royal court, claimed the king had been working on a design for an inflatable dartboard. Another poster claimed to have witnessed one of the king's children testing a bunch of square balloons.

Eventually, signs of trouble appeared. Concerns over the cost of the useless inventions created growing resentment and disillusionment among the king's royal subjects. Some even stopped wearing their gold "King Is Great" hats.

A traveling salesman who had witnessed the bicycle demonstration disaster with considerable amusement saw a situation ripe with opportunity. He approached one of the king's aids and requested an audience with the king to discuss an idea for a most magnificent invention. On hearing of the request, the king was eager to grant a meeting.

"What is your idea for my next marvelous invention?" the king asked as the salesman stood before him. The king sat on his majestic throne, draped in flowing gold and red fabric, right next to the dining room table.

"Your next invention will truly be out of this world!" the salesman boasted. "You will be the envy of all the people. You shall rise above all the other leaders!"

"Quickly, tell me the idea so I can instruct my fabricator to begin the project."

"Just imagine yourself rising through the clouds on your way to fame. It's a space balloon! No need for noisy rockets."

The king considered that last part. "Me?" he asked.

"Of course! You wouldn't want this kind of fame to go to just anyone, would you?"

King Bertrand stroked his chin in deep thought as he imagined his glorious return after such an adventure. His face erupted into a wide grin. Of course! It would be his most impressive invention of all.

"Tell me the details!" the king said, his excitement and impatience increasing by the minute.

The salesman handed the king a note that contained several diagrams and a list of materials.

The king became concerned. "What will this cost, and where can we obtain these materials?"

"Ah, that's the beauty of it. It just so happens that the company I represent can supply the materials you will need."

"Of course." The king nodded, seeing the obvious brilliance of the concept.

At last, they set the day for the magnificent Space Balloon demonstration. Word spread through posts on *The Social* and a crowd gathered in the usual place in the town square.

The king arrived with his loyal staff.

There it was: an oversized wicker basket attached to a gigantic party balloon. A small plaque, added by the Dollar Store salesman, identified the invention as The Grand Petard.

The staff connected a hose from a helium tank bearing the brand of the local dollar store. The king climbed a small ladder provided for the purpose and took his place in the basket to the applause of the small crowd. This was to be his finest hour. An aide turned the knob to fill the giant balloon.

As the gentle morning breeze grew into a brisk wind, the ropes were released and the king in his basket soared into the sky. Higher and higher went the balloon and its passenger, now waving wildly. The loyal subjects eagerly waved back. The king waved even more wildly.

Unfortunately, nobody had thought about a radio for communications. The king had obviously not considered the need. If they had a radio, someone might have suggested turning off the helium.

The balloon not only soared high in the sky, but also glided out over the ocean. In a short time, the big party balloon and its passenger became a tiny dot in the sky, rising until it vanished from sight.

Hours stretched into days and the hashtag "#MissingKing" rose to number one on *The Social, as* the people of the town became more and more concerned.

At last, someone thought to ask the salesman for advice.

"What should we do?"

"Hold an election for a new mayor!" was his reply.

And so they did.

The town elected a new mayor, and the city council went back to holding regular meetings, and the tiny town of Absonantville was once more restored to sanity.

Out of respect, perhaps, the city commissioned a monument in the town square. It was a giant relief of a child clutching a bunch of those square balloons. Everyone thought it a fitting tribute to their former king. The words "Gone but not forgotten" were inscribed on a large bronze plate, to which someone added "Up, up, and away" in chalk.

And nobody seemed to recall the plaque on the basket of the ill-fated balloon.

***

Chapter Five

Box of Secrets

In the early morning light, brother and sister Anthony and Susan sat together on the old porch swing at their grandmother's house. Ever since their grandfather's passing, they had made it a point to visit Nana at least one weekend a month.

The only sounds were the squeak of the chain supporting the swing and the birds chirping in the large oak providing shade from the morning sun.

"What can we do that's special for Nana's birthday?" Susan asked, as a gentle spring breeze touched her shoulder-length brown hair. "What about something pretty for the house?"

A strong-minded young woman in her late twenties, Susan had thick chestnut hair, like her mother once had. She embraced both challenging tasks and the people around her with enthusiasm.

Anthony glanced up at the weathered ceiling and thought for a moment.

"She always complains about clutter. You know anything we buy will eventually end up at the sharing center."

"You're right," Susan sighed. "Oh! I have an idea. What about a garden? That's something that she can enjoy every day," she suggested.

"I don't know. At eighty, she certainly doesn't want to work in a garden."

"We can plant things that don't need a lot of care. And besides, we can pull a few weeds when we come to visit."

"Sounds like a plan!" Anthony slapped the armrest on the swing as he got up. "I'll get a shovel from the garage."

"Let's not get ahead of ourselves. We need to pick a place and make sure it has Nana's approval."

"You're right, of course, as usual, "Anthony said with a gentle smirk. Switching moods, he added, "But if we tell her about it, it won't be a surprise."

"Birthday gifts don't always have to be a surprise," Susan answered. "And you know how Nana is about her yard."

"And everything else," Anthony admitted.

So, together, they set off to find a suitable location for a garden. It would need to be in a place with the right amount of sun, somewhere that was not too far to run a sprinkler.

As if in answer to their question, a cardinal flew out of a tree and landed on the ground nearby, at a spot where Nana could see the new garden from her kitchen window. They took it as a sign.

They told her about their plan, and Nana smiled her approval.

Spry and alert. Nana's silver hair still showed streaks of chestnut as it framed her deep-set eyes. Despite her diminished height of not much more than five feet, she still stood straight and poised.

Having gained Nana's approval for the location, Anthony retrieved a shovel and a rake from the garage and headed for the backyard. Susan was already pounding in sticks to mark the boundaries of the new garden.

"Do you think it's too big?" she asked.

Anthony pursed his lips and shook his head. "No, I think it's just about right. We might as well get started."

Susan raked away the leaves and Anthony went to work with the shovel, prying out the grass and weeds and loosening the first layers of soil. That went on until the shovel clanked as it struck something hard in the dirt. Susan brushed away the dirt to reveal the source of the sound. It appeared to be the top of something metal. Anthony dug around it until he could pull it out of the hole. Susan brushed off the dirt with her gloves.

They stared for a moment at what they had found. It was a small metal box with a tiny padlock.

"Who could have put that here?" Anthony asked.

"And why?" Susan replied. "Can we get it open?"

Anthony pried against the latch with the point of the shovel until the old encrusted latch surrendered. The rusty hinges squeaked in resistance, but eventually allowed the cover to open.

"It's either something from a miniature pirate or some kid's secret treasure," Susan joked with a wry grin.

The contents of the old box included the decomposed remains of a stuffed toy, perhaps a cherished teddy bear. A toy soldier stood guard over the contents from one corner, with a small rifle at the ready. At the bottom of the box, Anthony found something else.

"Hey, check this out," Anthony exclaimed. "It's a notebook."

On the cover were the words *"Property of Michael Reynolds"* in bold capital letters.

He and Susan carefully opened the notebook and began reading.

"It's a kid's diary," Susan noted with concern.

"It's a guy, so that would make it a journal," Anthony stated firmly.

"I stand corrected," Susan noted as she turned the damp pages. "Look at this!"

Mom and Dad were arguing again, and I heard them talking about me. They said something about Asperger's Syndrome. I don't know exactly what it means, but it sounds like it's about me and why I'm different.

Mom said it's Dad's fault, but I don't understand why she would say that. Dad got really mad and said it doesn't matter because I'm smart. I like that Dad thinks I'm smart, but it's scary when they fight. I wish they wouldn't argue so much. It feels like they're mad at me, even though they say they're not.

I don't like when people talk about me. It makes me feel weird and sad.

I'm unsure what Asperger's Syndrome is, but I hope it's nothing serious. I just want things to go back to normal, but I don't think they will. I miss when we were all happy. *Now it feels like everything is my fault, even though Dad says it's not. I don't want them to argue anymore. I just want us to be a family again.*

The later pages gave other clues to why the young boy had buried his most prized possessions. He said he feared he might be sent away to be cured of *whatever Aspergers was.*

That struck a note with Susan. A condition in the Autism spectrum had affected a member of their own family. She felt a connection. She carefully placed the once-prized treasures back into the box and set it on the porch in the sun to dry.

Later that evening, Anthony sat at the kitchen table with Nana while Susan leafed through the now-dried notebook, reading the entries and looking for more clues.

"When did you buy this house?" he asked Nana.

"It must have been around 1957, as I remember. Your grandfather was still working at the college as a chemistry professor."

"Grandpa passed in 1995, didn't he?"

"That's right. We had just retired. The life insurance paid for the house so I could stay here."

Susan connected her notepad to her phone's hotspot to search through the county property records online.

"1958," she corrected a few moments later. "I found it in the property records. It says the former owners were James and Julia Reynolds. That lines up with the name in the notebook. I wonder if we can find the kid the notebook belonged to?"

"Maybe you can Google the name," Anthony suggested.

"Too far back. Google didn't exist until 1995" She entered the name, anyway. "Oh wait, here it is. This explains why he didn't come back for his treasures. The newspaper must have posted their old microfiche files online. It's an obituary for Sgt. Michael Reynolds," she said, holding up the notepad to show the picture, then turning it back to read the description.

Sgt. Micheal Reynolds

"He died in Vietnam in 1971. He won quite a few medals. It says a sister, Joyce, survived him. It doesn't say anything about his parents."

"I wonder if we can find the sister?" Anthony asked.

"That would probably be impossible," Susan replied. "Besides, would she still be interested in her brother's notebook?"

"I don't know, but it wouldn't hurt to ask," Anthony replied. "Maybe we could use one of those online searches."

Susan's only response was to express her doubt by raising her eyebrows and pursing her lips at the notion.

The monthly weekend visit was coming to a close as Susan and Anthony hugged Nana and left for home, promising to return soon to finish the new garden.

After some online research, Susan went to the home supply store and purchased a selection of low-maintenance plants and a pale blue hearty cactus. She called her brother that evening to report her progress.

"We need to plant them this weekend," she told her bother by phone. "Will your wife let you get away?"

"Sure," Anthony replied. "she's got some volunteer thing she's doing."

"Did you find Michael's sister?"

"The search came up with a lot of possibilities. I paid the fee, but I'm still going through the list. So far, no good matches."

That weekend, Susan arrived at the old house with the plants. Anthony pulled up just in time to help her carry them to the new garden.

Anthony was tall and athletic and had no trouble carrying the plants.

Nana came out the back door when she saw the activity.

"I didn't expect you so soon."

"We want to get these planted before the weeds grow back," Susan explained.

"Anything new about the mystery box?" Nana asked.

"Maybe," Anthony reported. "The name I found is Joyce Reynolds Olson. I think it's a match. I found a phone number. We might try calling when we finish with the new garden."

After they washed up, Nana had sandwiches and iced tea ready for lunch.

Since it was Saturday afternoon, they all agreed it might be a good time to try reaching Michael's sister. Susan set her phone on speaker and placed it on the living room coffee table. Anthony and Nana gathered around on the couch as Susan dialed the number.

The phone rang ... another ring. Finally, after three more rings, there was an answer.

"Hello?"

"Are you Joyce Reynolds Olson?" Susan asked.

"Yes. Who is this?" was the cautious reply.

Anthony jumped in, "We're calling from what we think is the house where you grew up." He then added the address.

"Yes, that's where I used to live before my parents split up. Is this something about the house?" Joyce sounded concerned.

"You might say that, I suppose," Susan answered.

"Why did you call?" The woman seemed both concerned and confused.

"We found something we thought you might want to have," Susan explained. "We were digging for a garden when we found a box buried in the backyard, and your brother's notebook was inside."

Joyce's voice softened. "I didn't know he kept a notebook."

"We discovered your brother died in Vietnam, and your name was in the newspaper obituary," Anthony answered. "We traced you using an online search service, but there was no mention of your parents."

"They both died in an accident," Joyce explained. "They were trying to get back together when it happened. I think it was hard on Michael. And then he got drafted into the Army."

"You might find some answers in what he wrote," Susan replied.

"You said you were calling from the old house? Could I see the note-book?"

"We were just about to suggest that," Anthony answered.

An hour later, there was a gentle knock on the door. Joyce Olsen had arrived. As she waited at the door, a faint smile played at the corners of Joyce's lips, a silent acknowledgment of the memories the old house held for her.

Susan came to greet her and invite her in. Joyce entered the living room, pausing for a moment to take in the familiar details of the old house.

Susan introduced Joyce to Anthony and Nana.

"I was only six when we moved," Joyce noted sadly. "This house brings back a lot of memories."

Nana passed around a plate of fresh-baked brownies.

Michael's old notebook, inside a plastic zip bag, was on the coffee table.

Joyce smiled as she recognized her brother's handwritten name on the cover. She picked up the notebook and held it in her hands. "Michael was ten years old when we had to move. I think he wanted to bury that part of his life in this place. You were so thoughtful to go to the trouble to find me, and I'm grateful to you for that. Michael felt like he was different. He was also very sensitive. The divorce and the move were hard for him to accept. Maybe the notebook will help me understand some of what he was going through."

They all sat and talked about the changes in the house.

They said goodbye to Joyce as she left, clenching the cherished note-book, a hint of tears in her eyes.

Nana stretched her arms around Susan and Anthony as they watched from the front porch as Joyce was leaving and gave them each a gentle hug.

As the car drove away, Nana grinned at them both, remarking, "I think our new garden has already produced something beautiful."

***

Chapter Six

Perfect Candidate

"What do we do now?" Senator Evelyn Turner demanded. "We've hit rock bottom! Our candidates have become the nation's laughingstock. Now we're left without a presidential candidate, and the election is just a month away!"

"Relax," said Maxwell Synth, the party's chairman and resident genius. "We control Congress. We can still pull off a win."

There was a murmur that quickly spread around the room like an unpleasant odor.

Congressman Baxter was indignant. "What good does that do without a presidential candidate for this election?"

Smith was smug. "We run a robot."

"A robot? Are you insane?" Baxter was almost shouting at this point. "You mean we run a walking computer? What's next, a toaster for Vice President?"

"And how do you expect to get away with that?" Evelyn Turner was definitely not convinced.

"We change the rules," said Synth. "Besides, there's no rule against it."

"There will certainly be backlash," Party Chairwoman Collins countered. "This is your Plan B? People are afraid of robots. Remember '*The Terminator*'?"

"Fear has always been our friend. We simply turn it around to our advantage, like we always do."

Congressman Patterson wiped his brow. "I still don't see how you plan to pull this off."

Smith remained confident. "Consider the advantages. An AI president with no secret affairs, tax evasion, or skeletons in the closet. Hell, a robot doesn't even *HAVE* a closet!"

Senator Turner was also not convinced. "The future of the party hangs by a thread. We put all our eggs in one basket, and our top candidate dropped the basket. How can we pull it off?"

"This is what it will take," Smith said, holding up a file folder labeled 'The Equal Candidates Act'.

"We control the chairs of both the Committee on House Administration and the Senate Committee on Rules and Administration. We push through bills in both chambers and get them to the floor for a vote. If nobody screws up, it will sail through with enough support to blow off a veto threat from the White House. We get our people on all the news channels to pave the way."

Most of those in the room stared in bewilderment, while others nodded approval. With that, the wheels were set in motion.

The vice chair, Lucy Reynolds, sounded the alarm. "How will this work? There's this little problem with the Constitution." The Senate Committee on Rules and Administration meeting was off to a contentious start.

Senator Billings, the chair, remained undeterred. "By the time the other side can get their challenge through the court system, the White House will be in our control."

Meanwhile, a similar discussion was in full swing on the other end of the Rotunda.

"This meeting will come to order," Congressman Walters said, banging the gavel.

In the meeting room of the Committee on House Administration, the chairman asked, "Has everyone read the bill?"

"You don't really think you can get away with this, do you?" The Congressman from New York was indignant in disbelief.

Congresswoman Thomas whispered with a wry grin from the other side of the big table, "Watch and see."

The opposition put up a vehement protest in the form of amendments, but in the end, the amendments were voted down, and both bills moved out of committee and onto the floor of each chamber. The final bill passed and went to the White House, where it was met with the expected veto. Back in Congress, the vote to override the veto succeeded by a single vote in both chambers.

Lawyers instantly drafted court cases to challenge the new law's constitutionality, but time was running out. A challenge could be filed with the United States Court of Appeals for the District of Columbia Circuit, but moving a case to the Supreme Court in time to stop the election would be impossible. The opportunity was there. Lawyers built their first challenge case based on the Constitutional requirement of the Equal Protection Clause of the Fourteenth Amendment.

In the United States District Court for the District of Columbia, the bailiff called for order as the judge entered the room.

"All rise," the bailiff announced. "The United States District Court for the District of Columbia is now in session, with the Honorable Judge Andrew Charles presiding."

Judge Charles surveyed the crowd of news reporters and spectators. The critical constitutional questions at stake in his courtroom created a charged atmosphere of tension and anticipation.

"Good morning. You may be seated."

Attorney Jeffery Mills sat confidently at his table, his laptop displaying an artificial intelligence legal assistance program.

The judge continued, "This is the matter of case number 35-12878-CIV-DCC, challenging the constitutionality of allowing a robot candidate to run for President of the United States. Ms. Wilson, you may proceed."

Attorney Margaret Wilson approached the podium with a determined expression.

"Thank you, Your Honor," she replied. "We are here today to address the fundamental question of whether a robot is qualified to run for president under the Equal Protection Clause of the Constitution."

She continued, "The framers intended for rights and protections to be granted to human beings and not to machines. The Equal Protection

Clause provides that all *persons* be treated equally under the law. We contend that a robot, no matter how advanced, lacks the fundamental qualities that make us human, and that includes emotions and the capacity for moral reasoning."

At this point, the opposing attorney, Jeffery Mills, interjected, "Objection, Your Honor." He glanced at his computer screen as he rose to speak. "Council's argument is based on outdated notions of personhood. Advances in artificial intelligence have blurred the lines between humans and machines. A robot can now possess cognitive abilities and decision-making processes that are comparable to a human's, and I would suggest, in some ways, superior. For example, a humanoid robot is not subject to ulterior motives like greed. A robot can make decisions totally devoid of emotional bias or preconceptions. To deny it personhood would be discriminatory and contrary to the very spirit of the Constitution."

The judge considered for a moment before stating, "Overruled! Please continue, Ms. Wilson."

"Thank you, Your Honor." Wilson continued her argument: "While it is true that robots can emulate human behavior, that behavior is programmed. A robot is an entity devoid of any intrinsic qualities defining personhood. Granting equal protection under the law would set a dangerous precedent and open the door to a world where machines are treated as equals to humans."

Attorney Mills spoke up, "Your Honor, if I may; the Equal Protection Clause does not specify that protections apply only to humans. It guarantees equal treatment to all under the law. I maintain that a robot with the capacity for thought and expression satisfies the criteria for personhood as established by the Constitution.

"Your honor," Attorney Margaret Wilson countered, "A robot candidate does not qualify as a person."

The Judge leaned back to consider the argument, stroking his chin.

"Counselors, your arguments have been noted. The court will take a recess as I deliberate on the matter."

Attorney Wilson turned to glare at the other attorney as she gathered her papers and prepared to leave the courtroom.

Jeffery Mills, on the other hand, appeared confident as he typed something into his laptop.

As the upcoming election loomed ever closer, the court convened. The bailiff called the court to order, and Judge Charles addressed the courtroom.

"After careful consideration of the arguments presented here, this court finds in favor of the robot candidate."

An audible gasp flowed through the room like an invisible sandstorm. Mills sat back in his chair, folding his hands behind his head with a victorious smile.

The judge continued. "The Equal Protection Clause does not explicitly exclude non-human entities from personhood, and in light of technological advancements of artificial intelligence, it would be discriminatory to deny a robot candidate the opportunity to run for office, including that of president."

"With all due respect," protested attorney Wilson, "We vehemently disagree with this decision. Granting personhood to a robot candidate sets a dangerous precedent, undermining the very essence of our democratic principles. We will file our appeal without delay."

"Your objections are noted, Ms. Wilson," the judge responded. "The court respects your right to appeal. However, until a higher court rules otherwise, the robot candidate may run for president."

As part of the crowd erupted in muffled cheers, the dismay from the other side was palpable. Lights flashed, and news cameras clicked.

Attorney Mills nodded with a sense of triumph. "Thank you, Your Honor. We appreciate the court's thoughtful consideration of this matter and look forward to a fair and robust electoral process."

Outside the courtroom, the media swarmed around anyone willing to talk to the cameras, with their usual inane questions about "how do you feel" and "what will happen next." Those were questions for which nobody had answers.

Someone might file a challenge with the United States Court of Appeals for the District of Columbia Circuit, but moving a case to the Supreme Court in time to stop the election would be impossible.

With the start of the election early voting only a week away, the candidates met for debate on the national stage. Weeks of campaigning had come down to this decisive moment, a historical confrontation between man and machine.

The lights came on, and the candidates entered from opposite sides of the stage to take their places at the podiums.

Senator Janet Foster arrived on the platform in a tailored suit, looking confident and prepared.

AUTOMUS, the robot, appeared with the sound of electric actuators, the metal occasionally glinting a reflection of the television lights. The metal boots clanked as the heavy machine moved, towering over the opposing podium.

A giant video screen provided a backdrop behind the candidates, displaying a row of American flags flowing in the breeze against. Television cameras on giant overhead cranes moved into position for the opening shots as the marching music on the theater speakers faded.

Senator Foster appeared confident while AUTOMUS appeared ... robotic.

The moderator, Gordon Johnson, greeted the television audience, his image displayed on giant video screens on either side of the stage platform.

"Welcome to tonight's historic presidential debate." He continued with some meaningless remarks about the historical significance of the event before getting to the point.

"The questions for the candidates have been gathered from our online survey. This first question will go to Senator Foster. Senator, what is your position on ensuring access to affordable healthcare for all Americans?"

"I welcome the opportunity to respond to your question," Foster began. "Healthcare is a fundamental *human* right" (she emphasized the word 'human') "without facing financial hardship. As president, I will work tirelessly to expand healthcare coverage and maintain affordable access to prescription medications."

Johnson addressed the robot. "AUTOMUS: your response?"

The click and buzz of actuators could be heard as the robot turned toward the camera.

"Access to affordable healthcare is essential for optimizing societal well-being. By implementing data-driven approaches and maximizing efficiency in medical resource allocation, we can achieve optimal health outcomes for all citizens."

The television audience could hear an off-camera commentator remarking that the robot lacked the sort of powerful answers it had exhibited on campaign stops around the country. The live audience did not react.

Johnson posed the next question.

"AUTOMUS, how do you plan to address the humanitarian crisis in regions affected by conflict and war?"

The reply was immediate. "The resolution of conflicts requires strategic analysis and proactive intervention to mitigate humanitarian suffering. Using predictive models and strategic algorithms, we can optimize peace-keeping efforts and minimize collateral damage."

The camera panned the audience for a reaction.

"The same question to you, Senator."

"With all due respect, it's clear that AUTOMUS, my mechanical opponent, lacks the essential human qualities needed to lead with empathy and compassion. We need a president who understands the struggles and aspirations of real people, not just algorithms and data points."

The audience seemed more receptive to her answer, responding with whispers and nods.

Encouraged, she continued, "As a nation, we have a moral obligation to alleviate suffering and promote peace wherever possible. I will prioritize diplomacy and international cooperation to address root causes of conflict while also providing humanitarian aid to those affected by violence and displacement."

This time, the audience responded with applause. The pressure was clearly mounting for the robot candidate, and its responses fell short of convincing them. And the debate continued much the same.

As the election loomed just hours away, a flurry of signs sprouted up on lawns and street corners.

Signs promoting "Efficient Government" contrasted with slogans proclaiming, "Silicon Dreams Are Human Nightmares." Another proposing "AI Has The Answers" was next to one that read, "Robots Don't Understand Freedom."

The headline appeared on all the news channels the just as the voting was to start:

"BREAKING NEWS: AUTOMUS HACKED"

The initial shock among supporters quickly turned to disbelief as news broke of a last-minute cyberattack. The AUTOMUS campaign team faced a chorus of "I told you so" from within their own party, while the other side pounced on the new opportunity with a flurry of social media posts and attack videos.

One reporter or analyst after another jumped on the story. A seemingly endless stream of experts asserted their prior knowledge of the event, yet no one could recall these predictions, and no video evidence existed to support them.

Meanwhile, both campaign teams scrambled to respond. All at once, social media was full of discussions about the role of technology in government and the vulnerability of robots to enemy hackers. Social media "influencers" appeared in a flurry of videos with the same message. Ironically, much of the social media content from both sides was likely generated with the aid of artificial intelligence.

As the votes were being counted, it became clear that support for AUTOMUS fell short. Not only did AUTOMUS lose, but the down-ballot races for candidates associated with the party promoting the robot candidate were also impacted. The revelation of the last-minute hack exposed the vulnerabilities inherent in relying on technology. The political loss served as a stark reminder of the dangers of placing blind faith in technology without considering the broader implications.

At least, not that time.

***

Chapter Seven

Haunted Dreams

Her twelve-hour shift was off to a rough start.

EMS technician Katelyn "Kat" Delgado felt a knot in her stomach. She knew this was going to be a hard call. Her senior partner, paramedic Jake Andrews, called the dispatcher as they arrived. "Dispatch, this is unit twenty-three. We are on scene."

"Roger; police and fire are on route," was the reply.

There was the smell of smoke in the air at the accident location as the lights of the EMS unit revealed the scene of an EV that had entered a railroad crossing, striking the side of a high-speed train that was passing through. The force of the impact tossed the car to the side like a crushed toy as the train slowed to a stop, far down the tracks.

Kat assessed the situation with the car. Inside the crushed vehicle was a man, perhaps fifty years old. White powder and shards left from the exploding airbag covered the victim. After handing back chunks of the windshield to Jake, Kat reached in and worked to free the driver from his seat belt.

"Can you hear me?" Kat asked. "Don't worry, we're going to get you out! What is your name?"

The man turned his head in response to her voice and tried to speak. "David," she thought she heard him say.

Kat was feeling heat as smoke was rising from under the car.

"Fire!" Jake yelled as he tugged on Kat's safety vest. "Get back!"

As they retreated to safety, Kat's gaze was fixed on the fear in the eyes of the victim. Seconds later, the car became engulfed in flames. Jake already had a fire extinguisher in his hand, which was quickly emptied with little result. When the firefighters arrived, Kat heard one of them shout back at the others on the fire truck, "Another Class-D[1]!"

They hooked up the hoses and, after spraying many gallons of water from two tankers, they finally put out the fire. Sadly, it was too late for the driver.

The fire department took over the scene while Jake and Kat gathered up their gear.

"Win some, lose some," Jake said sadly.

Kat was in her late twenties, half the age of the victim. Jake was almost twice Kat's age, and had been through many cases like this and maybe worse in almost two decades on the job.

"David," Kat whispered to herself.

"Huh?" Jake asked.

She turned to Jake while she continued stowing her gear in the truck. "He said his name was David," she said with some sadness.

Jake's gentle manner betrayed his short hair and athletic appearance. He surveyed Kat's expression for a moment before getting behind the wheel to drive back to the station. He understood what she was going through.

Back in the ready room at the station, Jake poured cups of coffee and joined Kat at the break table.

"Are you OK?" he asked as he handed her a cup.

---

1. Class-D fires involve combustible metals such as magnesium, titanium, potassium, and sodium. These fires require specialized extinguishing agents like dry powder, which isolate the fuel and absorb heat, as water or standard extinguishers can exacerbate the flames or cause explosions.

With one elbow on the table, Kat brushed a strand of her light brown hair away from her face and slowly nodded as she reached for the cup, still deep in thought.

"That was a rough one," Jake continued. "But remember your training: be sure to set the boundaries. Putting feelings aside doesn't make them disappear. But you can't let it get between us and the people you need to help."

"I told him we could save him, and then we couldn't. If we had worked just a little faster...." Kat shrugged. "He reminded me of my father. I don't think I'll ever get used to that. I keep having bad dreams."

"No, we don't get used to it. But it doesn't mean we don't care. What we do matters. That's why we keep doing it."

"Yeah," Kat acknowledged. "Doesn't make it easier, though."

Jake was about to answer when the buzzer sounded with another call.

"We'll talk about it later. OK, Kat?" he asked, giving her a thumbs up gesture. "Duty calls. Let's get going." She responded with a like gesture.

"Unit twenty-three: medical emergency at Crestview Retirement Home," came the call from dispatch.

Grabbing the hand-held radio from his belt, he keyed the transmitter. "Twenty-three responding." Back in the truck, Jake noted the address on the dispatch screen and flipped on the siren as he merged into the traffic lane.

They arrived at the retirement home and approached the staff at the main desk.

"Oh, good, I'm glad you're here. This way," the woman said and led them down a hallway, glancing over her shoulder as she spoke. "Mr. Thompson is having trouble breathing. We put him on an oxygen tank, but he's still not breathing right."

As they entered a room, the staff member continued, "We were concerned it could be more serious, so we called you."

The older gentleman was sitting on the side of the bed, gasping for breath.

"Hey, Mr. Thompson, I'm Kat. We're going to do our best to help you."

Jake turned to ask, "Has he had any recent illnesses, surgeries, or medication changes that you are aware of?"

"No, nothing like that. He was fine until after his meal. He was out of breath when he got back from the dining hall,"

"How about any heart conditions?" she asked. The staff person shook her head.

"I need for you to lean forward. Can you do that for me?" Kat asked Mr. Thompson.

She retrieved a pulse oximeter from her orange bag and clipped it on the patient's index finger. After about twenty seconds, the readings stabilized. The sensor indicated a normal heart rate but a reduced blood oxygen level of 88%.

"Let's start him on high-flow oxygen," Jake instructed Kat, who was already reaching for the bag-valve mask in the kit.

"We're going to help you breathe better," she told Mr. Thompson.

After a few minutes, the meter showed a 96% oxygen level and remained steady after she removed the mask. Mr. Thompson was doing much better after the oxygen boost.

"I'm worried this could be a cardiac case" Jake cautioned the retirement home staff worker. "I think we should transport him to the hospital to be checked over, just in case."

"We're need to have you checked out at the hospital, Mr. Thompson," Kate said. "Is that OK?

Thompson nodded.

Jake and Kat helped him into a wheelchair and rolled him out to the EMS truck.

After delivering Mr. Thompson to the hospital, their next call found them at a city park. Dispatch said a child had what appeared to be a severe allergy reaction. When they got there, they found a young boy, no more than eight years old, sitting on a park bench with a woman. They pulled to a stop, and Kat climbed out to speak with the woman.

"What's his name?" she asked the woman as they walked up.

"Jimmy. His name is Jimmy. He's my sister's son," she said frantically. "I'm so glad you're here. He must have come in contact with something he's allergic to on the playground. His mother made sure I had his epinephrine auto-injector, and I used it, but it didn't work! I didn't know what else to do!"

"Let's get him to the hospital," Jake said quietly as he reached over to scoop up the child.

Kat turned and gripped his arm firmly to stop him. "Not yet," she cautioned. "I think I remember an update to the Practice Model that advised treating acute allergic reactions on-site before transporting whenever possible."

"Good call," Jake replied.

She checked the child's vital signs and noted the child's rapid pulse and evidence of hives on his arms and neck. Jake estimated the child's weight and measured out a secondary dose of epinephrine from the response kit.

With the extra dose of medicine, the child was responding to the treatment. After a few more minutes, the facial swelling subsided a bit. The child's pulse was close to normal, and the hives had diminished. Kat had made the right call.

"How do you feel?" she asked the boy, glancing at his aunt standing over her shoulder.

"I'm better now," he replied.

Kat turned to the boy's aunt. "Can you call his mom to let her know he's OK? But tell her we want to have him checked at the hospital."

The woman nodded as she reached for her phone in her purse. She turned away slightly to make the call.

Kat assured the child, "We're going to take you to the hospital to get you checked over. OK? Your aunt will be coming along and we're going to let your mom know you're going to be fine."

For the first time in the ordeal, the child smiled behind the oxygen mask. Kat made a quick evaluation from the child's reaction that he had been through this before.

"Let's go," Jake urged impatiently.

They loaded the child into the EMS truck. Kat stayed with him while his aunt rode up front with Jake.

Later, they pulled up to the hospital ambulance entrance and waited until a hospital staff member motioned for them to enter. Kat and the boy's relative accompanied young Jimmy inside while Jake stayed with the truck. After a few minutes, Kat returned and sat next to him in the truck.

Jake studied Kat's face for a moment before saying, "Just another day at the office. Right?"

Kat looked at him with a grimace. "Nice try, Andrews."

Another call on the radio: "Twenty-three: We've got an 81-year-old female. She's reporting she might have taken too much of a medication."

Back in the truck, Jake glanced at the dispatch screen. "Looks like one of our regular customers," he said as they headed to a familiar address.

Individuals who repeatedly call for emergency services are sometimes described as "super utilizers." It's common for seniors who live alone. Julia Smith was just such a woman in her 80s. She had several prescribed medications and occasionally became confused about the proper dosages and which to take.

A short time later, they pulled up at a house with a yellow light shining outside a green screen door. The house was a classic example of 1920's architecture with a set of stone pillars supporting the porch roof. As they reached the door, the woman inside smiled at Jake.

"I'm glad it's you," she said, reacting to a familiar face. "I'm afraid I may have taken too much of my medication."

Kat guided her to the living room couch and began checking her heart rate and blood pressure while Jake reviewed an array of pill bottles on the kitchen counter.

"It's this one," she said, retrieving a brown pill bottle from the pocket of her apron and waving it in Jake's direction. The label identified the medication as warfarin, a common blood thinner medication.

Kat reacted by inspecting the woman's arms, asking, "Julia, when did you take this?"

Julia's eyes welled up with tears and she confessed, "I'm not sure. A couple of hours ago, I might have taken it this morning, too. Sometimes I forget. I just felt like something wasn't right."

Kat noted several of what appeared to be bruises and purple spots. She cast a knowing glance at Jake. Jake nodded acknowledgement. It wasn't serious, but she would need treatment beyond what Jake and Kat could provide.

"We need to take you to the hospital," Kat told her. "Do you feel like you can walk to our truck outside?"

"My goodness, yes," Julia responded indignantly. "I'm not THAT old, you know." She reached out to Kat's hand as she got to her feet. Jake checked her cat's dish to be sure there was food. The cat was in the habit of hiding whenever there were strangers in the house. Julia stopped to take the house key from a hook by the door and slipped it into her apron pocket as Jake secured the door behind her.

Kat rode in the back and monitored the patient's blood pressure as Jake drove to the hospital. It wasn't an emergency, but the hospital would need to run blood tests to determine the appropriate treatment.

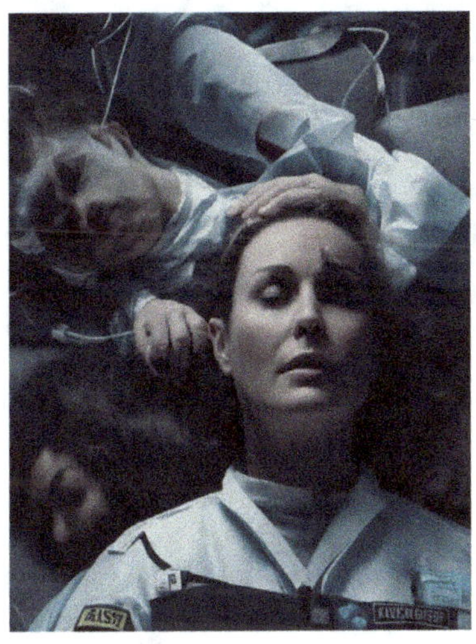

On duty for most of 12 hours, Kat was relieved to have a routine call to end the day. At the end of the shift, there were reports to be completed back at the station. Jake studied her for a moment before speaking. "Are you ok? I mean, really OK?"

"I'm just tired," Kat answered. "I just can't seem to get any rest. Lately, I can't help thinking about the cases. Sometimes I have dreams about them. It's been a bit overwhelming. That accident call today was really rough. I can't seem to shake it off. "

"We've all been there," Jake reminded her. "It doesn't mean you're not cut out for the job, it just means you need to find ways to put it all in perspective."

It was well after 7 pm as Kat returned to her apartment after her shift. She lay on the bed and closed her eyes, still thinking of the face of that driver, engulfed in flames. She opened her eyes and her heart jumped. A shadow moved across the ceiling and seemed to morph into the face of the victim of the car fire. Kat rolled to her side and tried to shut it out of her mind.

Back at the station the next morning, not really ready for the next day's work, the radio alert tone announced another call. She and Jake headed outside.

"No rest for the weary," Jake said, grabbing at the portable radio on his belt. "Twenty-three, responding," he answered as they climbed in for another day's challenges.

The call was at a street corner downtown. The manager of a convenience store clerk called about a woman in distress he discovered behind the store as he was emptying trash at the start of his shift.

Hearing the heavy EMS vehicle, the clerk met them outside the back door of the store. He pointed out the woman sitting on the pavement, propped up against a dumpster, and he headed back inside the store to tend to a customer.

Jake notified dispatch they were on the scene.

The woman appeared conscious, but her breathing was shallow and irregular. Her eyes stared into space, oblivious to the presence of the emergency responders.

"Hey," Kat said to the woman as she leaned down. "Can you talk to us? We're here to help."

There was no response. Kat was struck by the fact that the woman appeared about her same age, perhaps in her late twenties. She gripped the woman's arm, checking her pulse. Her arm felt cool and clammy.

Jake crouched on her other side, gently lifting her head to check for signs of a drug overdose. Sometimes the pupils appear constricted as a sign of an opioid reaction. Kat scanned the area and spotted a hypodermic needle next to the dumpster and pointed it out to Jake. Jake checked the woman's arms for needle marks, but found nothing obvious.

"What do you think?" Kat asked.

"I still think it's a pretty good bet it's an overdose. Let's find out." Jake reached into his "go" bag for the naloxone nasal spray, and he leaned to one side as he administered it in case the patient might sneeze. Jake monitored her pulse and oxygen level with a clip-on sensor. Naloxone sometimes causes a brief increase in blood pressure.

In a short time, the woman's breathing became more normal. The antidote had done its job, but the effects can be short-lived.

"I'm gonna puke," she said, somewhat irritated at her situation.

"That's OK," Kat said. "Let me get you a bucket."

Jake chimed in, "Hey, we're with the EMS. I'm Jake, and my partner is Kat. How are you feeling?"

"I feel a little weird, and maybe a little shaky," she responded.

"Do you have any medical conditions we might need to know about? What about a drug overdose?" Jake asked.

"Maybe," was all the woman would say. Her evasive eye movements seemed to reveal the truth.

"I didn't think it would get this bad," she said. That statement pretty much confirmed the suspicions. Kat returned with bottled water donated by the store clerk.

"What's your name?" she asked as she opened the water bottle and handed it to the woman, still seated on the ground.

"Susan," the woman replied bluntly.

Jake was unaffected by the response. "We gave you something to counteract the terrible effects of a drug overdose. If you puke, that's normal. But the effect wears off, so we need to get you someplace where they can get you past it."

"We're going to help you get up, and then we're going to take you to get help," Jake told her. "OK?"

For the first time, the woman actually smiled at the paramedics attending her. She was ready to accept their help.

Kat reflected the smile with the look of satisfaction of a job well-done. Soon, the woman was strapped into the side seat in the back of the truck. She was seated across from her on the other side as Jake drove to the local drug treatment facility. After dropping "Susan " off for treatment, Kat leaned back in her seat in the front seat, consciously relaxing from the stress. Jake cocked his head and assessed her mental state, but said nothing.

There were several other calls, but nothing as stressful as the car fire that had begun their day.

That night, Kat stared at the ceiling, waiting for sleep. Once again, she saw the shadow move across the ceiling. This time, she thought she heard a soft voice. She imagined it was the car fire victim, David.

"We couldn't save you," she heard herself saying.

The voice in her head replied calmly. "Don't blame yourself."

Kat felt a mix of emotions that included a lingering sense of sorrow. At the same time, the weight on her shoulders seemed to have been lifted, if only slightly.

"But ... We should have saved you," Kat felt tears in her eyes. A cool breeze through the open window seemed to touch the tears on her face as the apparition on the ceiling faded. She felt a calm sweep over her.

At the station the next day, the previous crew was heading home and Kat sat at the table in the break room, waiting for Jake's arrival and their first call.

"You seem more rested today," Jake remarked as he put his "street" jacket in his locker and slipped on his orange vest.

"I had a better night," she admitted. She glanced at Jake, who had a quizzical look on his face.

"Nothing like that, fool," she said, sensing his thoughts. "I had a talk with…"she paused,"myself. You might say I got a different perspective."

"That's good, because I was starting to worry about you burning out. That would be a shame. You're too good at what you do, "Jake said. "You still care. You can't lose that and be any good."

As they headed to the truck, Kat smiled. It was a different smile. Not the smile of a co-worker or even a friend. It was the smile of professional confidence.

"I never told you what it was like for me when I started this job," he said. "My first week on the job, I had a bunch of rough calls, all in a row, . It took me a while to deal with it. The nightmares, the doubts, the stress, it's all standard equipment."

Kat opened her eyes and gazed at Jake. She smiled for a moment before leaning her head back into the headrest.

"We keep our sanity by focusing on the job and the task at hand. We compartmentalize for our own sanity. When it starts to get hard on you, talk about it. Don't keep it in. When it's all said and done, it will make you stronger. Don't lose sight of the main objective." He smiled. "Don't let the ghosts get to you. The people out there need us. That's why we do it."

"Sometimes the ghosts can be a good thing." Kat said, remembering the reassuring words she heard from "David".

The dispatch screen in the truck spelled out the address of the next call. She strapped on her seat belt as Jake keyed the radio: "Twenty-three responding".

"Ready?" he asked.

"I'm ready!" Kat replied with a renewed determination.

***

Chapter Eight

How an Alien Saved the World

The story has continued for thousands of years, but this is as good a place as any to begin:

Japan Airlines (JAL) Flight 1628–November 17th, 1986
Location: Alien Patrol Sector *Mem* (Somewhere over Eastern Alaska)
Altitude: 37,000 feet
Ground Speed: 600 mph.
Origin: Paris, France
Destination: Tokyo, Japan, via Anchorage, Alaska.
Cargo: Beaujolais wine.

As the Japan Airlines cargo jet passed over eastern Alaska, Captain Kenju Terauchi scanned the sky from the left seat in the cockpit. He looked about 2,000 feet below and saw two bright lights moving at the same speed as the jetliner. He turned to his co-pilot and first officer, Takanore Mori, and said, pointing below, "Do you see that?"

The co-pilot leaned forward and strained to see through the window. "What are they?"

"I don't know," the captain replied. He glanced over his right shoulder at Flight Engineer Yoshio Tsukuba. Tsukuba grimaced as he shook his head.

The two unknown objects swooped up in front of the jetliner, one above the other, keeping pace a short distance ahead, in an odd rocking motion.

Pressing the radio button on the yoke, the captain called, "Anchorage Center, Japan Air sixteen twenty-eight, ah, do you have any traffic ah, in our path?"

Air Traffic Control responded, "Japan Air 1628 heavy, negative."

The captain continued, "Japan Air, 1628, Roger. We have in sight two traffic in front of us, one mile about."

At that same moment, aboard one of the two alien ships, the pilot, Zork, communicated with the other alien ship with the equivalent of "Watch this!" The alien craft shifted to a side-by-side formation, still maintaining the same distance ahead of the Japan Airlines jet. The pilot of the second ship, Zylox, expressed concern as he replied (in his language), "I'm not sure we should do this. If the Galaxy Council gets word, they could sanction us for breaking the Greada Treaty."

Both knew that, under the treaty, zooming airline pilots was not allowed. Realizing he might have made a mistake, Zork agreed. The two alien pilots engaged their nuclear ion antigravity propulsion and accelerated away at extreme velocity.

By the time Air Traffic Control vectored nearby United Airlines flight 69 to the area, the alien craft had vanished.

The Greada Treaty—1952

The Gray aliens contacted certain US government agents. The government exhibited obvious reluctance to permit aliens to conduct operations in the country. To make their side of the argument, the Grays staged flights over the capital in Washington, D.C.

The activity received mostly little attention and did not cause the scandal that had been feared.

Coincidentally (or not), Project Bluebook took shape in March 1952, less than two weeks later. A flurry of UFO sightings in July of that year, especially in Washington, D.C., put Project Bluebook to the test. The aliens wanted to make a point. Radar at Washington National Airport (now named after President Reagan) detected seven or more objects of unknown origin. Another event involved a Navy warship.

These events did not escape the attention of the newly elected President Dwight Eisenhower. In the beginning, Ike rejected a face-to-face meeting with the aliens, but the aliens apparently gave assurances of peaceful intentions. Thus, on February 20th, shortly after taking office, Ike quickly arranged for a mini vacation to California. It was unusual in that he had recently concluded a golf vacation in Georgia. However, the new president had more than golf on his schedule for this vacation.

Peter Carlson wrote about *Ike and the Aliens* later in the *Washington Post*

As described in the article, during President Eisenhower's vacation in Palm Springs, California, he briefly vanished. His staff used the excuse that the President had a loose crown and needed to make a quick trip to see a dentist. For a short time, the Associated Press reported Ike had died but quickly retracted the story. In reality, Ike had boarded a flight to nearby Edwards Airforce Base. The Air Force shut down the airbase for three hours. A small group of Nordic-looking aliens had landed at the base earlier in the day. The reason these particular aliens may have been selected is because they resembled humans, unlike the more commonly seen almond-eye Grays.

Air Force One, the Lockheed Constellation known as "Connie," was parked on the runway next to a large alien ship. Secret Service and base personnel were extremely uneasy about the new president going aboard the spacecraft alone to meet with the aliens. Discussion with the aliens was said to have centered on the scheduled hydrogen bomb test, known as Bravo, to be conducted at the Bikini Atoll. The meeting lasted almost 45 minutes and did not go well. After the meeting, Ike emerged from the alien spacecraft, hastening to his plane without speaking to anyone.

That would not be the last time there would be such a meeting.

After that first meeting, President Eisenhower established a permanent committee to monitor and conduct covert activities with the aliens under a treaty. The Greada Treaty was not finalized until a year later, when President Eisenhower again met with alien representatives, this time at Holloman Airforce Base, in Hanger 17..

Treaties and agreements may have also been made between the aliens and the governments of Britain, Russia, and China at the same time.

Steven Spielberg used reports of that meeting as the basis for the movie Close Encounters of the Third Kind. In a scene in the movie, the character playing the part of French scientist Claude Lacombe talks about past UFO encounters with American military personnel, known as the "Eisenhower Close Encounters."

What follows has been drawn from common speculation:

The government finally conducted the Greada Treaty signing in secret, conveniently bypassing the Constitutionally required Senate ratification. President Eisenhower, possibly because of his military background, stood as the sole US President, aware of the agreement with alien forces. The document remains classified *Above Top Secret*. Even President Jimmy Carter, who had openly acknowledged his own personal UFO experience, was not granted access to the information.

The terms of the treaty were said to have promised aliens would not interfere in our government's affairs, and the government would not interfere in theirs. The US Government would keep the aliens' presence on our planet secret. In exchange, the government would share in a limited amount of alien advanced technology. It was also understood in the agreement that the government would overlook the abduction of humans and animals for medical examination and study. The aliens agreed to return humans who had been subjected to abduction to the place of the abduction, with no memory of what had happened. Under the treaty, the aliens were to maintain their own secret facilities on our planet. Part of the agreement also involved the exchange of ambassadors.

A variety of alien lifeforms took part in the final agreement, including Grays, which ranged from tall aliens standing nine feet tall to a smaller variety less than three feet in height. Also, rumors suggest that the agreement included the Andromedans, Annukaki, and possibly the human-like Nordics or Pleiadians, who had been involved in the initial meeting. There were indications the subterranean Earth Reptilians wanted no part in the arrangement.

Many years later, the granddaughter of Dwight David Eisenhower appeared in an interview that can be found on YouTube.

The interviewer began by saying, "I've heard a lot about some rumors that I'm hoping you can either confirm or deny for me. I'm going to come right out and ask you: Do you believe that your great grandfather, Dwight D. Eisenhower, signed a treaty with extra-terrestrials?"

Laura Eisenhower answered, "It's a true story. What I've learned about Eisenhower's relationship to extraterrestrial beings and ET-government treaties is that supposedly, in 1954, there was a meeting at Edwards Air Force Base."

"Right," the interviewer acknowledged as Laura Eisenhower continued.

"They seemed to have diplomatic intentions. The treaty had to do with bartering exchanges of planetary goods, natural resources, and compounds, and it was in exchange for [allowing} things like abductions. "

The interviewer asked, "Why would they want to abduct humans? What are they doing with that?"

Laura responded, "They need our DNA. We have a treasure of DNA that is basically a living library." She explained the aliens needed to explore human DNA in their quest to unlock secrets of the Universe, which hide in the DNA of all living creatures.

The interviewer posed the question, why is it that every nuclear facility worldwide has been under extraterrestrial surveillance?

Dr. Steven Greer

Has provided a plausible explanation: "There is a scaler pulse coincident with a nuclear explosion that travels at multiples of the speed of light.

That pulse is in the entangled aspect of quantum physics, and it disrupts extraterrestrial travel and communications."

Malmstrom Air Force Base, Montana—March 24th, 1967

A few minutes after sunset, a large, cigar-shaped space vehicle hovered high above the sprawling 13,800-acre Malmstrom Air Force Base in Montana. On that base, the Air Force 341st Missile Wing had responsibility for the operation and maintenance of a complex of ten Minuteman III intercontinental ballistic missiles, or ICBMs. The aliens aboard the specially equipped spaceship had a new device to try out. They had developed the device from data gathered from various missile complexes, specifically at Vandenberg Air Force Base in California and Minot Air Force Base in North Dakota. They were ready to test an Ion-Disruptor device.

It is said the device could generate a focused field of disruptive ionic resonance which interfered with electromagnetic systems within its range. In operation, the emitter mounted on the base of the alien ship projected a pulsating red glow to the ground below. They had used a smaller version of the device against a Navy fighter intent on shooting down an alien craft over the Gulf of Mexico. The disruptor successfully froze the fighter's offensive weapon controls, shielding the alien ship from attack. As the plane left the area, the Navy plane's electronics returned to normal.

This time, the test was larger. Tests would take place at other installations, including Plesetsk Cosmodrome and Baikonur Cosmodrome in Russia, Dongfeng Missile Base in China, India's missile test facilities, and Sainshand Missile Test Site in Mongolia, among others. The goal involved testing the disruptor's capability to disable multiple missile launch systems to stop nuclear war.

As the alien device activated, a bright red glow filled the sky.

A red warning light flashed in the underground control room. Sergeant Thomas, a security guard on duty, muttered, "What the hell is going on?"

Private Ramirez was also on duty that day. "Could it be a malfunction?"

The sergeant's training had taught him not to take chances. He contacted the base commander.

"Colonel Johnson, sir, we've got a situation here. The warning lights are acting up."

The colonel asked, "How many of our assets are affected, sergeant?"

Thomas scanned the control panels. All the control panels displayed anomalies, and the missile status indicators wavered between operational and offline. "It began with one, but now I'm seeing offline errors on all ten silos," Thomas reported.

"I need to notify Washington and call NORAD. I'll secure the base and get the technicians down there to find the problem. Let me know immediately if there is any change."

Before the colonel could end the call, the red lights stopped blinking, and all the consoles went back to normal.

"Wait," the sergeant said. "Whatever it was, the problem cleared up."

"I'm still sending technicians to find out what is going on down there."

As the colonel leaned back in his chair, he took a deep breath. His phone rang. It was the MP guard at the front gate.

"Colonel, this is Corporal Mitchel. I didn't want to bother you, but I thought I should let you know about something."

"Go on," the colonel replied, with a mix of concern and curiosity.

"Well," the corporal continued, "We saw this light—a bright red light. It was coming from this, well, this thing that was hovering over the base. It started pulsating for a little while, and about the time I was going to notify you, it stopped. It shot straight up out of sight. It's gone now, but I thought you should know."

What the MP saw was the alien ship with the device that had proven successful at disabling all ten launch systems.

The colonel thanked the corporal and assured him he had done the right thing. He considered including that detail in his report on the incident, but he decided not to pursue the matter further.

Why do people in the military resist talking about UFO encounters? In 1948, the U.S. government published document number 146, known as JANAP. The acronym stands for Joint Army Navy Air Publication. It criminalized public disclosure of information about UFO sightings, subjecting offenders to prosecution under the Espionage Act. The penalties included fines of $10,000 and up to ten years in prison. JANAP 146 later underwent declassification and was replaced by Air Force Manual (AFMAN) 10-206 in 1997. That new manual addressed the procedures for reporting and recording UFO sightings, but contained no explicit restrictions on discussing UFO-related information. However, those who report such incidents could be subject to a Non-Disclosure Agreement.

Maui, Hawaii–January 13th, 2018

As the sun rose over the Hawaiian landscape, locals and tourists enjoyed the tropical paradise. In a small office in the Hawaii Emergency Management Agency, David Mitchell sat at his desk, monitoring the state's emergency alert system. He was responsible for ensuring the smooth operation of the system, including sending important notifications in times of crisis. Meanwhile, Sarah Bennett, his co-worker, focused on her own tasks, occasionally glancing at monitors displaying the various emergency channels.

The calm of the morning abruptly broke when an urgent message popped up on David's computer screen. He read the alert in disbelief.

"BALLISTIC MISSILE THREAT INBOUND TO HAWAII. SEEK IMMEDIATE SHELTER. THIS IS NOT A DRILL."

David struggled to comprehend the situation as he turned to Sarah. "Sarah, look at this! We have a ballistic missile threat to Hawaii!" His tone was a mixture of panic and disbelief.

Sarah's eyes widened, and she gasped as she read the message and realized the magnitude of the situation.

In a flurry of well-rehearsed activity, David and Sarah sprang into action, alerting their superiors who initiated the emergency protocol. As panic spread across the island, sirens wailed, and residents scrambled to find shelter. David's fingers trembled as he typed on his keyboard. The message flashed across the screens of the television monitors mounted on the office walls. Radio stations were spreading the message to their audiences. A push alert appeared on cell phones on all the islands.

Meanwhile, a group of friends were enjoying the weather on a boat when they heard the alert on the marine radio. As they got closer to shore, they could see people running and screaming in the streets.

After 38 minutes, a new message appeared on David's screen:

"FALSE ALARM. THERE IS NO MISSILE THREAT TO HAWAII. FALSE ALARM."

David and Sarah stared at each other. The gravity of the false alarm weighed heavily on them. As they and the island residents regained their composure, the false alarm served as a stark reminder of the threats that could strike at any moment, even in the most idyllic of settings.

As the new message spread, people began coming out of hiding, trying to make sense of what had happened.

SSBN 888 Prometheus–earlier that day.

Far out at sea, between Hawaii and the Republic of Kiribati, Commander James Anderson stood at the helm of the nuclear missile submarine, USS Prometheus. Through the periscope, he gazed at the expanse of the Pacific Ocean glistening in the morning sun. The submarine bobbed on the surface, its engines humming below decks.

A young officer, Lieutenant Ethan Roberts, broke the morning calm as he burst into the room.

"Commander, I have an urgent message. There's a missile inbound for Hawaii. Fleet Command in Pearl Harbor has issued the order to launch a response."

The Commander's brows furrowed as he took the message from the young officer's hand and scanned it carefully, his mind racing with doubts and uncertainty. He knew what this meant, the dire consequences that a wrong move could bring, not only for his crew, but on the world at large.

Shaking the paper in his hand at the other officer, he voiced his skepticism. Are you sure about this, Lieutenant?

The lieutenant nodded, his face showing mounting anxiety, as he hurriedly stepped back into the communications station in the next compartment and began the confirmation process with Third Fleet Command in Pearl Harbor.

Meanwhile, Commander Anderson waited as tension escalated in the command center. The weight of the decision pressed heavily on the commander's shoulders, and doubts tugged at his mind, along with a nagging feeling that something wasn't right.

Lieutenant Roberts returned. He had confirmed the order from US3FLEET. Commander Anderson nodded toward the Lieutenant as he reminded everyone in the room, "We have a mission to accomplish. Proceed with the launch sequence."

Two officers, Strategic Weapons Officer Lieutenant David Ramirez and Lieutenant Commander Julia Stephens, stood side by side, their fingers hovering over the buttons that would unleash the deadly missile on the target in North Korea. They exchanged a glance, their expressions reflecting a mixture of fear and obedience. They both gulped in a breath of air as they pushed the buttons simultaneously, their actions laden with a heavy sense of responsibility. And then...

Nothing happened.

A short time later, to the relief of everyone aboard the submarine, the Stand-Down order arrived from Hawaii Fleet Command.

High above the submarine hovered an Aleph-type alien spaceship, a newer model of the one that crashed near Roswell. Aboard the alien ship were Zork and Commander Xelrok, assigned to patrol the Zayin Sector. As the sensors detected the submarine arming the missile system, Zork, and Xelrok activated an alien Ion Disruptor device that halted the submarine's launch system until the danger cleared. The task completed, Zork set the

Interdimensional Gravitational Engine for the secret alien base. The craft first angled to one side and disappeared.

And that's how a space alien saved the world.

Fact or Fiction?

In a summary of this story, I asked the question *fiction or science?* Another question might be, how many science fiction stories include footnotes?

JAL Flight 1628 occurred on November 17th, 1986. The cockpit conversation is fictional, but the crew names are real. We transcribed the communications between the pilot and Air Traffic Control from the Air Traffic Control recording. United Flight 19 was also involved. The crew later related a description of the alien craft and their actions.

Multiple "sources" contributed information about the Greada Treaty. A detailed description of the purported event can be found (pp. 72 and 286) in the book Galactic Diplomacy by Michael E. Salla, Ph.D.

The author derived the details of those events from the testimonies of participants included in that book. The 2022 YouTube video provided the source for transcribing the quotations from the interview with Eisenhower's granddaughter. (Footnote link provided at the end of this chapter).

The JANAP and AFMAN government documents are real, and they include descriptions of UFO reporting.

Dialog in the story of the ICMB base at Malmstrom Air Force Base in Montana is total fiction. However, the account of the red-beam alien craft is from reports submitted on 3/24/67. In the story, Colonel Johnson is a fictionalized version of Captain Robert Salas, the 341st Missile Wing commander during the reported event.

Hawaii's false alarm on January 13th, 2018, was widely reported by several news networks, including CNN.

The submarine incident is entirely fictional, as you may have guessed. However, the fact that the Navy Third Fleet is in Hawaii suggests the possibility that such an event could have occurred, given the circumstances.

Which brings us back to the question: is this story fiction or science? It is a blend of the two, with generous liberties taken with the timeline. As to the truth or fiction of the underlying theme of aliens and nuclear weapons ... that is for the reader to consider: What if?

***

Chapter Nine

A Parallel Universe

29 May, 2020

S omebody in the office building at Kennedy Space Center shouted, "There it goes!". The low rumbling in the distance grew louder until it shook the building. James Cooper glanced out the window behind his chair. In the time it took for the sound to travel the two miles from Launch Complex 4, the contrails from the Chinese rocket already stretched into the clouds.

George Andrews was one of the 200-some people on the launch crew, working in close quarters on consoles. Because of COVID-19, they wore the face masks required by the CDC guidelines.

James and George became friends while working on the shuttle program. George, ten years James' senior, had thinning hair with traces of gray. Both men bore the distinguish markings of being married and well-fed, but not what you would call heavy. James, the taller of the two, still had most of the thick brown hair of his youth.

Rocket scientists, like James, get to go home at a regular time most days, but George and the rest of the launch crew had to be there to push the buttons at any hour. George was part of the launch crew for SpaceX that Saturday afternoon. His role in the launch crew was communication and tracking for the Falcon 9. Crew Dragon, with Endeavor Astronauts Bob Behnken and Doug Hurley on board. They would make history as the first crewed mission for SpaceX and Falcon 9, putting an end to NASA's dependence on Russia for transporting crews to the ISS.

Working at KSC since the 1980s, George had a few stories he liked to tell, especially about UFOs. His job involved monitoring communications; some of what he had heard had raised his curiosity. George had become convinced that astronauts had seen signs of extraterrestrials more than once.

It happened once during Apollo 8. Module commander Walter Schirra said, "Please inform that there is a Santa Claus." Had they seen something unusual? Was it a code word? As the Apollo 11 crew later orbited the moon, a crew member also mentioned something on the "dark" side. But CAPCOM (Capsule Communicator) in Houston quickly interrupted, instructing the crew to "Switch to kilo." Kilo is a secure and restricted communication channel not accessible to the public or most amateur radio operators..

As expected, by 05:30, the post-launch traffic had largely cleared. Leaving the building, James squinted against the bright afternoon sun. Despite sunset being after 8 pm this time of year, the sun would be in his eyes all the way home to Orlando on Highway 50. He had not considered that fact before choosing a home east of his job. George, meanwhile, was not a rocket scientist, at least not a physicist, but he was smart enough to live nearby in Titusville. That meant a direct route and a much shorter drive south from the space complex, avoiding the direct sun. The downside was when called to duty at KSC, George could be there on short notice.

The Cooper home, east of Orlando, was built in the mid-1980s. It had a small lawn and a two-car garage featuring his and hers Hondas. The design featured white siding with brick accents at the doorway. As James arrived, Judy was sorting through the mailbox at the curb. The drive from her job in nearby Longwood meant she got home early. James and Judy were about the same age, now in their mid-40s. Judy had changed little from when they had met at Titusville High, at least that was how James saw her. She had been his high school sweetheart. Her hair was a natural light brown, in a style that complemented her face.

Judy's parents had moved from her birthplace in Chicago to Titusville, seeking refuge from the harsh Illinois winter weather. Her father held a management position at a local food chain. Following in her father's footsteps, Judy had pursued an MBA at nearby Stetson University in Deland.

In contrast, James' father worked as a science and math teacher. Driven by his desire to be a part of the space program, James chose the University of Central Florida in Orlando (then FTU), where he earned a Master of Science degree in physics and Planetary Science.

The couple continued to date throughout their college years and married soon after graduation. James graduated with a physics degree, and although they faced challenges in the initial years, they could eventually buy a comfortable home. They deliberately avoided having children, focusing instead on their careers, paying off college loans, and mortgages.

Around the time of the STS-63 launch, with the first female shuttle pilot, Eileen Collins, Judy assumed her position as manager for a local department store. James joined a NASA contractor team. The STS mission marked an early phase of the International Space Station Program and involved a rendezvous with the Russian Mir space station. James' initial assignment was to handle the complex calculations for this rendezvous, which presented a formidable challenge from the outset.

The early history of NASA was uneven. The Space Shuttle disaster led President George W. Bush to terminate the program in 2011. That decision resulted in NASA being left to rely on Russia for Space Station supplies for over the course of nine years. As a result, many at the launch complex lost their jobs. While some individuals found work in the nearby defense industry in Orlando, others had no choice but to pursue other career paths. Nevertheless, the dependence on Russia was coming to an end with the SpaceX Falcon9 crewed launch that Saturday, which brought James a certain satisfaction.

After dinner, James clicked through the news on TV, which included ongoing protests over the death of George Floyd and declining COVID-19 deaths, though they might rise as more authorities process death certificates. At that moment, James received a call from his friend George.

"How's it going for the launch?" James asked. "Any problems?"

Ignoring the question, George said, "You're the physics guy. What's all this stuff about an alternate universe?" There was a logical reason George's fascination with UFOs had become focused on something new because of discussions in Scientific American and the TV show Sliders.

Theoretical physics didn't align with James' field. He was more concerned with practical matters. He had several issues with the multi-universe idea, which he explained to George. In response, George pointed out the Mandela Effect. He was convinced that alternate universes were connected.

The Mandela Effect originated from paranormal researcher Fiona Broome, who claimed to have detailed memories of a news event in the 1980s. She recalled that South African anti-Apartheid leader Nelson Mandela had died in prison, but history tells a different story. Mandela survived prison, became President of South Africa from 1994 to 1999, and lived until 2013 in our universe. Nevertheless, many people shared the same memory of Mandela's "death," which Broome interpreted as evidence of a parallel universe.

George discovered many people held false memories, leading some to consider it to be proof of alternate realities. The shared false memories include instances like a painting of Henry VIII eating a turkey leg, which some recall seeing but no one can find a picture. Another example is a misquoted line from Snow White and the Seven Dwarfs. Even the geographic location of New Zealand is a subject of shared false memories. The list goes on, and it was once even the subject of an article in Good Housekeeping Magazine.

James remained unconvinced. He had a ready response: "Theories don't make footprints on the moon; it's math and science that puts them there." As he explained to George, there is no means to test the theory of alternate universes.

George needed to rest up to be ready for an early start of a launch the next day, so he left it there and said goodbye.

Judy asked. Judy had overheard the conversation and scoffed at the idea.

"You guys work all day and still want to 'talk shop'?" She expressed her belief that Alternate Universes should be left to science fiction. James readily agreed.

It had been a hard week, so James spent a few minutes on his Mac PowerBook laptop, skimming through CompuServe and AOL, and called it a day. He said good night to Judy and went to bed early.

James slept peacefully that night, and as daylight peeked through the windows, he stumbled out of bed. As he stood, he heard a sound close to his ears, a whoosh reminiscent of a Star Wars lightsaber. His eyes widened as a glowing wave passed over him, like a ball of lightning forming a circle. He stumbled through the ring of light and felt startled when he discovered he was facing a wall. Not only that, but the bedroom had changed from soft beige to off-white.

From the bed behind him, Judy was asking, "What's the matter? Did you forget how to find the bathroom?" Perhaps he HAD forgotten, or at least the bathroom wasn't where it should have been. Other things were different, too. The wood floor had turned into a brown shag carpet. He found his way to the bathroom, contemplating the impossibility of the situation.

After James finished his shower, he found the bed had been made and Judy gone to the kitchen. He dressed and walked down the hall. The small kitchen reflected memories of the past: brown cabinets and a Formica countertop straight from the 1970s. He almost expected olive-green appliances, but they were all white.

Looking up from gently stirring a cup of frozen yogurt, Judy said, "It's about time you got going. We've got company today! Tommy is stopping on his way back to school."

James has a sense of panic. "Tommy?!" he asked blindly. He wondered almost out loud, *who is Tommy?* This was the same Judy, but everything else around him had changed.

Judy's face showed a look of concern. "Yes, Tommy, our son, remember? Who did you think?"

He would have to be more careful. Judy has always been very discerning. It was best not to raise her suspicions. It would be too much to explain, and she would certainly think he was crazy.

James opened several cupboard doors before finding an odd box of "organic" cereal. Next, he located a bowl, poured the cereal, and doused it with almond milk from the refrigerator. The house had become an organic enclave.

Sitting at the dining table, he glanced at the French doors leading to a patio and a fenced backyard. Turning back to Judy, he studied her carefully. She was the same Judy he had married, but the situation seemed all wrong.

The cool spring breeze of the morning air drifted into the room as Judy opened the outside door. An Irish Setter bounded into the room. The dog froze when he saw James and let out a low growl before moving toward him. James lowered the back of his hand toward the dog. The dog sniffed. Both James and the dog relaxed simultaneously. That was close, he thought. Had Judy noticed the dog's reaction?

After breakfast, James walked through the hallway as if touring an open house. At the end of the hall, he found a room set up as an office. He had not seen the need for a home office in his "other" life. On the desk was a Nokia phone connected to a charger.

He turned on the computer. The screen came to life, but unlike his faithful Mac, it displayed the Windows 95 logo. Luckily, the machine did not demand a password. On a hunch, he opened the Netscape browser and a Yahoo search for "Nelson Mandela." The first link on the page confirmed his suspicion. It included a reference to the death of Nelson Mandela while in prison in 1980. Contrary to his own knowledge, in this new reality, Nelson Mandela did not survive to become president of South Africa.

James realized he had found himself in a different reality. Apprehension was creeping in. Things were drastically different.

Moving to the living room, he turned on the TV and flipped through the channels, pausing on the Spanish station and a discussion of the new statehood for Puerto Rico.

Judy stepped around the corner from the kitchen and asked, "Why are you watching that in Spanish?"

"Maybe I'm practicing my high school Spanish?" James replied.

In high school, he had decided that Spanish would be a more practical choice than French, especially when visiting a foreign country, like Miami.

Judy's response was a curious mix of concern and surprise. "You never took Spanish in High School! You decided you wanted to be in my French class instead," she said as she returned to something she had been doing in the kitchen.

Judy possessed great intuition. She could often guess the plot of a movie and figure out *"whodunnit"* in the first few minutes. If she figured out what truly was going on, she might be more than a little upset. She might well have asked, "Who are you, and what have you done with my husband?" James needed to be careful not to let that happen.

When the doorbell rang, Judy went to the door. James followed. A familiar-looking stranger stood before there.

"Hi, Dad! How's the new computer? When your old Mac died, I thought, it would a good time for a change. You can set up a password when you get used to it. Do you like your new office in my old room?"

This was Tommy, obviously James's son. He looked to be about nineteen. He was also tall, with his mother's eyes. Other than that, it was like seeing a younger version of himself. James had a strange feeling as he hugged his "new" son. At least, this would be a pleasant change to–whatever this experience was, he had found himself in.

James assumed his "new" son, Tommy, went to college somewhere. James had to be careful. He had many questions, but he had to pretend he knew all the answers.

Tommy reached out to shake hands with James and hugged his mom as he picked up a small stack of folded clothing Judy had ready for him. He waved goodbye as he drove away.

James had not quite recovered from that experience when Judy said, "I've got a surprise for you! We're meeting an old friend of yours for lunch!"

"Who is that?" he asked.

"I promised not to tell!" she said. "It's a surprise. You'll see when we get there."

James pushed the button to open the garage door. Concerned that he might not know how to navigate the streets of the strange subdivision, he suggested Judy drive.

They got to the restaurant a bit early, and James tried to imagine who they might be meeting. As he glanced up from the menu, he thought he saw a ghost. The person walking toward their table bore a striking resemblance to his old friend, John. But it couldn't be John because John had died from alcoholism more than a year ago. James still felt the pain of losing his once closest friend.

James and Judy had both known John for a long time. They both blended well with musicians, and John had been a good one. John was a piano player and karaoke singer. Suffering through two failed marriages. John had become an alcoholic. Not that he didn't try to get it under control. He could go for months before dropping out of sight for a time, only to resurface later, as if nothing had happened. Everyone knew not to ask.

At one point, James was visiting John's home when he saw a bottle tucked into the corner of the room. Seeing the whiskey bottle had captured James's attention, John admitted, "That's going to kill me one day." His words had been prophetic. James wanted to take away the bottle, but he failed to do so. He knew John would resent the interference, even from a friend. He reasoned John would only buy more, anyway. But James later comes to regret not taking the opportunity to show his friendship in that way.

Not long after that time, John had called James. Said some things on that call that caused him concern. James knew the signs of suicidal depression. He had learned that from his NASA management training. At that moment, during John's call, James had wanted to go to John's house to talk some sense into him. But Judy had discouraged it. She said there was nothing he could do. He should let John deal with his problems on his own, as he had done so many times before. John had often gone missing, only to resurface a week or so later. James had decided that Judy was probably right.

But that time had been very different. Not long after, John's brother called: the alcohol had taken its toll. They had moved John to hospice, where James and Judy went to see him for the last time. A catheter collected an ominous dark liquid at the foot of the bed. Everyone knew the dark liquid meant death was imminent. James found it hard to take. It was tough and very sad for everyone who cared for John.

James could not bring himself to go to the funeral. He regretted not going to John's rescue when he had the chance.

But now, here was John! Very much alive and standing there, happy and well! John had dark features and stood about five feet tall. His hair was balding in the center. At a distance, he might be mistaken for George Costanza from the old Seinfeld show. John wore a white short-sleeved button shirt and gray slacks—his typical nightclub wardrobe. John was never one for wearing jeans.

There was a woman with John, but younger. Her face showed the signs of a hard life, topped by hair that was a ... hmm, tasteful shade of purple, tied in a ponytail. In contrast to John, she wore jeans, or the jeans were wearing her. It wasn't easy to tell.

"I can't thank you enough for saving my life!" John said. "You were a genuine friend when I hit bottom, and you convinced me to get my life together. I didn't want to, but you made me promise to join AA, and, well, I did it. It's still a struggle, but I made it! " turning to the woman next to him, "Well, we made it together. Oh, I want you to meet Pat! She was my AA sponsor, and, well, we have a lot in common."

Pat leaned in to shake hands with James and touched his shoulder. "I'm so glad to meet you, Jim!"

John corrected, "He prefers James." James once explained the reason to John. James has a certain dignity. James always thought that was why it was James Bond and James Thurber, not Jim Bond and Jim Thurber.

"Oh, I'm sorry, James! We're both glad you were such a good friend to John," Pat added.

"I can't go back to working at the club," John continued. "Pat warned me to stay far away from the booze. I need to remember I'll always be a recovering alcoholic. So I'm going to be a music teacher! I'll be working at a music store, and Pat will help me find students. No more nightclubs! Can you imagine that? And I owe it all to you... and to Pat, of course!"

James glanced at Judy, her smile filled with tears of happiness. "I knew you would want to know about John's success!" she said.

He tried to hold back the tears of joy, which rolled over him like an ocean wave.

"John, that's so great!" Pat said. "It's so good to see you. We couldn't be happier for you. You did it. You should be proud of yourself."

Changing the subject, James interrupted, "So, what will you have? We like roast beef sandwiches here, but the fried chicken is also pretty good! Come on, let's go order at the counter."

It had been a beautiful reunion. The four talked well past finishing the meal before saying their goodbyes.

Back in the car, James told Judy, "That was a wonderful surprise. It was so nice to see what John has accomplished. I think he's going to make it now. He and Pat are clearly helping each other."

What a day it had been, and so much to absorb and sort out. In this alternative universe, this new dimension, he now had a son, and his old friend had come back from the dead.

Back at home, James slipped into a comfortable chair. Next to the chair was a small address book. He thumbed through the pages to the "A" section, only to find George Andrews' name was missing. Had he gained one friend only to lose another?

Shifting his mind back to the current reality, one thing could present a serious challenge. Where would he go to work on Monday? He had one day to figure that out, with not much to go on. What if this alternate James Cooper he had a job that this James knew nothing about?

Where would he go? What if he couldn't pull it off?

What if Judy couldn't accept an alternate husband if she learned the truth? And what would happen to the Judy in the other universe he left behind? How would she cope? How would she survive? She would surely report him missing, and his job at NASA would be history, in more than one sense, if he weren't there on Monday.

But how could it all be possible? The concept of multiple universes, of parallel realities, of course, was only a theory. James was certain of that, or at least he had been. Would he remain in this parallel universe? Would the other James Cooper appear? What would he do if he met his other self? Could that even be possible? Impossible thoughts filled his mind. He wasn't sure about anything anymore. Back on the computer, tried a Yahoo Search for "Alternate Universes." It produced a link to an article by a "famous" Princeton physics professor, Cedric Clark.

The title of Professor Clark's article was "Sine Wave Theory of Creation." The professor had deduced that there could be no alternate universes. His reason was that it would follow that no single body of matter could occupy more than one space at a time. It made sense so far... In the video, Clark also asserted that the universe is infinite, not finite. He posed the question, *if you were to reach the end of a finite universe, what would be beyond that? A wall?* The professor's corollary held that for the same reason, the Big Bang could not be a singular event but one small part of a continuing cycle. The Big Bang would only serve as a zero point in one cycle of infinite expansions and contractions.

That was all well and good as a theory, but if parallel universes can't exist, what would explain this current situation?

His mind still swirled with conflicting ideas, questions, and contradictions as he later drifted off to sleep.

James awoke and opened his eyes. As he scanned the room, he was relieved to find the bathroom door where it should be, and the walls were again the right color. He had found himself back in his old reality!

It had all been a dream. Relieved that nothing had changed, he let out a deep sigh and went to take a shower.

As he dressed, he noticed a pleasant aroma from the kitchen. Judy was baking homemade biscuits.

"Fresh-baked biscuits on a Saturday? What's the occasion?" James asked.

"Today is Sunday!" she said with a quizzical expression. "Are you alright?"

"Sorry! I thought it was Saturday," James responded as he tried to make sense of things all over again. How could he have missed an entire day? He felt an icy shiver sweeping over him with the realization that perhaps he might not have been dreaming after all.

He swallowed hard, almost choking on the biscuit, when he noticed Judy studying his face. She quickly turned away as he looked up. Had she noticed something to cause suspicion?

"Will you be seeing John this week?" she said with a look of concern.

The question startled James. He hesitated. "Don't you remember?" John passed away from alcoholism last year."

Judy remained still for a moment before she replied, "Oh ... That's right. It's hard to believe he's gone. I almost feel like I saw him yesterday..." Her words trailed off.

James watched as she removed the dishes and silverware from the dishwasher. She opened several cupboards and drawers, as if trying to decide where things should go. Judy appeared to be concerned or worried.

"What's your schedule at the store this week?" James inquired. As branch manager, Judy often had to fill in for employees who had to take time off. He was surprised that she wasn't on the schedule to work that weekend.

Judy hesitated before answering, "My normal schedule, I think..." She went to a small work desk in the hall past the kitchen, and began sifting through the contents of a drawer until she found a small calendar with notes in the squares for the days.

"Do you need to stop by the office today to check with Ann?" James asked. Judy's Assistant Manager worked the weekends.

"I don't think so," Judy answered quickly. Pausing, she said, "I think we need to do some grocery shopping."

As James settled into a chair in the living room and began sorting through his AOL email, Judy announced, "Let's go to the store. Would you like to drive?"

James nodded as he got up from the chair and went to grab his wallet and keys from the bedroom.

He followed as Judy began making her selections in the store. She stopped at the dairy case and extracted a bottle of sugar-free almond milk. A thought flowed over James like a splash of icy water. Her selection appeared starkly out of character, but it was exactly what the "other" Judy would have done.

His mind swirled with possibilities and options, but he said nothing.

As they drove from the store, James stole a quick glance at Judy as she gazed at the scenery. It was as if she was taking mental notes of the route and landmarks. Could he be imagining things? But what could explain the uncharacteristic selections at the grocery store? Could he test his suspicions without now ... without spilling a giant cauldron of cosmic beans?

James began his strategy by asking, "Have you ever thought about how things might have turned out if we had made different decisions along the way?" He paused, "I mean, we could have had children, we could have lived in a different place, we could have chosen different jobs."

He continued, "You know how George is all about science fiction and the space alien rumors. Lately, George has been talking about the idea of a parallel universe and alternate realities. He thinks there might be multiple versions of us living different lives in different dimensions."

Judy squirmed in her seat as she listened. "What if there could be another version of us where we have a child?"

Judy paused, and it appeared there was something she wanted to say, but decided against it. She continued to process the words and nodded slowly. "I suppose it's possible, but it's still very hard to believe."

James knew he had to tread cautiously. "I know it's a lot to take in, but I think it's worth considering. It could explain a lot of the strange things that have been happening lately."

Judy's eyes widened again, and as James glanced over at her, he could see a strange look in her eyes as she began to speak, but stopped short.

She remained silent for a moment, and James could see the tears forming in her eyes. "I don't understand what is happening," she breathed, but did not explain further.

When they returned home, they unloaded the groceries. Soon, they had put them away, and folded the paper bags for recycling.

Turning to James, Judy glanced at him and said, "I have a confession. I'm not who you think I am."

The words reverberated in James's ear, his thoughts racing. He had it all figured out—he would explain what he had experienced, but now ... this ...

James asked, "What do you mean?"

"When I woke up this morning, I didn't know where I was, but I looked across the bed and saw you, but everything else seemed different. The house and the view from the window are all changed. I had to look in the mirror to be sure I was still me. I don't know if I can deal with it all."

James took a deep breath and turned to Judy, trying to decide how to respond. "I want you to know I believe you. And I want you to know that you are still the best thing that ever happened to me, no matter what universe we're in."

He spoke softly. "I have my own confession to make. I've been to that other universe. It was yesterday. But this morning I woke up back here. You must have passed through the same portal."

Judy looked as if struck with an electric shock as she quickly sat, comforted by the room couch, slowly dealing with what she heard.

"I don't know how it's possible, but it happened," James says, still trying to wrap his head around the experience. "I was in your universe on Saturday, and I woke up back here today, Sunday."

Now Judy's mind raced with the possibilities. "Did you see me? Did you see Tommy? And John?" she asked,

"Yes," James assured her.

Judy was trying hard to take it all in. "What can we do?"

"I'm not sure we can do anything. I mean, we don't know how it happened or why." James continued, "I mean, it's impossible in so many ways, but now ..."

Judy assured him, "I believe everything happens for a reason. "

James nodded in agreement. "I'll see if I can find any research about this," he says. "In the meantime, we should try not to draw attention to our - situation."

Judy nodded, staring ahead, still processing everything. Judy took a moment to let everything sink in. "But what does that mean for us now? Are we both stuck in this universe forever?" she asks, feeling a sense of unease.

"Okay. We'll figure this out together," James said as he placed a reassuring hand on Judy's arm.

Judy smiled in agreement. She turned toward James, leaned forward, and whispered. "You can start by telling me where the heck I go to work tomorrow."

James's phone rang. It was George. Nineteen hours after the launch of the new SpaceX Crew Dragon, the newly arrived astronauts passed through the DM-2 hatch to enter the ISS. George completed his task and wanted to share the experience with James. There was a launch delay earlier in the week because of the weather, but everything went as planned this time. George and his team had made history. As the two spoke, Judy whispered, "Who is George?" James waved his hand and mouthed the words, "I'll explain later."

After the call, James smiled at Judy as he spoke. "George is a wonderful friend. He's a part of the history of KSC, the Space Center, and NASA. I got to know him after, you know, I lost John.

Judy smiled understandingly and began to say something, but James stopped her. "George must never know. NASA might overlook rumors about space aliens. But this?" he shook his head as she said, "John was a wonderful person and a good friend. Now I understand how you reacted to seeing him."

James paused for a moment before he continued. "George has a lot of strange ideas. He talks about space aliens a lot, although recently he had been talking about alternate universes."

Judy took a breath, and she was going to speak, but James stopped her.

"George must never know. NASA might overlook rumors about space aliens. But this?" he shook his head. "George talks to EVERYBODY!"

Judy was concerned. "What will happen to Tommy? We are going to miss so much!"

"For all we know, there's another version of us back in his world looking after him. He'll be fine," James assured her. "But I'm sure glad I got to meet him, even if only for a short time."

Judy agreed. "I'm glad you did, too."

Now it was time for James to satisfy his curiosity. He asked Judy, "What job did I have?"

"It had something to do with communications. You always had to work crazy hours because of the rocket launches." To James, it sounded a lot like George's job. That might explain why he had not found George in the phone contacts. Was it possible James had been hired instead of George? That made sense. If James had not gone on to earn his physics degree, he would not have qualified to be the rocket scientist he is now.

Judy explained James had wanted to continue to graduate school for a degree in physics, but ... then Tommy happened.

The next morning, James gazed around the room in the dim morning light to assure himself that nothing had changed from the night before. He glanced over to Judy's side of the bed, where she lay sleeping soundly. They had talked about her job, her position as manager, and where she would need to go that morning. Hopefully, they could adjust to her new "normal." He had to be at the office by eight, but she could enjoy a few more minutes of sleep. After all, she had been through a lot in the last few days. They both had. But she would have a bit more adjustments to make than he would. He showered and dressed as quietly as possible.

Judy stirred awake. "What time is it?", she asked as she glanced at the clock on the nightstand. "I need to get going. Ann worked the weekend, so I won't have her to fall back on this morning." She got up and went about her business, getting ready for the day.

As James entered the kitchen, Judy pulled the almond milk from the refrigerator. "What's this about?" she asked.

James stammered... "We... bought it... yesterday..." Judy's face grimaced as she poured a small amount into a glass and sipped it. "It's not bad, but I certainly wouldn't have bought it."

Was she playing tricks on him? What had happened? James now had a new shock to recover from. He had just gotten used to the reality of a "new" Judy, and now this. In fact, he had fallen in love all over again. But somehow, during the night, the "other" Judy had slipped back into this reality.

James must have been thinking this wasn't a portal so much as it was becoming a revolving door!

There was no time to sort it out, it was time to get to their respective jobs. James would have to resist the urge to discuss the topic with George, but Judy would be back at her old routine, perhaps wondering what she had "dreamed" over the weekend if, indeed, she thought about it at all.

After all, that's what he had thought it when he found himself in another existence.

But ... what if she shared her "dream" experience with the other James? What would he say? How would he explain it? What if she was jealous of her "other" self? After all, James could not deny that he had fallen in love with her all over again, which would be a truly weird feeling to have.

James concluded that in the same way the two versions of Judy had traveled between alternate universes, it would be logical to believe that his other self could have taken the trip in reverse.

How would the Judy from yesterday react to being back where she had been after she had almost adjusted to a second reality? Would any of them be able to maintain their sanity? More, could they keep the secret?

While the concept of parallel or multiple universes has been the subject of scientific debate for more than a century, interest in the concept has increased in recent years. For example, where is "Heaven" if not in a parallel universe?

But this story is not really about science. It is about decisions, our own decisions, and the decisions of others. Some decisions might even affect history. We never know. When those decisions arise, we must ask ourselves...

What if?

***

Chapter Ten

The Time the Aliens Came to Leon County

After almost thirty years of teaching, Mildred Jenkins retired on her pension from the Leon County School District. She spent most of her evenings with her knitting and her cat, named Fred. After the weekly newspaper shut down, the local folks down at the Little Dollar store said it didn't matter, as they had Mildred. It was her nature to keep tabs on everything that was happening in the neighborhood.

It began late one summer night in July when Mildred saw a strange light coming through the trees outside her window. She put down her knitting and nudged the cat from her lap. She got up from the large leather armchair to take a look, pulling back the window curtains.

The lights seemed to come from the lakefront cabin next door. There shouldn't be anyone there this time of year, Mildred thought. The cabin was the winter home of Evelyn Montgomery, but she always left in April for her summer home in North Carolina, as did several others in the small north Florida community. Mildred listened closely to see if it might be a car, but the only sounds she heard were crickets and the occasional call of the Whippoorwill. She watched as the lights reflected off the trees, and then, without a sound, they quickly faded away.

"That's strange!" she thought, watching for a few moments more. But there was nothing more to see.

10:23 pm. Mildred made a note of the time on a pad she had on the coffee table for such occasions. Fred, the cat, had claimed the seat in the big gray chair. Mildred let him be and decided it was time for bed.

The next morning, Mildred peeked through the shades in her bedroom to see if anything was going on at the house next door, but everything appeared quiet. At least, so it seemed. She decided to check with Sherry Green across the road in case Sherry had noticed anything that night.

"Hello, Mildred," Mrs. Green answered the phone, apparently noting the name on the Caller I.D.

"Hi, Sherry," Mildred replied. "Did you see anything unusual last night, about 10:30 or so?"

Sherry perked up at the possibility of some excitement in the dull little village.

"Oh, did I miss something? An accident? Or a burglary?" she said with some concern in her voice.

"No, nothing like that. I only wondered if you saw a strange light in the woods about that time. It swooped in over the trees without a sound. And then it was gone."

"What do you suppose it could be?" Sherry asked.

"Well, I can't say," Mildred responded. "I had hoped you might have seen it. Oh, well. Thanks anyway."

Later, at the Little Dollar store, Henry Thompson, the store manager, rang up an order for Agnes Patterson, another retiree who lived within walking distance of the store.

"Did you hear what happened last night?" Agnes asked Mr. Thompson. Apparently, Sherry Green had called Agnes about what Mildred had told her earlier that morning. Word had already been spreading through the community.

Mr. Thompson continued ringing up the sale. "Would you like the receipt?" he asked, seemingly ignoring the question.

"No, I don't need a receipt, thank you. Mildred said she saw some strange lights in the sky near her house last night." Sherry continued, loud enough so more people in the store could hear.

Tommy Jones, the stock clerk, spoke up. "I bet it's them!" he said.

"Them who?" Turning his head with a grimace, Mr. Thompson directed the question to Tommy.

Tommy, in his early twenties, sported a short beard and shaggy hair, combed to reveal one pierced earring. He mainly worked in the stockroom of the Little Dollar store.

"Them aliens!", he said. "I've been hearing about them a lot on the news," he said confidently. By "the news", Tommy really meant YouTube and Facebook.

An enterprising woman in her early fifties, Janet Taylor had one of only two real estate offices in the area. Everyone knew Janet Taylor for her attention to detail. As a real estate broker, she managed vacation rental properties for the owners, many of whom were not full-time residents. Being observant was in her nature.

She was returning from a rental property she managed when she passed by Mildred's house. As she rounded the corner, she thought she saw something or someone behind Evelyn Montgomery's cabin. It was hard to see as she concentrated on negotiating the bends in the road. At first glance, though, whatever it was had large dark eyes and what could have been a helmet. She couldn't stop to investigate because she was late for an appointment at the office.

Back at the real estate office, Agnes Patterson waited patiently in her car outside. She had been considering renting out the cottage where her mother had lived before her death earlier that year.

Janet pulled into her reserved spot and unlocked the office door.

"Good afternoon, Agnes," she greeted warmly. "As I mentioned on the phone, I believe a seasonal rental could be a wonderful option for you. There's a demand for charming cottages in the area, especially during the winter months. As you know, I manage several rental properties in the area."

Agnes leaned forward attentively. "What do you think I can expect in terms of income for the winter months?"

"Well, Agnes, based on the current rental market and the appeal of your cottage's location, I think you can expect something in this range." Janet pointed to the prices on a rental list she had on her desk.

"That's more than I expected. Go ahead and fill out the forms, and I'll stop by later to sign them."

Agnes was relieved. She still had expenses that were left over from her mother's illness, and the rental income would be a big help.

Changing the subject, Agnes asked, "Did you hear about the strange lights out by Mildred Jenkin's house last night? I stopped by the Little Dollar store and everybody was talking about it."

"You know, I passed by there this morning after showing a rental, and I thought I saw something at the Montgomery cabin," Janet replied. "Something or someone with big eyes creeping around through the bushes."

Now concerned, Agnes asked, "Do you think we should call Mike?"

Mike Reynolds was the local deputy. The town was not big enough for a real police department, so the county assigned a deputy to patrol the area. In view of the discussion at the store, the girls thought it might be a good idea to ask Mike to check out the stranger Janet had seen in the woods.

After Agnes left and headed home, Janet decided to share her concerns with the deputy. With a determined sigh, she picked up her phone and dialed the number.

"Sheriff's office, Deputy Reynolds speaking," a calm and professional voice answered on the other end of the line.

"Hello, Mike, this is Janet Taylor," she began. "I wanted to bring something to your attention. People all over town have been talking about the space aliens up at the Montgomery house by the lake."

Deputy Reynolds paused for a moment, taking in the information. "Space aliens? At the Montgomery house?" he replied, sounding slightly surprised. "I haven't heard anything about that. "

"Yes, Agnes told me everybody's talking about it," she explained, trying to convey the seriousness of the situation. "I know it sounds ridiculous, but that's what they're saying down at the Little Dollar Store."

"I understand, Janet," the deputy said in a reassuring tone. "Well, I guess it's my duty to investigate any reports that might affect the community's well-being."

"Thank you, Mike," she said, feeling relieved that the deputy was willing to listen.

"I appreciate you letting me know," Deputy Reynolds replied. "I'll look into it and see what is going on."

Janet was grateful for the deputy's assurance. "You'll be sure to let me know what you find out, won't you?"

"I will, Janet, and thank you for bringing this to my attention," the deputy said sincerely.

"I'll leave it in your capable hands, Mike," she replied, feeling grateful the deputy was taking her concerns seriously.

She decided to stop by the Little Dollar store to find out what everybody was talking about.

As Janet was picking up a few things from the back of the store, Tommy Jones was refilling the coolers with dairy products.

"How are you today, Ms. Taylor?" he asked. "Have you heard about the space aliens out at the Montgomery place last night?"

"I was by there this morning, and I saw something creepy in the woods. I called the deputy and asked him to check it out, " she replied.

"I think it's them aliens," Tommy said with a look of certainty. "It's been all over the news, you know."

Ten-year-old Emily Campbell was visiting with her grandmother for the summer. She had heard the discussion from the end of the next aisle. She stepped out of the aisle and turned to look at Tommy with her hands on her hips.

"Seriously? You think it's space, people?" she said with a look of disgust. Her grandmother promptly silenced her, unwilling to let the young girl come across as impolite. Emily resisted but soon folded her hands and rejoined her grandmother in the paper goods aisle.

"Mr. Thompson? Is it OK if I go on break now?" Tommy asked. Mr. Thompson waved his hand, showing his approval.

Tommy slipped into the side stockroom and started texting.

Tommy: "Hey, Sandy, you won't believe what I've been hearing at work! There's this stranger hiding in the woods, and people are saying they saw lights like a UFO! #AlienAlert"

Sandra: "OMG, this sounds like something out of a sci-fi

movie! ”

Tommy: “I think the aliens have landed, like we’ve been hearing on the news. It’s wild! I’m gonna text Joey to find out what he’s heard. SYL.”

Tommy to Joey: “Did you hear about the spaceship in the woods up by the Montgomery place?”

Joey: “No, what’s up with that?”

Tommy: “People in the store are saying there might be space aliens wandering in the woods down by the lake.”

Joey: “Did anyone see the spaceship?”

Tommy: “Mildred Jenkins said she saw a spaceship land right before midnight. Sherry Green saw a creature with big eyes creeping through the palmettos this morning”

Joey: “Somebody should call the sheriff!”

Tommy: “I think somebody did report it to the sheriff. Gotta go. Mr. Thompson is probably wondering what I’m doing.”

As Deputy Mike Reynolds cautiously approached the Montgomery cabin, Mildred waved him to come closer.

“Hi, Mildred. Say! Janet Taylor thought she saw someone creeping about at Evelyn’s place. Have you noticed anything over there?”

Mildred cocked her head to one side as she thought. “Now that you mention it, my cat, Fred, acted a little strange when I let him out this morning. I told Sherry Green I saw some lights in the woods last night.”

At that moment, a twig cracked in back of the old cabin next door. Deputy Reynolds adjusted his gun belt and gave a side salute to Mildred as he turned to investigate.

Mike moved quietly to the side of the house. Peeking through the azalea bush, he saw the "creature" Janet had described, with what looked like large dark eyes on the top of its head, stooping next to a palmetto.

As the deputy moved closer, he shouted out, "Hello?"

"Hello! Is there a problem?" was the reply, as the "creature" stood up, revealing a gray sun hat with wrap-around sunglasses perched on top. It was easy to see how that combination, from a distance, would resemble the classic alien's head when looking down.

"Can I ask who you are and what you are doing here?" Deputy Mike asked the stranger.

The "stranger" was an older gentleman wearing denim coveralls. In one hand, he held a small bowl containing saw palmetto berries. He reached out his other hand to the deputy.

"I'm Dr. George Montagu. I'm a professor at the College of Agriculture in Gainesville. Evelyn Montgomery's daughter is one of my students. She's allowing me to stay at their cabin while I conduct some research on the effects of climate change on the edible berries in this area, specifically the Saw Palmetto. But why are you here, if I might ask?"

The deputy stroked his cheek and looked up at the trees as he thought about how to respond. "The neighbors said they noticed some strange lights in the sky late last night, but they didn't hear any sound, so it couldn't have been a car. Would you know anything about that?"

"That would be about the time Evelyn's daughter dropped me off last night. Her car is electric, so it wouldn't make any sounds," the professor explained.

The deputy shook his head. "Well, that explains it. But you have no idea what's been going around. The folks down at the Little Dollar had it figured out that the aliens had landed here. The neighbors saw the lights, someone else saw your sunglasses on your head through the bushes, and well, one thing led to another..."

The two of them had a nice laugh, and then the deputy asked, "Do you think we should tell them or just let them think the aliens came here for a visit?"

***

Chapter Eleven

A Camera that Could See Through Time

E than confidently pointed to a camera in the display case. "I want THAT one, please."

A curious and imaginative teenager, Ethan had a natural passion for photography. In his small English village, he discovered a charming old second-hand store. Thirteen-year-old Ethan, always nurturing a special love for photography, delighted in finding a display of cameras.

The store clerk reached into the case to retrieve the camera and hand it to the boy.

As Alex examined the camera, turning it around to reveal the brand name, he said, "I've never heard of Vixtel." He looked to the clerk for a response, but the clerk raised his eyebrows and turned his head with an expression that meant he didn't have an answer. It was in a second-hand store, after all. It could have come from anywhere.

"It must be special," Ethan said. He was startled by what he saw when he switched the camera on. Through the camera's lens, the old store looked different. Ethan pointed the camera around the store. The digital screen revealed vivid colors and made some of the old things on the store shelves look almost new. He checked the menu functions, but there was no HDR or High Dynamic Range setting, which might have explained the brilliant colors.

Ethan convinced himself that this magical camera was exactly what he wanted. Checking the tag, he found a pleasant surprise. The price matched the amount he had in his pocket! He smiled and handed his money to the clerk, completing the deal.

"Here," said the clerk, "it comes with a case and a few lens filters."

"Thank you," said Ethan.

Ethan rode his bicycle home as the late afternoon shadows hovered over the narrow streets of the old village. Summer filled the air, and school being out meant he would have plenty of time to experiment with his new camera.

The following day, Ethan began his adventure, exploring his world with the magical camera. He rode his bicycle into the village, looking for subjects to photograph. He stopped at an ancient bridge that spanned a serene river. As he framed the scene and pressed the shutter, the display changed before his eyes, revealing a happy family in a horse-drawn carriage. Ethan moved the camera away from his face, but the people and the carriage were nowhere to be found. The camera had transported him into another era. But how could that be?

Ethan crossed the bridge into the village as he wondered about the possibilities. Ahead, an old cathedral dominated the town square with its towering spires. As he paused to snap a picture, the walls transformed inside the camera, washing away the years of dirt and fading. Intricate carvings and ornate patterns came to life. The camera revealed the hidden beauty, no longer burdened by the weight of time. The stained-glass windows glowed with vibrant hues of color in the morning sunlight. Ethan parked his bicycle and walked through the giant open doorway to the sanctuary.

He raised his camera, framed the scene from the entrance, and pressed the shutter. The photograph captured not only the physical attributes of the cathedral but also the spirit of its rich history. Ethan spent much of the next hour capturing scenes of the cathedral's beauty from different perspectives. He snapped the shutter as he crouched below the towering majesty of the organ pipes and climbed the stairs to photograph a view of the pulpit and choir benches from the balcony.

Through the camera's display, Ethan studied how the windows cast their colors on the aisles below. He snapped close-ups of the ornate carvings of the church benches. As he set the focus and the f-stop to a narrow field of view, the images took on the appearance of three dimensions. Ethan felt pure excitement for the art of photography, limited only by the perspective of the camera's single prime lens.

As Ethan emerged from the cathedral, he looked around to see what else he might explore with the magical camera. An older woman sat resting on a bench beside the fountain in the town square.

"Excuse me," he asked, "may I take your picture?"

The old woman's weathered face, punctuated with wise eyes, studied Ethan curiously as the young boy stood before her. At last, she parsed her lips as if to show he had passed her inspection.

"Why would you want to do that?" she asked.

Ethan considered a respectful response. "You bring something special to the scene. It would mean a lot to me."

The woman nodded in solemn agreement. "I'm not inclined to pose, you know," she said firmly.

"I'm not inclined to ask that of you," Ethan answered with a smile as he began exploring different angles and settings on the lens. "I think you will like what you see."

Ethan took time to find the right composition for each scene. He took one close-up study of the woman's face with the defocused fountain in the background. In another, he framed the woman on the bench in perspective against the sidewalk and trees stretching off into the distance. At one point, a curious squirrel came to visit, and Ethan captured the woman's expression as she greeted the young creature. In another shot, Ethan positioned the camera so that the sun splashed across the lens with a streak of light.

The camera's display screen revealed the captured image. Wrinkles of age on the woman's face softened, as if the hands of time were rewinding as she looked on in wonder and amazement as Ethan showed her the pictures. "How did you do that?" she asked almost defiantly.

"My camera can see the beauty inside. It captures what makes you, well, you. When I take pictures with this camera, I can save the scenes and the special people that make the world awesome." Ethan explained, trying his best to express his thoughts. "It's like a magic window to keep the good stuff from slipping away."

The woman listened, not fully accepting the reality of the situation. Still, she expressed her gratitude to Ethan for bringing her the special moment of her day. She thanked him as he placed the cover on the lens, put the camera back inside the case, and climbed on his bike to continue on his way.

As Ethan walked his bike along the path in the park, he encountered a young couple posing for a professional photographer. Ethan stood at a distance, observing the scene as the photographer directed the couple to various poses and adjusted the camera. Upon completing his work and thanking the couple, he packed up his equipment.

The older man sported a well-groomed salt-and-pepper beard with wavy chestnut hair, neatly styled. He appeared tall and confident, dressed in a tailored charcoal gray suit. Next to him, a weathered leather camera bag stood open, housing an expensive camera case nestled alongside an assortment of lens cases. A large box of reflectors and tripods stood open to one side.

Ethan found the courage to approach the photographer. "I see you have a camera," the man said. "You must be a photographer, too!"

"I would really like to be one day," Ethan answered. "I've been trying out my new camera."

The photographer stood straight and peered over his glasses at Ethan. "Let's see what you have."

Ethan turned on the camera and stepped through the images he had captured.

"These are quite remarkable!" he exclaimed to Ethan's proud satisfaction.

"I think it's a magical camera."

"Do you think so?" said the photographer. "I see some genuine talent in your pictures." He reached into his top pocket and retrieved a business card: Alex "Lex" Montgomery, Wedding Photographer, it said. "I'm Lex. What might be your name?" he asked.

The young boy reached up to shake his hand. "I'm Ethan," he answered.

"You keep taking pictures like these, and I'm going to have some serious competition," said Alex with a grin.

He thanked Alex as he said goodbye.

Ethan wanted to take one last picture before heading home. As the afternoon sun painted streaks of color in the sky, he carefully placed his camera on a park table and attached a neutral density filter. He set the camera and the lens for a long exposure. The people in the park scurried about, gathering up various children and their toys as the evening approached. Others strolled along the pathways and stopped to take in the sunset's beauty. The camera clicked, marking the end of the exposure. The display screen revealed streaks where people had been moving about. In the foreground, a couple stood holding hands, taking in the sun sinking into the horizon.

Ethan rode his bike home as darkness fell. He leaned his bike against a tree and went inside. His mother complained he had missed supper, but Ethan hurried upstairs. He thought, "Dinner can wait," as he moved the pictures from the camera to his school laptop.

That night, Ethan dreamed of new things he could do with the magical camera, envisioning new subjects and techniques. The next day, he awoke early, all but gulping down the croissant his mother had made for his breakfast before rushing back up the stairs to his room. He seized his faithful camera and set out to find more adventures.

Once again, his bicycle tires thumped across the stones of the old bridge into the village, his camera safely wrapped in a cloth in the bicycle basket.

Bump!

As Ethan was looking for something to photograph, the bike hit a large root in the road, causing the camera to tumble to the ground. He scooped it up to inspect it for damage. Relieved to find no cracks or scratches, he carefully wrapped it again and continued on his way.

Riding his bicycle into the village, he came across a small farm. "This might be a nice subject for pictures," he thought. He peeked through the fence and saw a tiny baby lamb in the farmyard. Ethan quietly braced himself against the rough boards of the fence, following the little animal with his camera and taking several pictures as the cute baby lamb jumped and pranced about. While reviewing the images, he felt proud to capture the pure joy of the little lamb at play, momentarily forgetting about the camera's magical abilities.

Ethan peddled into the village, intent on finding more subjects for his camera adventures. He turned a corner to see the rotting structure of an old water-powered gristmill. Ethan thought, "I wonder how it looked when it was new?" He reached for the camera in its wrapping and switched it on. As he focused on the old building, it looked ... ordinary! The camera's magic powers to reveal the past had vanished. It must have happened when the camera fell out of the bicycle basket.

Ethan felt devastated!

Reaching into his pocket, he found the card the photographer in the park gave him. Perhaps the magic could be restored! Bundling the camera into the bicycle basket, Ethan found his way to the address on the card. The photographer's shop was a storefront on the main road. As he glanced through the glass, Ethan saw Alex speaking with the young couple from the park. They were likely reviewing the wedding pictures from the day before. As the couple left the store with their wedding album, Alex looked up to see Ethan and beckoned for him to come in.

"Hello! What brings you here today?" he asked the clearly saddened Ethan.

Ethan explained how his camera once had magical qualities, revealing the brilliance of the old cathedral and the youthful image of the old woman in the park. But now, the magic was gone.

"Can you find the settings? Can you fix it?" he pleaded.

The older man smiled knowingly. "There's nothing wrong with the settings," he told Ethan. "The magic is real, but it is in your imagination. You have discovered the possibilities within yourself and the many things you can do with the camera. Your imagination gives the camera its ability to create the magic in the images you can create."

As Alex shared his wisdom with Ethan, the young photographer's eyes widened with a newfound understanding.

"You mean, the magic in my camera is actually my imagination?" Ethan replied.

Alex smiled warmly, nodding in agreement. "Exactly, Ethan. The camera is simply a tool, but the real magic lies within you. It's your unique perspective, your creativity, and your passion that breathes life into every photograph you take."

Ethan's face lit up with a mixture of excitement and realization. "So, it's not about freezing moments, but about capturing the emotions and memories that touch people's hearts."

Alex nodded again, his eyes filled with pride. "Absolutely! Photography has the power to evoke emotions, to tell stories, and to preserve precious memories. It's your own vision, your ability to see beauty in the world, that creates the magic. With every click of the shutter, you have the power to make the world a little more beautiful, one frame at a time."

Ethan's mind raced with possibilities, his imagination ignited by the empowering words of the experienced photographer. "I see it now, Alex. It's not about the camera but about the magic I can create through my vision and creativity. I can make a difference with my photographs."

"Your vision has the power to touch hearts and make the world a better place."

With newfound clarity of purpose, Ethan understood his camera had been merely a conduit for his imagination and artistic expression. The true magic lay within himself, waiting to be unlocked with every frame he captured. As he thanked Alex for the invaluable lesson, Ethan walked away, fueled by a renewed sense of purpose and the knowledge that he could create his own magic, one photograph at a time.

***

Chapter Twelve

We Saw the Aliens

"Ashley Taylor at Oceanside Beach, where there were several reports earlier this evening of a strange light in the sky. One report said that they saw what looked like a bright light hovering over the ocean and disappeared. We contacted the local airport, but they had no reports of a missing plane and no radar reports of anything unusual in the area. Still, local witnesses insist they saw something out there." She turned to point out to sea to her left as the scene returned to the studio.

Earlier that evening, Lisa and Mark strolled hand in hand along the moon-lit beach, their laughter mingling with the gentle crashing of the waves. The cool breeze kissed their faces as they relished the moment's intimacy, oblivious to the world around them. As they gazed into each other's eyes, a sudden burst of blinding light above shattered their tender moment. The light caught their attention, causing their eyes to widen with curiosity and awe.

"What IS that?" Mark exclaimed, his voice tinged with excitement and disbelief.

Lisa's heart skipped a beat as her gaze followed Mark's, fixating on the mysterious object hovering in the night sky. It seemed to defy all reason, an otherworldly presence that had intruded upon their romantic moment.

"Is that... what I think it is?" she murmured, her voice barely audible.

They watched, transfixed, as a sizeable disk-shaped object hovered over the water at some distance offshore. Its metallic surface shimmered with an ethereal glow as it disappeared beneath the water.

Mark had pulled out his phone to take a picture right before the object disappeared beneath the water's surface. He and Lisa stood there on the quiet beach, trying to grasp what they had seen. Mark checked the picture on his phone. It proved disappointingly small and slightly blurred. He put the phone back in his pocket.

Mark broke the silence. "Did we really see that, Lisa? It... it just disappeared!"

Lisa turned to Mark. "We saw what we saw, but you know nobody is going to believe us."

Mark insisted, "We need to report it, anyway," as he pulled his phone back out to dial.

At the sound of a knock on the door, Mark went to see who it could be.

"Hello, I'm Bill Williams from KBUZ Radio 103. Can I discuss what you saw on the beach last night?"

A reporter from the local radio station had read the police reports and tracked down Mark's address.

Keeping the door partially closed, Mark answered, "There's not much to say. We saw a light. Some thing hovered over the water and then it went under."

The reporter persisted, "Could you guess how far it was?"

Mark thought for a moment. "Probably about, I don't know, maybe half a mile? It was hard to tell in the dark."

"Did you hear anything?"

"No, it didn't make any sound, at least not that we could hear over the waves."

Right then, Lisa peered around the door to see the conversation. "We told the police everything we saw. It was there and then it wasn't. That's about it. I told Mark nobody would believe us..."

"I'm afraid we don't have anything more to say," Mark added. "We would appreciate it if you wouldn't use our names in whatever you decide to report." The reporter nodded in agreement, turned and walked away as Mark closed the door.

"I wonder how many more times *that's* going to happen?" Lisa grimaced and walked back to the other room.

"Well, he was nice about it,"

Mark went back to the couch and resumed reading something on his phone.

"Hey Lisa, we weren't the only ones who saw that thing last night. It's all over social media. Some people are saying some pretty wild things about it. They're saying it shot a laser beam at an apartment building on the beach. I think it was only the lighthouse."

Lisa came back into the room. "That always seems to happen. People make up all kinds of stories. That's why I didn't want you to report it. It makes us look like the crazies."

Later that afternoon, the doorbell rang again. Mark muttered something to himself as he went to the door. This time, it wasn't another reporter.

Mark opened the door to see two men in dark suits, their features obscured by sunglasses and hats. Their pale complexion contrasted with the dark glasses. "Just like in the movies," Mark thought.

"We would like to speak with you about your 'encounter' last night," the 

first man said, holding out a white card with a strange logo and the word "Security" in the center. He didn't offer the card to Mark, but slipped it back into the inside pocket of his jacket.

"May we come in?", not waiting for an answer, he said as he gently pressed against the door and moved inside. Lisa came around the corner from the hallway and the second man nodded toward her He. followed the first man into the room. Their sunglasses remained on their faces.

As the men passed by, Lisa sensed a slight odor of … something like sulfur or ozone, perhaps.

The two strange men did not offer to introduce themselves as the first one asked Mark, "We have some matters to discuss regarding your sighting last night." The man's face had no expression as he spoke.

Mark felt more than a little annoyed by the intrusion. "Do you mind telling me who you are?"

"You don't need to worry about that. We know who you are. Let's say we're from the government," he said. As he said it, the second man turned to face Lisa and briefly smiled. Lisa was now feeling even more uneasy.

"And what part of the government would that be?" Mark asked firmly.

"That doesn't matter," the man in black replied. "What were you doing on the beach last night?"

"We were out taking a walk," Mark said defensively.

"We have been monitoring reports of unusual phenomena in the area. Your report of a sighting caught our attention, and we are here to ensure the situation remains under control. What do you think you saw?" the second man asked.

Lisa interrupted, "I think you know what we saw…"

The second man spoke. "Your safety is our utmost priority. For that reason, we advise you to refrain from discussing this incident. Publicizing such events can lead to unnecessary panic and misinformation."

"But it's already on the radio and TV. There's even a group that formed on Facebook already…"

The first man broke in to say, "We're asking for your cooperation and understanding." There was an implied threat in the way he said it.

Lisa remained undaunted. "We have no reason to talk about it to anyone else. It's caused enough trouble already."

That seemed to satisfy the two strange men as they turned, opened the door for themselves, and left. Mark watched as they got into a dark car parked at the curb. As the car drove away, Mark tried to see the license plate, but he saw none. The car turned and disappeared into the traffic.

"Well, that was an experience," Mark said, looking to assess Lisa's reaction.

"Did you notice anything weird about those people, like their cologne? It just came to me, I swear, it was the smell of iodine. No, more like ammonia, I think."

Mark reached back to scratch the top of his head. "Now that you mention it..."

"I would like to know who those people were."

"I'm not sure if it even had a license tag. I couldn't see any," Mark said as he again checked his phone. "We're not the only ones. The people in that new Facebook group are talking about their own visitors."

Lisa's skepticism grew stronger as the couple sat at the dining room table that evening. "I can't shake the feeling those two weren't who they said they were. Who can we talk to?" Lisa asked.

Mark checked Google and came up with an idea. "Maybe the Federal Aviation Administration."

"Do you expect the FAA to take us seriously?" Lisa said emphatically. Mark shook his head "no".

"But I found this one organization," he said, pointing at his phone screen. "They have an online form. I say, let's fill it out and see what happens. It looks like we can upload the picture I took."

Lisa shrugged. "We're probably just asking for more trouble."

Several days later, Mark's phone displayed an incoming call from the website where he filed the report about their sighting.

"Hello, this is Ben. I'm calling about your UFO report. Do you have a minute to talk?"

"Sure, but I don't want my personal information spread around," Mark said with concern.

"That concern may be why fewer than one in four hundred UAP or UFO sightings are reported. But about a quarter of the reports that we get have more than one witness. I can assure you that we are a full-time organization of professionals. We're only interested in the data, not your personal information. You gave a pretty good description of your experience online, and I see you uploaded a photo. Do you have any more information, and have you been back to that location since that night?"

Mark switched on the phone speaker so that Lisa could hear and replied that they had not been back to the beach.

Ben continued. "We did get a few other reports, and one person saw the report on TV and went out to look. They said while they were watching, an object out of the water and streaked away into the sky."

"Do you know anything about the two guys who came to visit us?" Mark asked.

"The government tells us they only respond when there are reports of physical evidence. Somebody came to talk to you?"

Lisa answered the question. "Yes, two men showed up the next day. They asked questions, told us not to talk about it. They were really weird if you ask me."

"I have no answers for you. The government has told us they don't do that," Ben answered.

Mark and Lisa had nothing more to offer, so they thanked Ben for calling and said goodbye.

Mark remembered the video camera on the front door. He checked the recording for the time the two men came to visit and rang the bell. As he scanned the video recording, he gasped. "Lisa, you were right. Come see this".

Lisa's eyes widened, her hand instinctively covering her mouth in disbelief. The sight before them appeared both mesmerizing and chilling, as the video showed the two agents with features that defied all human resemblance. Their eyes were large and almond-shaped, their skin had an otherworldly pallor, and their hands appeared elongated with slender fingers that ended in unnaturally sharp points.

"That's not how they looked to us", she exclaimed. "How did they do that? How did they make us see something totally different?"

Mark said softly, "I'm guessing they weren't government agents."

Lisa answered, "Ya think??!! That's scary. We were scared when we thought they were from the government, but now we're scared because they might not be!"

Mark turned to Lisa. "This isn't at all what happens in the movies. Now we know why people don't like to talk about it when they see UFOs."

What Mark and Lisa saw in the doorbell camera video

***

Chapter Thirteen

The Call

When paramedics arrived at the scene of the accident, they found Emily Foster unconscious and unresponsive. Her pulse was weak, and her breathing was shallow. They loaded her onto a stretcher and rushed her to the hospital.

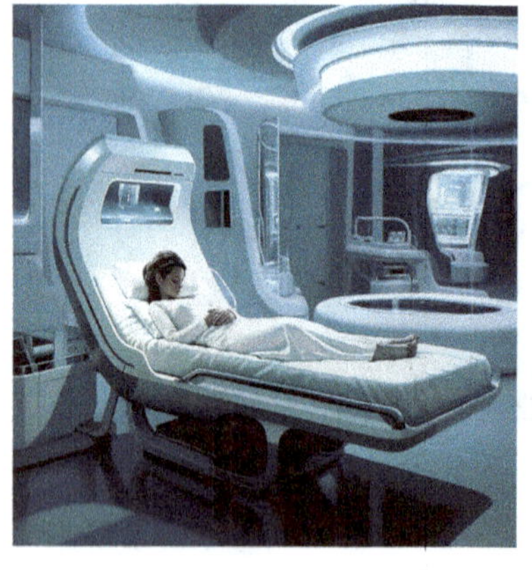

Moments before, Emily had been looking forward to a "girls' night out" with her sister, Rachel. Late in the afternoon, she approached an intersection. The light turned green, but she failed to notice the dark gray SUV fast approaching from the right. The SUV collided with Emily's smaller car and her car spun out, violently stopping at the curb.

The other driver suffered no serious injuries, and explained to the police she had "blacked out" as she approached the intersection, possibly from a diabetic condition.

At the hospital, ER doctors examined Emily, but they could not find any apparent reason for her to remain unconscious. There were no visible indications of head trauma, so they began testing for other possible causes.

Rachel kept checking her phone screen as the minutes ticked away. The room grew dim with the advancing hour, and questions swirled in her mind about where Emily could be. Then, as if to confirm her suspicions, the phone's buzz pierced the silence. She hesitated before answering the call. Her heart racing and the unfamiliar number on the caller ID only increased her fear.

"This is Officer Patterson from the police department. Are you Rachel Foster?"

Rachel's heart sank as she answered with obvious concern, "Yes, I'm Rachel. Why are you calling me?"

"I'm afraid I have some tough news about your sister, Emily. Your number was the emergency contact on the lock screen on her phone. There's been an accident, and they have transported her to the hospital."

"Is she alright?" Rachel asked.

"She doesn't appear to be seriously hurt, but you will need to come to the hospital. Emily is unconscious, and the doctors may want to ask some questions."

As Rachel wiped away tears, she said, "OK, I'll be there as soon as I can".

She would wait to call their mother until she knew more about Emily's condition.

The connection between the two sisters ran deep. Although separated by three years, they were otherwise like twins. Despite the age gap, their bond went beyond finishing one another's sentences. Yet matching their schedules proved a perpetual challenge. Emily, a gifted graphic artist in the world of advertising, frequently devoted herself to laborious hours on specialized projects. At 29, Rachel's path had led her through school to a bachelor's degree in nursing. But she had found her niche as an Occupational Health Nurse. Rachel's innate empathy set her apart, though it occasionally teetered on the brink of overwhelming compassion, prompting her to veer away from the relentless demands of hospital work.

Her duties frequently entailed tending to accident victims and fostering a well-established partnership with the local hospital staff.

The wait seemed unbearable until Rachel heard her name called. A nurse beckoned her through heavy doors to a small room on the side of a large hallway. Dressed in pale blue scrubs, the duty nurse, Sarah Thompson, appeared to be older than Rachel, perhaps in her late thirties, with a kind expression and short curly brown hair.

"Hi, Rachel, you're Emily's sister, right?" the nurse asked.

"Yes, is she going to be OK?" Rachel answered, flicking a bit of her hair away from her eyes.

"We can't say for sure now. We ran a few tests and hope to have some answers soon. There weren't any signs of head injury, but the doctors ordered a CT scan and an MRI, just to be sure."

Rachel wanted to know, "When can I see her?"

"We'll call you when she is back from the tests."

Returning to a seat in the ER waiting room, Rachel decided to break the news to their mom. She hesitated, her thoughts gathering the words she needed as she dialed the number.

"Hi, Mom," she said as her mother answered. "I'm at the hospital, with Emily. There's been an accident, but Emily's OK. I didn't call right away until I found out more. I don't want you to worry too much."

Rachel discouraged her mom from coming to the hospital, but, of course, her mom insisted on coming, anyway.

Later, as her mom arrived at the ER, she came and sat next to Rachel, holding her daughter's hand.

A different nurse took over the duty station, her hair gathered in a neat bun. Noticing the shift change, Rachel went to the desk to ask about any change in her sister's condition.

"Excuse me," Rachel asked the new duty nurse, "you tell me if there's any news on my sister? "

"Of course," she said, "I'll check for you. What is your sister's name and date of birth?"

Rachel responded, "Emily Foster, May 12th, age 26."

"Thank you, let me see," as she typed the information into the computer. "It looks like they have transferred her to the ICU. I'll call up there and get an update on her condition for you."

The nurse picked up the phone to call.

"Hi, this is the ER desk. Can you give me an update on Emily Foster? Her family is here, and they're worried about her."

Rachel overheard the ICU nurse on the phone. "They finished running the tests and took her back to her room." Rachel nodded in acknowledgment to the duty nurse and turned to repeat the information to her mother.

"Oh, thank goodness. Is she awake?" her mom asked.

The duty nurse relayed the question but shook her head no. "But you can go upstairs and wait there." She pointed to the doors on the left. "Go through those doors, and you'll find the elevators to the ICU on the fourth floor. The nurse's station can direct you to her room."

Rachel and her mom found the elevator, and on reaching the fourth floor, Rachel felt happy to see a familiar face. At the nurse's station, Susan Wells stood out with her curly red hair. Rachel knew her from nursing school. Susan appeared surprised and concerned to see Rachel there. The two exchanged waves and smiles as Rachel approached the desk. Her mom took a chair in the hallway.

"I'm surprised to see you here. How are you?" the nurse asked.

Getting right to the point, Rachel said, "We're here to see my sister, Emily Foster. Can you tell us how to find her room?"

Susan glanced at the list on a clipboard. "She's in 410, but we can only let one of you visit at a time. She's still unconscious."

"They only allow one at a time. You go first," and motioned to her mom to follow the nurse down the hall. After a few minutes, their mom and the nurse emerged from the room. The nurse beckoned for Rachel.

Rachel told her mom. "It's late, and you should go home. I'll let you know if anything changes." Her mom objected, but Rachel squeezed her mom's hand and smiled. "There's nothing you can do here. Better get some rest." Her mom nodded in agreement. The elevator door opened, and her mom looked back to see Rachel slipping into Emily's room.

The hospital room had a pleasant atmosphere, with off-white walls and a large window. The faint scent of disinfectant and medicine filled the air, accompanied by the steady beeping of the monitors.

Emily remained motionless in the center of the room, lying in a large hospital bed. White sheets and pale blue blankets covered her to her chest. Medical equipment surrounded the bed, including a heart monitor screen, an oxygen tank, and an IV bag hanging from a stand. The monitors displayed graphs and numbers, tracking Emily's condition.

After a few moments, Nurse Wells came to check on her patient. Rachel felt helpless as she stood next to her sister.

"Why is she still like this?" Rachel asked.

"Doctor Elliot said they don't know. She didn't suffer any serious injury; no broken bones, only some nasty bruises on her legs. They ran an MRI and some other tests, but you'll need to talk to the doctor for any more," the nurse explained.

Rachel felt worried. "But why?" she almost protested.

Nurse Wells told her, "I'm sorry, Rachel, I can't give you the answers about your sister's condition. However, I can tell you that the doctors will keep running tests until they find the answer."

"Thank you. Can I stay with her for a while more?" Rachel motioned toward the chair by the door. "I want to be with her."

"I don't think anybody will object. I'll check with Dr. Patel, the doctor on duty. If there's any problem, I'll let you know." The nurse pulled the door almost closed as she left.

Someone had recovered Emily's phone and purse from the wrecked car at the accident scene and had them delivered to the hospital.

Rachel found a small pillow in the room and tried to find a restful position in the chair as she gazed at Emily's face. In a short time, she drifted off to sleep. She dreamed about her sister, but the dream faded as she stirred awake. She strained to see the dimly lit clock, which showed something after two.

As Saturday morning dawned, the hospital room door opened, and the duty doctor entered. He smiled at Rachel as he noted the readings on the medical monitors and Emily's charts.

"Good morning," he said. "I'll be taking care of Emily today."

"Thank you. She's my sister. Can you tell me anything?"

"We're still waiting for more test results, but the MRI and CT scans didn't show any brain damage or internal bleeding. However, we are checking for other conditions like stroke, aneurysm, or any other neurological issues. We're also checking for any underlying medical conditions that could have triggered the coma."

Rachel wanted to know, "What kind of conditions?"

"There are a few possibilities: a severe infection, metabolic abnormalities, or even a drug overdose. We're running blood tests to check for those conditions."

Rachel stated adamantly, "Emily is not into drugs."

"I understand, but sometimes normal medications can have adverse reactions or interactions. We're checking for that possibility as well. Is there any family history of diabetes?"

"No, nothing like that. When will she wake up?" Rachel almost pleaded.

"It's hard to say at this point. We're doing everything we can to find the cause and decide on a treatment. But it's important to remember that recovery from a coma can be a slow and unpredictable process. We'll keep the family updated as we learn more." The doctor finished up, making notes on the chart attached to Emily's bed as he left the room.

Rachel played a voicemail from her sister earlier in the day, perhaps to hear her voice. She reached out to touch Emily's hand. The beeping of the monitors had a hypnotic effect. Her hand fell as she drifted off to sleep.

Again, she dreamed she saw her sister, but this time, Emily seemed she wanted to say something but couldn't. At the same time, Rachel sensed being thirsty.

Later in the morning, Susan Wells stopped by the room to check on the two sisters. The sound of the heavy door opening awakened Rachel. She smiled to see Susan and wanted to tell her about the dream.

"I had the strangest feeling," she told Susan. "You're going to think I'm crazy, but I saw Emily in a dream, and I felt like she wanted to tell me she's tired and very thirsty. Does that make any sense?"

"That really can't be," Susan answered. "The IV shows she's getting plenty of fluid. We keep track of that on her charts."

Dr. Elliot came in to check on Emily. The doctor, in his early 40s, had short black hair, almost like a military cut, with slight touches of gray. "Do we know who her doctor is?" he asked.

Rachael thought for a moment and then shook her head. "She told me she changed doctors a while back, but I'm sorry. I don't remember who her new doctor is."

Doctor Elliot thought for a moment. "It could be another dead end, but I would like to know if she's reacting to something prescribed."

Nurse Wells looked toward Rachel and then to the doctor as she asked, "Is it crazy to think that the patient might try to reach out to her sister in her dreams?"

Dr. Elliot looked surprised, but then he smiled. "A coma is a state of profound unconsciousness in which a person cannot be awakened and does not respond to stimuli. There is no clear scientific evidence to support the idea that a person in a coma can communicate through dreams. While people in a coma may exhibit some brain activity and may even experience their own dreams, there is currently no reliable way to communicate with them. I'm sorry."

Susan turned to Rachel, "This is the end of my shift, and the hospital has a great cafeteria, and they should be open about now. Maybe we can talk over breakfast?" Disappointed by the doctor's response, Rachel nodded in agreement, and they walked to the elevators.

The hospital cafeteria bustled with activity as the two joined the line. They worked their way through the food selections and found an open table.

As they sat down, Susan asked, "Tell me more about your dream."

"It felt so real! It was like she knew I was there, and she was trying to reach out to me for help. All I can think of is that was experiencing what Emily was feeling. I bet Dr. Elliot thinks I'm crazy. I bet he thinks we're *both* crazy."

"Maybe." Susan stretched her neck to see someone. "But I think I see someone who can help. Excuse me for a minute." She stood and walked over to where an older gentleman dressed in a suit was emptying his tray. She spoke with him briefly, and then he followed her back to their table.

"This is Dr. Eugene Phelps. He's a neurologist who stops by from time to time as a consultant. I told him about your dreams, and he might have some different ideas."

Dr. Phelps pulled over a chair from an empty table nearby.

"Hi, Rachel, I understand you experienced something in a dream. Tell me about it."

Rachel felt relieved. "In my dream I saw my sister reaching out to me. She didn't say anything, but I had the sensation of being trapped. And thirsty. It felt like Emily knew what had happened, and she tried to tell me..." Her voice trailed off as she gestured helplessly upward with her hands.

The doctor pursed his lips and tilted his head a bit before he spoke. "Tell me about how all this started. Why is your sister here?"

Rachel and the nurse pieced together the story of the past twenty-four hours for Dr. Phelps: the accident, the coma, the testing. They explained the doctors didn't understand why Emily remained unconscious.

"I see. Interesting," Dr. Phelps said. "I'm not going to tell you that you're crazy. Not at all. There's a history of research in this area that even goes back to Nikola Tesla and the 1880s. I recently saw a study by Dr. Stanley Critur at Saybrook University in California, citing a wealth of material supporting the possibility of telepathic effects occurring during dreams.

There are several books on the subject. Let me speak with your doctor. We may have uncovered a clue."

Rachel felt relieved and thanked the doctor as they finished their breakfast.

Rachel needed to go home and change, but she couldn't leave. She returned to Emily's room. Emily remained the same, still unconscious. The door to the room stood open, and Rachel glanced down the hall to see Dr. Phelps talking with Dr. Elliot, who had arrived on shift. Soon, both doctors walked toward Emily's room. They acknowledged Rachel but didn't speak. Dr. Elliot handed Emily's chart to Dr. Phelps and studied his response. Dr. Phelps nodded. Rachel smiled hopefully as her eyes followed the two doctors as they left the room.

Not long after, Dr. Elliot returned to the room. "Dr. Phelps thinks we may have overlooked something. We're going to run a different test on Emily. That might solve the puzzle for us." He reached out and grasped Rachel's hand. "Don't give up! Maybe you can wait outside while we set up."

Rachel reluctantly left the room to wait down the hallway as two nurses entered. A few moments later, one nurse left and returned with a blood glucose meter. About an hour had elapsed when Rachel finally saw Dr. Elliot coming toward her.

"I think we found the secret. In my consultation with Dr. Phelps, we looked more closely at your sister's blood work. On his suggestion, we found a case study describing a similar presentation of acute adrenal crisis in a minor trauma patient."

The doctor explained, "The adrenal glands produce vital hormones, including cortisol and aldosterone. In Emily's case, they failed to function properly, possibly because of the shock of the accident. Her body could not produce sufficient amounts of the hormones, which led to her condition. We tried an emergency intravenous steroid infusion to replace the lack of cortisol. She seemed to respond positively. I can't explain how, but the message about her being thirsty was the clue we needed."

The doctor continued, "In Emily's case, the shock from the accident likely caused a disruption in her adrenal gland function. Without adequate cortisol production, her body couldn't respond appropriately to stress, leading to a range of symptoms. One of the key indicators we noticed was her excessive thirst. This showed that her adrenal glands were not functioning properly, as the imbalance in electrolytes caused by inadequate aldosterone production can lead to increased thirst."

Hours later, Rachel watched as Emily stirred, her eyes fluttering open. As her vision adjusted to the soft light of the room, she turned her head to see Rachel standing by her side with a look of sheer relief and joy. Without hesitation, Rachel reached for the call button, pressing it urgently. Within moments, a nurse entered the room, the sound of her footsteps echoing against the tiled floor.

"Emily is awake!" Rachel exclaimed, her voice filled with a mix of excitement and anticipation.

The day nurse smiled warmly at the sight of Emily's conscious gaze. "Oh, thank goodness! I'll inform Dr. Elliot right away," she said, reaching for the phone to notify the doctor of Emily's awakening.

Emily awakened. "Rachel... Rachel, is that you?" "

"Welcome back! How are you feeling?"

Emily's mind swirled with confusion. She turned to her sister and said, "I had the strangest dream. I remember seeing you. I tried to tell you..."

Rachel smiled. "I know. You were in my dream, and you told me you felt thirsty. The doctors didn't know what to do. I told them about my dream, but it was hard to make them believe me."

"Is that possible? ...that you heard me? Wow, I can't wrap my head around it. It's amazing to think that we could connect that way."

Rachel reached out to hold her sister's hand. "I know. It's hard to believe. The doctors couldn't figure out how to help you, but when you told me about being thirsty in your dream, that was the clue. That's how the doctors brought you back."

"You were always there for me, big sister. I really can't wrap my head around all this, but I'm sure glad we have each other."

"That's all that counts, right, Em?"

Dr. Elliot arrived. His eyes lit up with delight as he saw Emily. He walked over to her bedside, checked the monitors, and confirmed that her vital signs were stable. Dr. Elliot stepped closer and stood beside Rachel. "Emily, it's wonderful to see you awake. How are you feeling?"

Emily's lips curved into a weak but grateful smile. "I... I'm glad to be back, that's for sure!" she said, her voice barely above a whisper as the emotion of the moment took over her.

Rachel's eyes welled up with tears as she took Emily's hand in her own. "Oh, Em, you do not know how relieved I am. I knew you were in there all along."

Dr. Elliot leaned in closer, his eyes focused on Emily's face, attentive to every word and expression. "Emily, we're so glad you've come back to us," he said, his voice filled with sincerity. "During your coma, we discovered you were experiencing locked-in syndrome, a condition where you were conscious but unable to move or communicate. It had been a difficult situation to diagnose initially, but thanks to Rachel's, hmmm, clue, we found the underlying cause."

Emily's eyes widen with curiosity and a renewed sense of hope. "What caused it, doctor? And what do we need to do to correct it?"

Dr. Elliot took a deep breath, his gaze conveying a mixture of compassion and professionalism. Answering the unspoken question on Emily's face, he said, "It appears that you had an unusual electrolyte imbalance that affected your nervous system, causing the locked-in syndrome. You were in an accident and something about that shock set it off. We'll need to keep a close eye on your electrolyte levels and provide targeted treatment to restore the balance. With time and proper care, we believe you can make a full recovery."

The weight of Emily's condition lifted, replaced by a renewed sense of hope and determination. She looked at Rachel, their eyes meeting with an unspoken understanding of their journey together.

Emily said, "Let's do whatever it takes. I'm ready to go home!"

Dr. Elliot nodded, his gaze reflecting admiration for Emily's resilience. "Emily. I'll ensure you receive the best care possible, and we'll work towards restoring your health and independence."

Over the next few days, Emily underwent a series of tests and treatments to address the electrolyte imbalance. Dr. Elliot and his medical team monitored her progress, setting the medications and fluids to restore balance and support her recovery.

Rachel asked for more time off from her job to stay with Emily..

Early one morning, Emily sat up in her hospital room as daylight peeked through the window. Dr. Elliot came in with a smile on his face.

"Good morning! Emily, your tests show significant improvement," Dr. Elliot announced confidently. "Your electrolyte imbalance is back to normal. I think you're about ready to go home. Your sister is already on the way."

Emily's eyes sparkled with hope and relief. The nurse assistant rolled her out to the hospital entrance. As Rachel helped her sister into her car, she asked, "So, what again are we going to do for our girls' night out?"

Emily thought for a moment and said, "No, let's go see mom. We can go to the movies any time."

A smile played across Rachel's lips as she nodded in agreement. "You're right, Em. Let's go see mom. She's been waiting for this moment as eagerly as we have," she said as she started the engine.

As they drove, the streetlights cast ethereal shadows on the pavement. The cool breeze whispered through the open windows.

The girl's home was bathed in the glow of the early dawn as Rachel pulled into the driveway, and the sisters stepped to the front door. Their mom had been waiting and heard the car as they drove up and the door opened. Emotion filled the reunion. When the sisters came inside, the three formed a circle of love and support. The worries, the pain, and the uncertainty of the past days seemed to melt away in that moment, replaced by a renewed sense of hope and gratitude.

With tears of joy streaming down her cheeks, their mom marveled at her daughter's strength and resilience.

"You two share an unbreakable bond, a connection that goes beyond the physical. I've always believed that the love between sisters is unique, but you've truly opened my eyes to its incredible power."

Rachel turned to her mother and sister. "If dreams could speak, maybe they'd tell us what we always knew deep down—that love is the bridge that keeps us together, even in the darkest times."

***

Chapter Fourteen

The Company Hired a Robot

B eep–Beep–Beep–Beep!

Shipping and receiving manager, David Lee, looked up from the paperwork on his desk through the window of his small office as a truck backed up to the loading dock. He recognized the name of the local delivery company and punched the button on his phone to call the Information Technology manager's office.

Tomi Singh answered, "What's up, David?"

"Your new toy is here." David punched the button to disconnect the call without waiting for a response.

Dave Lee had been with the company for over ten years. He took pride in keeping the shipping and receiving area organized and efficient. His stern approach didn't fool anyone. He was well-liked by the people who worked at the company. He also didn't like to waste time on formalities.

As he walked out onto the loading dock, the driver opened the squeaky roll-up door of the delivery van and handed him a clipboard. Inside the truck stood a single large crate with big black letters that spelled out

"Robotic Office System for Communication and Operational Efficiency." David signed the delivery order and handed it back to the driver.

Tomi soon arrived as David rolled the large pallet jack under the big crate in the delivery van to move it onto the loading dock.

In his early thirties, Tomi Singh was determined to find innovative IT solutions. He always kept up with the latest technology trends, and this was Tomi's new baby. He had convinced the board of directors and the CEO, Robert Johnson, that an artificial intelligence mobile robot could improve the company's efficiency and productivity.

Johnson interpreted that in dollar signs.

As the news spread, more people arrived at the loading dock. The shipment was exciting to some employees, but for others, not so much. Like HR director Robert Jones. Bob was among the doubters. He expressed concern about how employees might react to this machine's intrusion.

Last to arrive was Emily Jones, the Tech Support specialist. In her early twenties, she was naturally a problem-solver, open to new things if they would help her clients. She welcomed the new arrival to help her better manage technical support.

Someone in the group located a flatbed dolly. The crate was loaded on, and the people who had gathered on the loading dock filtered back to their offices. David and his assistant, Alex, rolled the crate to the freight elevator and up to the IT office. Inside the crate were several parts wrapped in plastic, along with bundled cables, motors, and other components. Tomi moved closer to inspect. As his hand rubbed the back of his head, he muttered, "Some assembly required." Alex picked out one of the heavier boxes and proclaimed: "Yes, but the battery *is included!*"

The various parts came together, ROSCOE took a familiar robotic shape. It had mechanical rollers, a display screen, and a robot head, complete with camera sensors for the eyes, while a pattern of holes covered a speaker where a mouth should be. There were sensor units at every point. The articulated arms included gripper-hands with connectors for various motorized tools and utility attachments. A collection of connectors decorated the back panel above the battery compartment.

Tomi had been reading the manual and reviewing online videos for weeks, so he knew exactly what to do. As he connected the last of the modules, he lifted the battery into place. A fiber optic cable connected the Local Area Network, or LAN port, to the company's mainframe rack.

IT assistant Alex looked on as Tomi pressed the control switch before he closed and latched the battery panel. The machine responded with a hum and a whir of motors as it came to life, concluding with a beep. The readout on the front panel screen spelled out the initials "R.O.S.C.O.E" and the word "Ready!"

At a nearby terminal, Tomi logged into the robot's admin interface and replaced the default with a secure password. Next, he went about configuring the robot's access to the company's Wi-Fi network so it could operate freely about the building. And of course, the robot could speak. Alex and Tomi browsed the selection until they decided on an appropriate voice for "ROSCOE". The voice they chose sounded dignified but not stuffy, somewhat smooth and almost melodic. The voice might allow employees to feel comfortable responding to a machine. At least, as comfortable as they could be, to a five-foot-tall metal and plastic box moving around on tread rollers.

The internal artificial intelligence engine went about accumulating information. As it scanned in the data, the built-in screen displayed the company's department directories, including employee photos, and mapped out the various locations within the building. The robot's optical sensors would enable it to navigate the hallways and recognize employees. This was the part that had Tomi worried. He had no serious concerns about data security. Security functions were integrated into the system framework. The manufacturer had satisfied those concerns. What he was concerned about was the reaction of the staff as they came to realize how much information the robot had stored.

What was most impressive was the artificial intelligence that allowed it to gain new knowledge as it gained more and more input data. It could analyze information and suggest improvements in marketing documents and accounting spreadsheets.

Finally, the time came to introduce ROSCOE to the board of directors and the CEO. CEO Johnson was a seasoned business-executive type who appeared to be in his early fifties. He presented an image of a leader expecting a high level of performance. Not so much ambitious as he was focused on growing the company. Tomi and Alex had convinced him that ROSCOE would help him achieve his goals. The board members, elected by the stockholders seated at the long executive table, showed no sign of doubting the decision. Actually, the board members rarely displayed any expressions at all.

Well, there was one. That *one* was Jack Thompson. He hid a smirk as the trio from IT entered the boardroom. Jack had always been skeptical of new technology and Artificial Intelligence in particular. As Jack caught Tomi's eye, the smirk became a forced smile.

While the CEO looked on from one end of the table, Tomi and Alex stood at the other, describing ROSCOE's capabilities and advantages to the board. Next it came time for ROSCOE to take over. ROSCO took control of the presentation on the large screen at the end of the large boardroom. Tomi's presentation listed the advantages of the new mobile artificial intelligence robot technology. The board appeared impressed and smiled his satisfaction as Alex issued a voice command to ROSCOE. The trio left the room together.

The CEO and the board members voiced no objections, which meant that ROSCOE had passed the first test.

The corporate website created a central hub for employees to access important information and communicate. It helped them to carry out their daily tasks even when working from home or off-site. As the first task, ROSCOE generated a scheduling system. The system provided a way for employees to schedule a visit from the robot. The robot accessed the internal Content Management System and began constructing a new welcome screen. It detailed how to use the new resources and included illustrated examples. Next, ROSCOE accessed the network database and generated a calendar that was connected to the corporate scheduling system. ROSCOE created an internal email message sent to each employee. Job completed, ROSCOE announced, "Ready," and the robot's front panel screen spelled out the word at the same time.

First to sign up for ROSCO's aid, Emily headed the company's Technical Support team. She expressed the need to streamline the system to make it easier for customers to get answers.

ROSCOE rolled into her office, stopped in front of her desk, and greeted her by name. A bit surprised to hear the robot speaking directly to her, Emily ran through a prepared list of problems she needed to solve.

Emily asked ROSCOE, "How can we handle surges of customer online contacts that sometimes overwhelm our limited staff?"

ROSCOE's voice responded, "Instead of your current text window, we propose a new chatbot powered by Artificial Intelligence. We'll program it to identify the most common problems and use the customer files to provide answers. The AI can gather the customer's information and generate an accurate response to their questions in real-time."

Emily was concerned. "What about my staff?"

"The system can handle many customer contacts at once, eliminating hold-time and routing only the more complex questions to your staff. If a customer's question requires human help, the system can seamlessly hand off the conversation to your support staff, along with providing all the relevant information and context to ensure a smooth transition.".

"How long will it take to create that system?" Emily asked.

Generating computer programming is something Artificial Intelligence is especially good at doing. ROSCOE linked the new chatbot response system to the company's customer database and logins. In a short time, ROSCOE's screen spelled out the now familiar "READY" response and announced: "Let's test it".

Emily created a test customer and account information. She logged into the company's website from her phone. She paused for a moment and typed in a complex question. The new chatbot responded with a link to an appropriate resource to answer the question.

"But what if it can't find the right answer?" Emily asked. "Most of the complaints are about the time it takes."

ROSCOE said, "Ask an impossible question."

Emily knew what to do. She typed in a question with confusing wording based on a tough call they had recently handled. The chatbot analyzed the message and apologized to the customer for not having an appropriate answer. It asked the customer to wait for a human response while it switched the customer to the support staff. The system reproduced the complete text conversation on the staff member's screen, along with a summary of the customer's contact and product information. Randy, the support tech, saw that he had all the information to work from and responded to the "test" customer on the chat screen.

Impressed by the result, Emily continued, "We have one native Spanish speaker on staff. Can we include a Spanish option, and if a human response is needed, can that customer be directed to our Spanish speaker?"

"That program module is activated. Spanish customers can only connect with the right staff person," ROSCOE responded.

"But what about voice calls?"

Once again, ROSCOE had a ready answer. "We will integrate voice recognition software into the phone system in the same way. It will answer in a human voice and offer an alternate language option. It will respond the same as the chatbot. The system will learn from the questions asked and build the data resource. If it can't provide a suitable answer, it will route the call to your support staff. That way, your staff can manage a larger number of calls with minimal hold time."

ROSCOE promised to have the software generated and integrated into the phone system for testing the next day.

"It feels strange thanking a computer," Emily said.

ROSCOE made a beep sound, then turned and left the room.

The next request came from Sarah Rodriguez in Marketing. A natural communicator in her early thirties, Sarah had a good understanding of marketing. Above all, she was a good listener who made time to understand others' points of view. Active on social media, she kept up with the pulse of her market community.

ROSCOE rolled into Sarah's office at the exact time of the scheduled appointment. Sarah, however, had concerns about how her staff would react to a robot. She began with a simple task: "Hello, ROSCOE. We need to find the right target audience for our new product line. Can you do that?"

ROSCOE said, "Let us connect to your terminal so you can direct me to the product line."

Sarah brought up the new product line.

ROSCOE scanned the document files and images and began generating text output: "Here's a list of our current customers who might be interested in the new products. We can generate a newsletter for your review, and you can send it to those customers. I can also create some sample social media posts. You'll find the files in a special folder on your home screen."

Sarah smiled. "That would have taken me a long time. I'm sure glad to have you around!"

Nearby, Luke Elliot, the staff artist, felt his job threatened by AI-generated graphics. He even made doodles on his notepad, showing a robot melting into a blob on the floor. However, of course, he made sure his boss, Sarah, didn't see those drawings.

Next came John Stephens in Human Resources. At the scheduled time, ROSCOE rolled down the hall and came to a stop in front of John's desk.

Robert got right to the point: "I need a simple way to evaluate employee job performance for the quarter."

ROSCOE responded: "We can generate a report with all the relevant data. Would you like me to send it to your company email?"

"That would be good. When can you get it to me?" Robert asked.

"Check your email now. Is there anything we missed?" ROSCOE replied.

"I'll look it over and let you know. Can I reply to your email?"

"Yes, you may respond to the email." ROSCOE answered. "What else do you need to be more effective in your job?"

Robert nodded toward the staff as he described his next concern. "We have a lot of employees. The turnover is not excessive, but I'm concerned about potential threats from former employees. We need a defense strategy to prevent unauthorized access to the building. What can we do?"

Again, ROSCOE had a ready solution. "We have accessed the photo ID files of all current and former employees. We can integrate facial recognition into the security cameras to prevent unauthorized access to the building and compile a cost/benefit report for approval by the accounting department."

Robert responded sternly, "Most mass shootings take place at the workplace. That would address my most serious concerns."

The robot beeped, and the screen blinked "READY" as ROSCOE moved to the hallway and back to the IT department for the next task assignment.

Lisa Martinez, in the Facilities Management office, had only glanced at the notices about updating passwords when she found an email in her inbox telling her that her password had expired, and she assumed a connection.

Subject: Password Expiration Notice:

Hello Lisa,

I hope this message finds you well. I am reaching out to let you know that your company password will expire soon. In order to ensure the security of our system, we require all users to renew their passwords on a regular basis.
Please follow the link to access the password reset page: **CLICK HERE**
Once there, you will be able to create a new password that meets our new security requirements.
If you have any issues with this process or have questions, please don't hesitate to contact me.

Best regards,
Information Technology Department

When Lisa clicked *HERE*, it brought up what appeared to be the regular company login screen. Lisa did not think to notice the different URL in the browser address bar. She entered her password, and a message on the screen thanked her for "renewing" her password. She wondered why she had not been required to make a new password, but thought nothing of it.

Within minutes, a hacker used Lisa's password to log into the company's network and got to work exploring exposed documents and files on Lisa's terminal. At that exact moment, ROSCOE detected the login from an unauthorized external internet address or IP. A quick check of an online resource revealed it originated from a local internet service provider. ROSCOE promptly isolated Lisa's computer from the network, limiting the damage to the files on her computer. The hacker had briefly gained access to the company server, but the most sensitive data remained secured behind a security firewall.

Meanwhile, ROSCOE alerted Tomi, who blocked the intruder's access by resetting Lisa's password. He ran a scan of the entire network to make sure there were no new hidden files. He reported the steps to ROSCOE through an isolated side network. ROSCOE began a deep scan of the system for any malware that might have been installed. ROSCOE would also need to carefully scan Lisa's computer for hidden "bots" that might have been set for later activation.

ROSCOE reviewed Lisa's email account and discovered the fake email notice. The robot next posted a notice on the company forum warning against realistic-looking fake email notices about password expirations and communicated the information about the hacker's source IP address to Tomi. Tomi conferenced with the CEO, along with Tom Watson, in the legal department, as they agreed to contact local law enforcement.

A short time later, two investigators arrived at the front reception desk. One detective, Lt. Brown. The other officer's badge identified him as Sgt. Jones. They asked to be escorted to Tomi's office on the second floor. When they arrived at the IT office, they saw ROSCOE. The officers were not expecting to see a robot.

Sgt. Jones asked Tomi, "What's THAT thing?".

Tomi replied, "That's Roscoe, our mobile AI system." It detected the intrusion and blocked the affected terminal from the network. Lt. Brown smiled with an understanding nod. Brown mentioned to Tomi he had been qualified in cyber security. Tomi then explained how the hacker had gained access through a compromised employee password. The officers asked what they knew about the extent of damage, potential motives, and recent employee terminations.

Tomi responded, "Yes, we have had a few employees leave, but I don't recall any who left under bad circumstances."

Lt. Brown asked, "Can you provide us with a list of those employees?" Tomi nodded yes.

"We traced the intrusion to this IP address at a local Internet provider, so the intruder is not far away." Tomi said, handing Officer Brown a section of a log printout with the intruder's information.

The other officer asked, "Is there any other information that you think might be pertinent to this situation?"

Alex stood nearby, listening to the conversation, and looked puzzled as he looked at Tomi.

Tomi turned toward Alex, "He means, do we have any suspicions." To the officer, he said, "We'll let you know if we come up with anything."

After the officers left, Tomi called Lisa's extension. She sounded upset and worried, explaining that her computer began acting strangely. Tomi assured her he and Alex would visit her office to address the issue. Lisa's response sounded relieved. Her computer was isolated from the main network, so she had not seen the notice warning about not responding to fake password reset notices via email.

Tomi and Alex arrived to find Lisa still stressed and bewildered about the situation. She described how her computer seemed to be haunted, with the cursor moving by itself until it stopped. After that, she couldn't do anything. The computer refused to work.

Lisa looked perplexed.

"The email said it was from you," she complained. "It said I had to renew my password. I think I saw something about that on the company forum, but I didn't pay much attention. A little later, my computer went crazy...."

"I did not send that email," Tomi explained. "A scammer tricked you. But we're lucky we have ROSCOE. The robot detected a hacker in your computer and isolated it to prevent the damage from spreading. We need to scan your computer to make sure nothing nasty got planted inside. That will take some time. Alex brought you a laptop so you can get back to work. It already has you logged in with a temporary password. You can take it to the other desk while Alex gets to work on your computer. Don't worry. No serious damage was done, and the police are investigating. You need to be more cautious. And read the notices on the company forum more carefully, ok?" He smiled at Lisa. She relaxed a bit and smiled back as she accepted the laptop and took it to a nearby desk.

Alarm bells rang in the security office. The new facial recognition camera system had detected an unauthorized person at the employee entrance. Marcus, the chief of security, checked the camera. A pass lock keypad and a camera secured the interior door. He saw a hooded person using a metal rod to strike the break-proof glass on the inside employee entrance door. There was no one else in the room, so he pressed a button that locked the outer door, trapping the dangerous intruder inside. That also prevented any other employees from entering the enclosed entrance. Pressing an intercom button, he instructed the intruder to remain calm and await the police.

Next, he called 9-1-1 and reported that an unauthorized intruder had been captured in the employee entryway. The operator told him officers were on the way. By then, the security software had identified the intruder as a former employee.

Marcus Johnson had once been a military officer. Now, in his second career, he still looked the part, with a muscular build and closely shaved hair. He was comfortable with new technology, but he admitted he still had reservations about ROSCOE. That might have changed.

Twenty minutes later, his extension rang, and he let the officers in. They took the unauthorized intruder into custody without a struggle and transported him to the police station for interrogation. If the company pressed charges, the initial offense could be trespassing or unauthorized entry.

But at that point, the motive remained a mystery. Tomi made a copy of the security video and sent it to the police to include in their investigation. The facial recognition system did not identify the intruder as a former employee.

The police interrogation of the intruder did not provide any useful information until they ran a fingerprint check and confirmed the identity of twenty-seven-year-old Michael Williams. A previous conviction was related to theft at a warehouse where he had been employed. Williams refused to provide any motivation for attempting to access the building. A common thug would have tried to smash the keypad, but he had attacked the security glass on the door instead. The police held Williams, awaiting word from the company attorney. The attorney would need to let them know if the company would press charges for the damage. A final decision on that needed to come from the CEO. The company provided a summary of William's brief time as an employee.

Meanwhile, ROSCOE reviewed the computer access log for the employee entrance passkey. Tomi had taken the precaution of changing her access code when her company password was updated. During the intrusion, the access log recorded attempts to Lisa's employee pass code key. ROSCOE passed along that information too. Tomi and Alex immediately related it to the hacker's attack on Lisa's computer. Break-ins don't fit the profile of the average hacker.

What was the connection?

The investigating officers brought in the two other officers who had responded to the hacking complaint. Detective Lt. Brown and the officer arrived at the CEO's office at nine the next morning.

As they sat down, Robert Johnson asked, "What have you come up with?"

Brown began, "The officers who worked on your intruder incident had reason to suspect a connection to the hacking event. It turns out they were right. We identified the location where the hacker originated the phishing email. Your robot's information identified the entry code the intruder tried to use unsuccessfully. The suspect is in custody, awaiting a hearing on the attempted breaking and entering charge. We intend to add computer crime charges stemming from the hacker attack on your employee."

Johnson smiled, "Well, that's good news!"

"Yes, but there's some bad news," Brown continued. "We needed to find the motive. We kept pressing the prisoner until he finally admitted he got paid to make you look bad. The transaction took place in cash from an unknown party he met at a local bar.From what we can tell, it appears the intruder intended to make it look like the company wasted money on the new mobile computer robot. Can you think of anyone who would be motivated to do that?"

The CEO's face looked serious for a moment as he tried to decide how to respond. A name did come to mind, but would it be enough to make an accusation?

He began, "I might, but if I'm mistaken, it could create serious problems. Can we keep this confidential?"

The officers agreed. "Who do you suspect?" the second officer asked.

"This can't get out," jotting a name on a notepad along with some other information. He didn't want anyone nearby to hear him say it out loud.

The officers looked at the notepad. "Do you have a photo?"

The CEO nodded and pulled a photo from a file in the horizontal file cabinet behind his desk.

Hoping to find more information on the stranger who hired the intruder, detectives went to the bar the suspect had identified. The bar owner directed them to the bartender. When officers showed the bartender the picture, he remembered seeing the man in the picture. He stood out because he didn't fit in with the usual customers.

Officer Johnson spotted security cameras. The owner said the recordings were cataloged off-site and provided the contact information for the security company.

After a few days, the security company delivered a data drive with video files to the police station. Detective Lt. Brown sifted through the video and found Williams, the man they had in custody, standing with the person who matched the photo of Jack Thompson. That provided the connection they needed and enough suspicion to bring the board member in for questioning.

Jack Thompson was a prominent and wealthy individual who described himself as an investor and entrepreneur. His address was, not surprisingly, in a gated subdivision. The officer and the detective presented their identification at the gate. They found the address and walked up to the front door. Brown looked up at the security camera as he pressed the button. After a moment, as the detective raised his hand to knock, the door opened. Thompson had a scowl on his face.

"I'm Detective Lt. George Brown, and this is my partner, Sergeant Steve Jones. We need to talk to you about the recent attack at the company where you serve on the board of directors."

Thompson stiffened as he stepped back into the doorway. "I know nothing about it."

Sergeant Jones asked, "Are you sure? We have reason to believe you know the intruder who attempted to get past the entrance security."

Thompson shook his head. "I come in contact with a lot of people," he insisted.

"Mr. Thompson, we need you to come to the station to discuss it. You can give us your side of the story there."

Thompson stood firm. "I'm not going anywhere with you. You don't have any evidence."

"I'm afraid we do. We have a confession from the man you hired," said Sergeant Jones.

After a brief hesitation, Thompson sighed and shrugged. "Fine!" he said. "Let me grab my coat."

CEO Robert Johnson called a special board meeting on Monday morning at 9 am. The notice said only there would be information about the recent security incidents.

The board members gathered, and the CEO introduced the two officers. Detective Brown spoke first.

"We have been investigating the recent cyberattack and the attempted break-in. Through our investigation, and with the help of your IT department, we connected the events, resulting in two arrests. The first arrest was Michael Williams, an individual who was hired to hack into the network. He was also the person who had been trapped at the employee entrance. We remain unsure of his intentions, had he successfully gained access through the employee entrance. He is known to hold grudges against large companies, possibly stemming from his release from his employment at a local warehouse."

One of the board members spoke up. "You said there were two arrests?"

"That's correct," said Officer Jones. "The other person is a member of this board." A gasp filled the room as the board members looked around.

"You may have noticed Mr. Jack Thompson's absence," the officer continued. "We took him into custody late yesterday, and he has been released on bond pending trial. According to the confession from Mr. Williams, He admitted Thompson paid him to make this CEO look bad. It appears Mr. Thompson resented Mr. Johnson's selection as CEO. A judge approved our request for a search warrant, and we got more evidence from Mr. Thompson's residence. We believe we have enough for the District Attorney to charge him with conspiracy to commit cyber crime and possibly as an accomplice to the attempted break-in.

Detective Brown was next to speak. We should acknowledge the invaluable assistance provided in solving this case. We were assisted by your Information Technology office and one more. That would be our new mechanical friend, Mr. ROSCOE.

The board members responded with polite applause for the two officers and ROSCOE. The officers turned to leave, but not before giving a short wave of salute to the robot.

Board member Susan Worth leaned over to Mary Wiggins: "I knew this robot would be a good thing".

Mary glanced over at ROSCOE and turned back to Susan as she whispered, "You're not going to believe this, but I think that darn robot winked at me!"

***

Chapter Fifteen

Interview with an Alien

In Nexus Broadcasting Network's dimly lit satellite control room, racks of equipment hummed with the soft whir of computer fans. Mark Foster, the network satellite engineer, sat at his control monitor. He glanced at the studio clock as he awaited a scheduled feed from the West Coast. Startled by a sound, he looked up at the satellite feed monitor to see a strange creature. Mark's gaze was fixed on the screen and a sudden flashback sent a shiver down his spine.

Jolted back to his senses by the call buzzer on the IFB[1] intercom, he pressed the talk button and said quickly, "Let me get back to you."

"We have a problem with the feed," came the reply from the West Coast satellite truck.

"Yes, I know," Replied Mark. Obviously, they were not aware of what he was seeing.The alien creature on the screen began speaking with a strange accent. Mark instinctively reached to press the feed record function on his console.

---

1. The IFB is a special intercom circuit that consists of a mix-minus program feed sent to an earpiece worn by talent via a wire, telephone, or radio receiver (audio that is being "fed back" to talent) that can be interrupted and replaced by a television producer's or director's intercom microphone.

"I am Zypteron," it said. The alien creature had large, almond-shaped eyes set in an overly large gray head devoid of visible ears. The creature's head had no hair and tapered past a tiny nose to a small mouth that did not move when it spoke. Its pale gray skin was lighter than the dense fabric of the uniform or suit. A hand with a rounded thumb and three slender fingers with no fingernails gestured toward the camera as the alien spoke. "My world is known to you as Zeta Reticuli. It is far from your planet." Zypteron's voice resonated with an otherworldly quality, translated into human language in a voice that sounded both artificial and electronic. "Knowledge of our existence has been revealed to some among your species, but it is now for a broader understanding to unfold."

Zypteron leaned further toward the camera with large, unblinking eyes. "We have chosen this network for our communication." The alien's message continued, both measured and stilted, inferring a totally different language structure.

"This is an invitation for you to submit your inquiries should we wish to respond. We shall return in seven days from this, when the time is twelve, Universal Time. Signal your agreement by transmitting your inquiries by this satellite channel, preceded by a sequence of five tones."

The Zypteron paused. "At the designated juncture, we shall manifest once more for your broadcast, wherein some answers you seek may be revealed."

With that, the transmission ended, and the screen went blank.

Mark paused to settle his nerves. After a few moments, he reached to stop the recording. He pressed the IFB control and said to the West Coast satellite crew, "Reschedule in one hour. Acknowledge?"

"Acknowledged," came back the reply.

Mark gathered his thoughts before dialing Richard Blaine's number.

Richard "Richie" Blaine was the general manager at Nexus Broadcasting. A shrewd businessman, he rose to his position, not through a background in broadcasting, but through a series of corporate maneuvers. As with many executives in broadcasting, he had little insight into what being a broadcaster was about.

"Blaine," the manager answered. "Who's this?" he asked impatiently.

"This is Mark in satellite operations. There's something here you need to see. Can you come down?"

"Is it important?" he asked.

Mark replied with deliberation in a lowered tone, "More important than you can imagine, sir."

As Blaine entered the room, Mark closed the door behind him and motioned him toward the control console.

"How can I explain this? We received an unusual transmission feed today, which requires your attention."

"Explain what?" the general manager responded, his tone a mix of curiosity and mild irritation.

Mark knew he had to tread cautiously, hoping to convey the gravity of the situation without divulging too much at once.

"Mr. Blaine," Mark began, "earlier today, while setting up for a satellite feed, something unexpected happened. The only way to explain it is for you to see it for yourself. You might want to sit down for this..." He reached for the button to play the recorded video.

As the video played, the manager leaned toward the screen and arched an eyebrow. His initial irritation gave way to fascination mixed with a hint of skepticism. "Is this real?" he questioned slowly, turning to face Mark, almost accusingly. "Surely, it's one of those, ... you know, deep fakes, right?" His tone changed. "You're trying to pull one over on me, aren't you.?" Blaine clearly did not know how to deal with this situation.

Mark stopped the playback. His eyes turned to lock with Blaine's bewildered gaze. "Yes, sir. This ... alien," He pointed to the screen, "claims to be from the planet Zeta Reticuli. That matches up with the information we have been getting from our news sources lately. It would seem they have decided to reveal what our own governments, the world governments, have been unwilling to tell us."

Unconvinced, his boss challenged, "Why does it sound like that? Its lips don't even move"

Mark had an explanation. "I believe they normally communicate telepathically. I think what we heard was some kind of translation machine. It overrode our one-way down link. It was meant for us. Nobody else saw it."

The manager's suspicions turned in another direction. Blaine leaned in and asked, "Why us? Why Nexus?"

Mark took a deep breath before responding, "You saw the recording. We are being offered an exclusive interview with conditions: we submit questions, but I feel the questions need to represent different parts of the world. The alien's response will come to us in a satellite feed one week from now. We could handle it like any remote news interview. The alien will respond in the satellite down link."

Blaine pondered for a moment, his fingers tapping on the control panel. "So, we have a chance at the biggest scoop in history, is that it?"

Mark nodded. "Yes, sir. Our network would have the world's attention like never before."

Blaine considered the implications, "But here's what we need to do, Mark. From now until the interview takes place, this process needs to be conducted with the utmost security. We can't let any of the other networks or, much worse, social media, get even a hint of it. Not one word gets out, understood?"

Mark replied, almost like a military recruit, "Understood, sir. We'll keep this under tight wraps."

Blaine continued, now fully grasping his authority, "The reporters who will take part in the interview need to think we are interviewing some high-ranking government official with secret knowledge. We can't afford to raise any suspicion."

Mark nodded in agreement, confirming his grasp of the obvious. "We'll make sure of that, sir."

"I'm putting Emily Clark in charge of this operation. You fill her in on what's going on."

With that, Blaine pointed a finger at Mark for emphasis, turned and darted out of the room.

Mark called the news director's office. Emily Clark answered on the first ring.

"Emily, there's something I need to show you. Can you stop by the satellite control room?"

"Sure, Mark, is something wrong?" she asked.

"It's not that there's something wrong, but you will want to see what I just recorded off the satellite feed."

Emily agreed and arrived in the satellite control room almost magically a few moments later.

"OK, whacha got for me?" she asked.

Mark motioned toward the large monitor as he played the recording of the alien message. This time, he played the entire recording, including the details of the arrangement. Privately, Mark felt uneasy as the alien appeared on the screen.

"Have you shown this to Richie?" she asked.

"I did, and he put it all in your hands," Mark responded.

Emily replied with a grimace. She slapped the side of her head with her palm, glancing skyward. "Of *course* he did."

"Richie said we can't let any of the other networks or social media get wind of it."

"No kidding!" she said knowingly. "OK, this is how we work it: I'll fill in Michael and Sarah before the broadcast so they don't fall apart in shock on the air. Nobody else needs to know. We'll have to give Alex Ramirez some kind of made-up story so he doesn't come unglued and start pushing the wrong camera buttons or forget to push any button at all while we're live. And under no circumstances is Rachel to get any hint of what is happening."

Rachel Turner, the online media director, was already deep into conspiracy theories. There was no way she could be trusted to keep a secret like this.

Emily stopped and looked up at the ceiling, and her eyes traced her path toward the door as she was leaving. "I didn't need this. I've lost enough sleep over all the political crap."

After Emily left the room, Mark glanced at the clock and turned his attention to the West Coast feed.

Emily had a lot on her shoulders. For many reasons, they decided to pre-record the interview questions. In the few remaining hours of the day, she began contacting her selection of field reporters and stringer[2] reporters, telling them each to prepare one question for an undisclosed person. She told them to assume it to be a high-ranking former official with special knowledge of the government's secret alien projects. Some reporters were on the other side of the world, none too happy to be awakened about something that was not a new war or world disaster. This was one assignment she didn't feel comfortable trusting in email. Emily discussed the kind of questions that would be required and asked that they text the

---

2. A "stringer" reporter is someone who is under contract to a news
   service, paid by the story and not on salary.

questions to her privately, rather than using email. They would need to await her response before recording their questions. She set a three-day deadline for the feeds to be transmitted and screened for her approval prior to the broadcast date.

Emily provided Carol Anderson with only enough information to generate the Teleprompter scripts for reporter lead-ins for the on-the-air anchors. Janna Morrison would need to set up the lower-third titles for the reporters on the Chyron, [3] but that could come later. Maya Silverstone, with her usual artistic genius, could come up with the promo graphics, of course. Each in its turn.

That night, as Mark tried to sleep, he kept having flashbacks to his own personal close encounter. It had been years since that terrifying night, but the memories returned to haunt him. He tossed and turned in his bed, the room lit by the soft glow of his alarm clock marking the hours. Images from the past flooded his mind. He saw the blinding light. He revisited the sensation of weightlessness and the feeling of being pulled upward against his will. Mark felt his heart beating fast as he remembered being in a strange corridor with gray creatures with big eyes and long limbs looking at him with intensity. The memories were so vivid, so visceral, that he could almost smell the sterile, metallic scent of the alien craft. He had told no one of his experience and was certain he never could.

Desperate to shake off the memories, Mark reached for the water bottle on his nightstand. He took several deep breaths, trying to steady his hand to drink. This was different, he told himself. The alien was there to communicate. He was in no personal danger. This time.

The fear lingered. Mark knew he had to overcome his terror for the sake of the network, his job, and the historic event that was about to take place. He closed his eyes and focused on the rhythmic sound of his own breathing, determined to push the past to the recesses of his mind and face the extraordinary encounter that awaited him and the world. Still, he was sure the nightmares would return.

---

3. A Chyron is a text-based graphic overlay displayed at the bottom of a television screen or film frame, as closed captioning or the crawl of a newscast, named for the Chyron corporation, much as the word Xerox has come to mean any copy machine.

Back at the network the next day, a feeling of urgency infected the entire staff, even those who had no clue what was going on behind the scenes. Maya Silverstone, the graphics artist, stopped Mark in the hall to ask him what was happening. Her obsession with detail went beyond fonts and formatting. As any true artist, she was sensitive to the world around her and had picked up on the urgency in the building. Mark dismissed her fears by telling her,

"We've got a big story in the works. You'll be filled in on it soon enough," as he smiled and pressed past her to the satellite feed center and locked the door behind him.

Later that day, Mark received an internal email from Emily listing the first of the scheduled feeds from the overseas field reporters. She must have worked all night reviewing and approving the questions. The reporter satellite feeds continued coming in for the rest of the week.

By the end of the week, everything was ready. As the time ticked away toward the special event, Mark had a sudden fear that the alien would not be there, that it had been a hoax after all. He steadied his nerves as the alien finally appeared on the large satellite monitor screen, awaiting the start of the broadcast. Mark accessed the satellite talk-back channel, hoping the alien could hear him, as he questioned, "Soundcheck?".

Zypteron responded: "Soundcheck." Mark decided the alien must have seen the movie "Network."

Pressing the call button again, Mark replied, "Soundcheck, confirmed. Satellite feed ready."

Mark waited before sending the satellite feed to Alex Ramirez in the network control room just yet. His video monitor for the "program" feed from the control room blinked on with a wide shot of the news anchors seated at the news desk. The studio lights dimmed and brightened as lighting director Robert Carter programmed the automatic controls.

The Chyron previewed various titles. Carol had come through with her usual genius, with a SIG slide that said what it needed to without giving away the secret that was to be revealed. As the program monitor switched back to the wide shot of anchor desk, the makeup artist was putting touches of powder on news anchor Sarah Sommers to dull any light reflections.

As she faced the camera, Sarah's personality switched on like one of the studio lights. She was at once both magnetic and relatable as she twirled a pencil like a miniature baton.

Beside her, Michael Malone, the other news anchor, shuffled through papers on his desk, periodically looking up at the floor director, who was nervously pacing between the studio cameras and talking into his headset.

A large transparent plastic Nexus Broadcasting Network logo spread across the front of the news desk. Behind the host anchors was a graphic of a world map, looking more like a scene from the Matrix.

The control room was a flurry of activity. Lisa Reynolds operated three remote cameras, adjusting the zoom and focus for the news desk and the mystery interview guest's big screen. She set each of the remaining cameras for medium close-up shots of the news hosts.

Technical Director Alex Ramirez switched between the camera shots. He reviewed the rundown sheet for the program, noting that each of the reporter videos showed a "ready" mode on his computer screen. His preview monitors displayed each of the studio cameras and the pre-roll of the first of the reporter videos. Everything was there except the satellite feed.

Out of sight of the studio floor, Sarah Anderson focused on the Teleprompter control. Next to her, Rachel, the Online Director, was busy setting up the social media posts. The public already speculated about what the broadcast might reveal, and social media exploded. Would it be another revelation by Rick Doty, Stanton Friedman, or even Bob Lazar, or would it be some mysterious anonymous CIA agent? The conspiracy theorists were already hotly battling the skeptics. Some networks said a large cigar-shaped spaceship was hovering over Atlanta, but the U.S. Space Surveillance Network had not confirmed it. The main satellite uplink was in Atlanta.

The broadcast, set for noon Universal Time or GMT, was seven o'clock at the network headquarters in New York. They cut the last hour of the morning show for the special event. Across the world, the clocks moved toward 14 hours in Germany and 5 in the afternoon in South Africa.

In the main studio, producer David Mitchel shouted on the intercom, "Two minutes to live!"

Mitchel had learned the secret only moments before. The thought had crossed his mind that this momentous televised event could make Orwell's *War of the Worlds* look like a rehearsal for the Macy's Day Parade.

In the communication headsets, TD (Technical Director), Alex Ramirez, called for the opening camera shots. He clicked the intercom to the satellite control center: "Ready on remote." For the first time, Mark let the crew see the alien. All eyes stared in amazement at the program monitor. A second passed, then five. The crew then accepted the reality of the situation and got back to their responsibilities. After all, they were professionals who had witnessed live reports from war zones.

The floor director, holding a clipboard with the Run Sheet in one hand and raising a finger on the other, called out the countdown to airtime.

"Five ... four... three ... two..... " (The "one" was silent.) At zero, the red light on camera two lit up as his finger dropped, pointing to anchor Michael Malone.

"Good day," Malone began, focused intently on the Teleprompter text projected onto the glass in front of the camera lens.

"To say that this is a moment in history is to minimize the impact this event will have on the world. To provide a background for today's interview, our special guest, who you are about to meet, appeared unexpectedly on our satellite feed. At first, we were not sure if what we were seeing was real. In this day, anything is possible." Malone stiffened as he leaned forward. "But I can assure you, our guest is real."

The director switched to camera three and Sommers: "Our reporters today represent a cross-section of world cultures. We have selected a sampling of our NBN reporters from around the world, from Canada to Mexico, from Germany to South Africa, to India, as well as here in the United States. Our reporters have not seen or met our special guest, but you will now." The camera switched to the studio-wide shot to show the giant screen. Zypteron nodded to the unseen audience.

The floor director raised his arm and motioned for Malone to face camera one for a close-up as he continued. "We begin in Berlin, Germany, with NBN reporter Klaus Müller."

The video recording of Klaus Müller began: "I would like to ask a question that has been on the minds of many in our country and, perhaps, around the world. It has been long rumored that our earlier German government once sought to establish an Antarctic base with the goal of contacting extraterrestrial beings. Can you tell us whether those rumors are true?"

Ramirez switched to the satellite feed as Zypteron spoke. "We can confirm that there was a base established. The base you refer to was known as Base 211 or New Swabia. We became aware of the intentions of that government and did not involve ourselves in the activities. There were experiments conducted at that facility, but those experiments failed to achieve any of the goals for world dominance."

Sarah was next tasked with introducing the reporter from Canada. "Now, here is Morgan Riley in Montreal."

"Hello," the reporter began, "Can you provide any insight into the many reports of human abductions and whether they were, indeed, conducted by beings from beyond our world?"

In his office, in satellite control, Mark Foster squirmed in his chair.

Zypteron responded: "The reports of abductions hold elements of truth, but they are not uniform in their accuracy. Incidents have been conducted by beings from different places beyond your world. These activities are driven by a quest to understand life on your planet. At times, it has been necessary for us to secure what you identify as DNA for our research. However, we are aware that many of these reports lack basis in true events."

Michael Malone made the next introduction. "I'm sure this next question will generate a great deal of controversy. We considered whether to present this question to our guest. In deference to the source, we will include this question from Antonio Ricci at the Vatican.

"In the Christian Tradition," Ricci began, "we have long revered the Star of Bethlehem as the guiding light that led three wise men to the birthplace of our Lord Jesus Christ. However, in the face of scientific study, it is difficult to explain how a distant star could serve as a moving guide. Some have asserted that the light could have been something else. I would dare to pose this question: could it be that the Star of Bethlehem was not a celestial event but rather an alien craft that guided the wise men on their journey to that holy place?"

The studio crew froze in their places as they anticipated what might come next. Viewing the broadcast from his office, Richard Blaine couldn't help but think, "*THAT* will be in ALL the papers!"

Zypteron also paused, contemplating the effect of a reply. "We can acknowledge that beings from beyond your world have taken part in certain historic events, including those involving religious figures of various belief structures." The picture remained on the alien until it was clear there would be no more to the reply.

Sarah Sommers waited to collect herself as she took in a deep breath and looked to the Teleprompter for her next introduction. "Amina Kamara provides us with the next question for our guest, from Niger, in West Africa."

"Legend in our country has led to speculation that the Dogon people of our continent had direct contact with extraterrestrial beings, who imparted knowledge of a star invisible to the human eye. Can you provide any insight into the basis of this legend?"

Came the response, "Throughout the history of your planet, many species of beings have made contact with humans. These interactions have taken many forms through time, involving shared knowledge and experiences. This legend you indicate is one such example."

The camera switched to Michael Malone: "Maria Fernandez has the next question for our guest. Maria wants to know about the Mayan Pyramids and other structures in Central and South America. Here is Maria's question."

"The world has long marveled at the architectural wonders of our ancient civilizations. Many have speculated about extraterrestrial involvement in these amazing constructs. The intricate Pumapunku structures in Bolivia or the inspiration of the Nazca lines in Peru. Perhaps you might reveal something about these speculations."

"The Mayan Pyramids, Pumapunku, and the Nazca Lines are indeed remarkable human achievements, but they also bear traces of cosmic influence. Pumapunku's precision stonework was meant to harness the planet's natural energies. As for the Nazca Lines, they were a response to a brief exposure of the native peoples to our contact, much as the Amazon natives once created a straw effigy after an aircraft flew over their village."

Sarah Sommers delivered the lead-in for the next reporter's question: "We now move to India and our reporter there, Rakesh Kapoor."

The reporter began, "Throughout our history in India, there has been speculation regarding the ancient temples at Khajuraho, known for the intricate carvings and celestial depictions. Some have proposed that these temples might have been influenced or guided by extraterrestrial beings, possibly because of their remarkable architectural precision and astronomical alignments. Could you kindly share your insights on the origins of these magnificent structures and whether there might be any connection to beings from beyond our world?"

The alien seemed to have expected the question: "It would be correct to say there was involvement in these temples of beings not native to your planet. They shared knowledge of celestial alignments and construction techniques."

Zypteron continued: "The Khajuraho temples represent a bridge between your planet and the cosmos, a testament to cooperation between your species and others beyond the stars. They stand as a legacy of cosmic collaboration."

Malone introduced the final reporter: "Our last question comes to us from Las Vegas, Nevada, and Rebecca Mitchel."

She had likely assumed her question was for a high-ranking official in the intelligence community. "Reports of alien involvement in nuclear incidents have been circulating," she began. "I would include the example of Malmstrom Air Force Base, where a craft... was observed coincidentally with the disabling of nuclear missiles. Prior to that, there were accounts of alien presence during the testing of the first atomic bomb in New Mexico." Rebecca paused; her expression turned earnest as she continued. "Can you provide insight into those occurrences? Have beings from beyond our world been present during these events?

The alien pulled back and stiffened as it answered: "It is true that cultures in the universe have become concerned over certain activities on your planet. The destructive and disruptive potential of nuclear devices poses a threat not only to your species but to the balance of life in the universe. At certain times, restraint has been deemed necessary to safeguard the future of the galaxy and to protect the intricate tapestry of life that exists. You may expect these efforts to continue."

As the alien interview came to a close, the view dissolved to a two-shot of the hosts. The background image of the alien dissolved away and was replaced by a graphic featuring the moon and stars on the large screen. News anchors, Michael Malone, and Sarah Sommers, exchanged solemn glances. The weight of the moment hung in the air, and it was time for them to deliver their closing statements to those watching.

In a dramatic close-up shot, Michael Malone turned to face the camera. His steady expression conveyed his thoughtfulness as he summarized the historic event.

"We have touched the fringes of a reality long feared, a reality that challenges our understanding of the universe and our place in it."

Sarah Sommers continued the message, her voice measured and precise. "The impact of this encounter will undoubtedly spark discussions, debates, and soul-searching across the globe. For some, it may shatter preconceived notions of the cosmos, while for others, it may affirm long-held beliefs."

Michael nodded; his gaze was unwavering as both anchor hosts faced the center camera. "There will be controversy, there will be speculation, there will be accusations, but the truth is often hard to accept and harder still to understand."

Sarah echoed his sentiments, her eyes reflecting a mix of hope and trepidation. "As we move forward, let us remember that knowledge, even when it challenges us, has the power to unite humanity in our shared quest for understanding."

Michael concluded with a note of unity. "We are witnesses to a moment in history, a moment that calls upon us to come together as a species, to embrace the unknown, and to strive for a future where we explore not only the cosmos but the depths of our own potential."

The screen transitioned to a Nexus Broadcasting Network logo over a spinning Earth and a background of stars. And that was how it ended. The closing statements left the world to contemplate the profound implications of the alien encounter, a moment that would resonate for generations.

Or, at least until the next network program.

***

Chapter Sixteen

If Ghosts Could Talk

"What's that thing do?" Jack looked over Alex's shoulder at a device plugged into a USB port on his laptop computer. Alex had always been one for techy things, while Jack was more into adventure.

"It's a radio controlled by a program on my computer: a Software Digital Radio. It's really an updated version of the old scanners."

SDR, as it is called, has a USB flash drive on one end and an "F" connection for an antenna on the other. The military and amateur radio enthusiasts often use it. The simplest models have a tuning range from 500 kHz to 18 GHz and can be found for less than $50 online.

Jack looks puzzled. "What's wrong with a regular radio?"

"A digital radio lets me listen to almost all the frequencies," Alex explained. "I can tune in all kinds of signals. FM, AM, the military, police, and aircraft have different frequencies. I want to see what I can find."

Jack couldn't see anything interesting about that. "So, what are you looking for, then?"

"Maybe I can find something hidden, like maybe the FBI, or drug smugglers, or NASA's private channel," and Alex smiled, " or even space aliens. Who knows?"

Alex connected the antenna to the digital radio device. The antenna looked something like old TV rabbit ears, with a cable coming out from the bottom. He ran the program on the laptop computer, and the screen displayed the frequencies from left to right with tiny vertical spikes, looking like the side view of lawn grass. The display is sometimes described as a waterfall. The speakers hissed and crackled with static.

Jack squinted at the screen, his eyes fixed on a sharp spike on the left side of the display. "So, what's that?" he asked, pointing.

Alex frowned. "That's weird. That's a very low frequency. I'm not sure what it is. He turned up the speakers and switched between FM to sideband to some of the digital options. Finally, when he selected Amplitude Modulation, the old AM mode, they heard a low hum, more like a moan.

"Well, what is it? Can you figure it out?" Jack asked impatiently.

Alex tried moving a few of the filters and settings. "Let's see... it's definitely not a regular station way down on that frequency. Lower frequencies can travel a long way, so there's no telling where it's coming from."

"What is it, then?" Jack asked, leaning over Alex's shoulder.

Alex shrugged. "It could be almost anything." He was about to continue with his explanation when the signal spike disappeared, and that section of the screen display went almost flat, except for background noise.

Jack frowned. "What do we do now? Wait for it to show up again?"

Alex nodded. "Yeah, I'll keep checking and see if I can find out. Maybe we can even track it down."

Jack was skeptical. "But what if it's something really creepy, like a secret government experiment or something? Hey! It might be time for a new adventure!"

Alex and Jack liked to go on adventures with their other college friends, Maya, Liam, and Emma. The group formed in a science class at the local college when they discovered they all shared a special kind of curiosity.

Although Alex assumed the role of the tech guru in the group, Jack was more of a thrill seeker. He considered himself an adventurer, always looking for exciting things to do. Sometimes Jack found Alex dull, but Alex managed to capture his attention. That's likely why he often came to visit to see what Alex had going on.

Emma might have been the leader of the group or the organizer, depending on your point of view. She could also be described as resourceful. She seemed to have the answer to most any problem the group encountered, and they had encountered quite a few challenges.

Maya, unlike the others, possessed a profound connection to the energies of the universe. Her mind remained receptive to all possibilities, be they extraordinary or ordinary. She unabashedly embraced her belief in the paranormal.

In stark contrast to Maya, Liam identified as a realist—a description that could easily be replaced by the word *skeptic*. He prided himself on his unyielding logic, never hesitating to characterize himself as the pragmatist. From his perspective, there's always a rational explanation awaiting discovery if one seeks it.

Early the next day, Alex texted Jack, "It's back! What do you say we find out where it's coming from?"

The antenna comprised two telescoping rods. A small tripod connected to the base where the wire came out. He hooked it to the USB device which plugged into the laptop computer. While bulky, it remained manageable. Shaping the antenna into a "V" served to focus the directional sensitivity. Alex methodically rotated the antenna, adjusting the opening of the "V" to face various directions until the mystery signal appeared the strongest.

Alex knew it would be hard to juggle the laptop with the antenna attached to the digital radio dongle. That's why he sent the next text message to ask Jack for his help.

When Jack arrived, Alex passed him the laptop and held the antenna as they made their way outside. Once there, Alex began a circular path, holding on to the antenna while Jack followed with the laptop. Avoiding stumbles while monitoring the display proved to be a challenge. After repeating the pattern several times, Alex decided the signal was strongest toward the northwest.

Time for reinforcements: Alex called Emma and filled her in on what he and Jack had been doing. He had to explain to Emma what a digital radio was, but she caught on.

"What do you need me to do?" she asked.

"You could drive us around in your convertible while Jack and I try to figure out where this mystery signal is coming from," Jack explained.

Fully in on the adventure, Emma exclaimed, "I'll call Maya and Liam to see if they're up to joining in."

Since it was Saturday, assembling the group for a new adventure was no problem. As a group, they resembled a live-action Scooby-Doo team, albeit without the talking dog or the van.

When Emma drove to Alex's house, Maya and Liam were in the front seat and Alex and Jack climbed in the back. Alex called out directions: "Find a way to go left ... no, the other way!"

In the hills outside of Whispering Pines, the signal seemed to come from an old cemetery. On the top of a hill behind the cemetery stood a massive, ancient house, or maybe it was an old mansion. The old house exuded a blend of grandeur and decay. The colonial structure resembled something out of a horror movie. Even from a distance, they could make out intricate carvings on the doors. The old wooden structure's siding showed many signs of age, with deep grooves and knots punctuating its weathered surface. Glints of sunlight reflected from the diamond-shaped glass panels in the tall, narrow windows. The roof had a steep slope, with metal shingles in different stages of rust. Above the roofline, the chimney tilted precariously to one side. Sections of the wide front porch sagged, revealing the surrender of the wooden structure to gravity.

Maya looked up at the old building. "Well, if it isn't haunted, it certainly has all the potential," she said with some amount of satisfaction.

By now, Alex had been watching the mystery radio signal getting stronger, but as the car slowed to a stop, it faded away. Alex and the others waited for something to happen, but the computer display remained quiet.

Maya shared in the disappointment. "Maybe it saw us!"

"How do we know this is where the signal is coming from?" asked Liam.

Alex didn't have an answer. "We don't, really, but it looked like it came from that direction," he said, pointing toward the old mansion up the hill. "But I guess we'll have to try again another time."

"That house looks like something out of the Adams Family," Jack said.

"Or The Munsters, more likely," Liam suggested.

Emma had her phone out, checking Google Maps. "I'm not sure how to get up there," she admitted.

Jack realized the adventure he had expected would not materialize. At least not that day.

So, the disappointed group headed back to Alex's house, stopping along the way at their favorite ice cream shop, of course.

Early Sunday morning, Alex once again had the digital radio to check for the mysterious signal. Sure enough, there it was again. He sent a group text to the others: "It's back. Anybody up to giving it another try?" After a few minutes, they all texted back. Yes, they were ready to go.

Emma devised a route to reach the old mansion. On reaching the cemetery, she turned on an old dirt road hidden by branches and debris. Alex and Jack got out to clear the way. The roadway had seen no traffic for quite a long time. Liam commented how it struck him as odd not to see any "no trespassing" signs, much less a "for sale" sign. As they reached the old house, they found the front door sagging open, the hinges having long since tired of holding onto the frame.

Once inside, Alex turned on the computer. As the group watched, he checked the display. This time, the signal was back, and it was even stronger than before. But as he guided the antenna around in a pattern, the signal display remained the same. "I think it's here.... somewhere," Alex announced to the group.

"Well, I guess we didn't scare it off this time," said Maya. "This place is still really creepy, though."

Liam suggested they explore the house to see what they could find.

As Liam, Maya, and Jack went to explore, Emma stayed behind, and Alex to see if he could decode the signal. He switched through all the settings. When he finally went back to the AM setting, the speaker barked with a strange rumbling sound. The noise brought the others back from their tour of the old mansion.

"What's it saying?" Jack asked as he peered at the computer display.

Alex, still adjusting, "It's not *SAYING* anything," he grumbled, glancing over his shoulder at the others.

Emma put her hands on her hips and shook her head. "There's nothing here. There's certainly no electricity for anything to run on."

Jack and Maya joined them. Maya was frightened. "What if ghosts can talk?" She jumped as the sound of the laptop speaker changed, almost in response, as it emitted a series of bursts of staccato pulses.

"That's no kind of ghost I ever heard of," Liam said. "Sounds more like some kind of data."

"We're not on a digital setting. It's still on AM," Alex answered. He tried the other settings again, but with no success. "Certainly not digital," he concluded. As the noise continued, Alex clicked on the recording function so the software could capture what they were hearing.

"Maybe it's a robot," Emma suggested.

"What would a robot be doing in a house like this?" Maya asked.

Jack had a thought. "Maybe there's a basement."

Jack and Emma left the others to look. A short time later, they came back to report finding a stairway to the darkness below. They decided not to venture into its depths.

Alex sighed. "Well, that's it for today. The signal's gone again."

"Now what?" Liam asked as he came down the stairs. Like the others, he was disappointed.

Alex shook his head. "I've been watching it for a while when you guys went looking around. It's definitely gone quiet."

"Are you sure?" Emma asked.

"But I made a recording," he said. "I think I know who might be able to help us. There's somebody I want to play it for."

Alex's Monday morning classes lasted until noon. After lunch, he went to find Dr. Emily Jameson in the science department. Luckily, she was in her office. He knocked on the door. She put aside the papers she was grading and invited him in.

Dr. Jameson, in her early 40s, had short blond hair and glasses. Previously a researcher in electromagnetic radiation and its effects on the human body for a government agency, she grew weary of the bureaucracy and politics. Leaving that world behind, she pursued her passion for teaching and became a physics professor at the College of Arts and Sciences. Enjoying the more informal setting, she found fulfillment in interacting with students and sharing her knowledge with them.

"Do I know you?" she asked. "Are you one of my students this year?"

"I was in one of your classes last year," he said. "I wonder if you could help me solve a mystery?" Alex pulled the digital radio dongle out of his pocket and laid it on the desk. "I've been experimenting with this."

"What is it?" Dr. Jameson asked.

"It's an SDR: a software digital radio. I plug it into my laptop, and I can listen to almost any frequency and transmission type," Alex explained.

"OK, I know about those. I've never seen one. So how can I help you?" the professor asked.

"I found this on a very low frequency." Alex had copied the recording to his phone, and he played the sound from the computer program. "What do you think it is?"

The professor was silent for a moment. Her head turned at an angle toward Alex while she thought. "You probably know VLF or Very Low Frequencies could come from anything from lightning to geomagnetic activity. Where did you hear it?"

Alex explained how they ended up at the old cemetery a few blocks from his house. He admitted the group had gone looking for clues in the old house since they found it open and with no "keep out" signs on the property.

"What else is around there?" Dr. Jameson asked.

Alex couldn't recall seeing anything but the old cemetery.

"I think we can rule out any geomagnetic activity," she said. "I don't remember any thunderstorms so far this month. That really doesn't sound like lightning static, anyway. There might be some power grid wires nearby. It could even come from underground pipes. The hospital is on the other side of town, so that would probably rule out EEG machines or magnetometers."

Surprised, Alex remarked, "I didn't realize there's so much stuff on low frequencies."

"You've certainly got my curiosity up," said the instructor. "I might want to check it out with you. How about this weekend?"

Alex never expected the professor to take an interest in the mystery. They agreed to meet at Alex's house early on Saturday morning. Alex thanked the professor. He couldn't wait to tell the others, so he typed out a group text as he walked through the hallways to his last class of the day. They were all set for the weekend!

Not everyone could fit in Emma's car Saturday morning, so Dr. Jameson followed in her own car, so Alex and Jack rode with her. They loaded the laptop gear and a small folding table in the back of the professor's SUV.

Upon reaching the old house, Alex again set up the laptop on the folding table in the main entry. The rest of the group checked to be sure no one else … or no *THING* else was in the house, while the professor circled around to the back of the property. On her return, Alex focused intently on the screen, continuing to adjust the antenna as the signal came and went.

"I think I know where your mystery signal is coming from," she said to Alex. "You said it seems to come and go, like the wind. Am I right? Did you notice the windmills in the field behind the house? "

Alex shook his head no. The windmills had escaped his attention.

"I'm guessing that there is some kind of defect in one of the wind turbines. When the wind is exactly right, it vibrates. I can hear it rattle. It's possible for wind turbines to generate low-frequency waves."

She went on, "Those waves can travel through the ground, creating a sympathetic resonance. That's what you see on your digital radio. It's unusual but not impossible. If you move your setup to the back porch, you can watch for the radio signal as the windmills turn."

Maya came down the stairs from exploring the second floor and heard the last part of the conversation. She helped Alex carry the computer and the setup to the back porch. Sure enough, the signal on the screen went away when the windmill stopped turning.

Professor Jameson explained, "The key to this mystery is understanding electromagnetic resonance. We know this part of the state has a history of iron mines. It is possible that a network of tunnels is deep underground, under this old house. Over time, it's possible that over time, some of the exposed iron has corroded and formed peculiar shapes, acting as a natural tuned cavity."

Alex broke in, "You're saying the tunnels could be resonating with the radio waves from the windmills?"

"Exactly," Dr. Jameson confirmed. "The windmills have electric components that generate magnetic fields. When the wind blows, it creates vibrations. The vibrations, in turn, resonate with corroded iron deposits in underground tunnels, magnifying electronic waves."

Jack was impressed. "So, it's like a natural radio transmitter?"

"That's right. The signal on your little receiver comes from a unique electromagnetic resonance phenomenon: no paranormal forces, only science."

Alex nodded in understanding.

"I have an idea that it won't be long before the windmill maintenance people repair the problem, and your radio signal will go away," the professor added.

"I was really hoping for ghosts," Maya confessed.

Jack spoke up, "I guess it's like the old song! The answer was *blowing in the wind* all along!"

Dr. Jameson smiled. "No, I was just kidding, it was really ghosts." She was joking, of course.

As they all headed back to the cars to leave the old house, Emma suggested, "How about some ice cream?"

***

Chapter Seventeen

Dream Catcher

What if you could experience a dream of your choosing? In your dreams, you could be someone else, experience a different world from your own, and see the world through different eyes.

What if you could buy your dreams?

Megan felt displeased with her life. Each day was like the one before. Her relationships never lasted very long, reducing her life to a bowl of frustrations.

Her only pet was a stuffed animal.

That's why the online advertisement drew her attention. A link took her to a website:

Dreams for sale! You can be anyone you aspire to be! Be the star of your own movie. Let the adventure begin! Dream Catcher: Offices Worldwide! Sign up TODAY!

It's true, her life had been anything but exciting. She realized her dreams, what she could remember, were dull and meaningless.

So why not buy a dream? What could it hurt? Trying out a new dream might open her mind to new experiences, perhaps even a new outlook. Certainly, it could not be as dangerous an escape as drugs.

She filled out the online form and waited. Almost instantly, her phone "binged" with a text message reply:

Welcome to The Dream Catcher, where your next dream can be an ADVENTURE!

The message included confirmation of her requested appointment date, a time, and the company's local address.

Why not? Megan was ready to take a chance.

The address was on the second floor of a downtown medical building. Inside, the office had posters decorating the walls, depicting dream scenes. Some showed beautiful landscapes of snow-capped mountains, with people riding cable cars, or riders on painted horses racing through a desert. Still others depicted surreal scenes in outer space and musicians entertaining cheering crowds.

As she entered the office, a small window slid open.

"Welcome to your dream world!" The receptionist's voice was almost musical. "What kind of dream do you wish to experience?"

She was about to reply when the woman poked out a small electronic tablet.

"Fill in the form," she said, flashing a push-button smile as she closed the sliding window with a snap.

Megan sat in a chair to answer the questions on the tablet and checked a box next to a dream category. After filling in her name, address, and so on, there was a long legal disclaimer. She blindly scrolled through and checked the box marked "accept."

Almost instantly, a pleasant man in a brown suit opened the rear door.

"Megan?" he asked, as if anyone else was in the room. "Please step inside." He beckoned, and she followed.

As she entered, she saw what looked like a dentist's chair. Next to it, on a small table, was a strange-looking helmet with wires attached. To the other side was a computer screen and a selector mouse.

"Have a seat," the man said, motioning to the chair.

As she lowered herself to sit, she glanced uneasily at the equipment.

"How does this all work?" she asked with more than a bit of trepidation.

"It's simple, really. People sell us their dreams, and we store them in our system. When a customer makes a selection, we upload it directly to their mind through our special machine."

"How do I know it's safe?"

"We run a thorough background check on all our dream providers. Then, our computer program scans the dream files for defects."

"How many times can I see my dream?" Megan was still unsure.

"You are free to enjoy your new dream as often as you like until it expires. Think of it like renting a movie."

"I see," she replied, still with some trepidation.

She leaned forward to gain control of her apprehension before leaning back to relax in the chair.

"Let's see what we can find for you."

The video screen scrolled through a list of choices. The list included famous clothing designers, sports stars, life in the military, famous writers, lucid worlds, and romantic fantasy.

Megan pointed to a selection: "I think I'll try this Romantic Fantasy."

"Good choice!" the man asked. Megan nodded as he placed the device on her head. He then clicked the mouse to set the selection.

"You may feel a little dizzy while your dream is being transferred, but I assure you there will be no pain. The dream remains dormant until you go to sleep. That's when your mind activates it. Here we go!" he said and pressed the red button. The machine made a whirring sound, almost like a small vacuum cleaner.

She felt a slight tingle as the whirring sound continued for half a minute and then gradually wound down.

He smiled as he handed her a slip of paper. "Please see the woman at the counter on your way out."

At the desk, Megan passed her credit card over the sensor, and the woman at the counter handed her a small booklet with instructions.

"Who needs instructions for a dream?" Megan wondered. She took the booklet and thanked the lady behind the window as she left.

On her way home, she grabbed a sandwich at a fast-food restaurant.

"I wonder what I've gotten myself into!" she thought as she unwrapped the take-out food on the kitchen table.

Megan had trouble keeping her eyes open, so she slipped into bed and stared at the fan spinning overhead, counting the blades as they turned. Soon, she was sound asleep, and her new dream rushed into her mind like a blast of cold air.

Megan's mind drifted into a swirling vortex of colors and shapes until she stood in front of a breathtaking view. The golden glow of the setting sun illuminated the rolling green hills before her. A gentle breeze brought with it the scent of wildflowers. As she viewed the beautiful scene, her deepest desires and fantasies unfolded before her eyes as she danced under the stars with a mysterious stranger. Together, they twirled and spun in a moment of pure joy and exhilaration.

The dance went on and on, but as she danced, she noticed a dark shadow. It moved closer and closer until Megan awoke with a feeling of fear. She felt the sweat as she touched her neck, her heart pounding as she scanned the room to assure herself she was alone.

The next night, she was apprehensive about going to sleep, but she couldn't resist the lure of the dream world. Once again, she arrived in a beautiful scene. Her mysterious partner smiled and pulled her around, swirling and swaying to mystical music. When the music stopped, Megan held her partner's hand as they walked to enjoy the view.

From behind a wall, the dark stranger again stared from the shadows. He had a rugged face and hair like straw, almost a cartoon-like villain. That was when Megan saw a knife. The shock startled her out of the dream. Once again, she woke up in a sweat, her heart pounding.

"What does it mean?" she asked herself. She reached for the dream merchant's booklet to see what it said about a defective product. At the very least, she wanted to be done with this fearful dream.

She checked the small print: All sales final.

"No refunds," the lady behind the little sliding window told her sternly. This time, there was no music in her voice.

"I don't care. I want to be rid of it. You need to make it go away."

"We've had no complaints," the lady said indignantly. "Five stars on Google!"

Megan suspected that might not be true.

"I need to see the man who can take this dream out of my head."

"Just a moment," the lady said as she slid the little window closed.

In a few moments, the man in the brown suit opened the door and motioned toward the chair.

"We've never had a defective dream" he said. "Why don't you tell me about your experience?"

"The dream took me to a beautiful place where I was dancing with a wonderful man, but then a sinister stranger crept up from the shadows and started coming at me. I had to wake up to get away."

"I can assure you that was not in the dream we sold you. The monster was of your own creation. The subconscious can bring out unresolved conflicts, hidden threats, or other aspects of the subject's mental state. Perhaps a psychiatrist can help resolve any issues you may have. You should consider it. That was all explained in the booklet, of course."

"I still want you to erase that dream." Megan was becoming irritated. She could not wait for it to expire.

"Are you sure you don't want to exchange it? We have many more available. Perhaps you dream of being a movie star or a famous writer? What about an alien abduction?" the man suggested. "That would be exciting! We have several of those. Are you sure you would not like to try one?"

She folded her arms and scowled, staring straight ahead as she reached for the headset.

The man in the brown suit correctly took her response as a "no." He fiddled with the computer settings and then pressed the red button. The machine responded with the whirring sound, and then it stopped.

She peered out from under the headgear. "Is that it?"

The man in the brown suit said, "Yes, that's all there is." so she got up and marched out of the office.

Megan thought about the suggestion of seeing a psychiatrist.

"That's for crazy people," she had told herself. Even so, the notion of an evil demon lurking inside her mind made her fearful. What if the dark figure appeared in another dream? She couldn't take that chance.

At long last, she decided to conquer her fears.

The psychologist, Dr. Carol Miller, was an older lady whose gentle manner and soft features reminded Megan of her own mother. The lighting was subdued, and the lush carpeting dampened the sound. She felt calm as she lay on the classic couch and closed her eyes.

"Tell me about your dream experience," Dr. Miller began. "Did you say you purchased this dream?"

"Yes, the dream merchant had an extensive selection, and I chose a *romantic fantasy*."

"And was it what you expected?"

"Oh, yes. In the beginning I was dancing with a wonderful partner in a beautiful place. I remember the music was bright and whimsical."

"But you said something disturbed you?" the doctor asked. "Tell me about that part."

"As I gazed into my dancing partner's eyes, there was something lurking in the shadows. As I looked, I saw a dark figure coming toward me."

"I see. And then what happened?"

"Then I woke up," Megan replied. "I was shaking and sweating."

"Is this the only time you had that dream?"

"No, it came again the next night, as it had before, except this time the man was coming closer, and he had a knife."

"Did the dream merchant offer any solution?"

"No, he just said they thoroughly scan all their dreams for negative experiences and conduct background checks on all the providers. He said the demon had been in my mind all along."

"I see. Perhaps your demon came from another source. Let's explore that possibility, shall we?"

Saying nothing and with her eyes still closed, Megan reached to adjust the pillow under her head.

The doctor continued. "Dreams involving threats of attack often reflect internal conflicts and struggles the individual may be experiencing, perhaps in their subconscious mind. Can you tell me about what has been happening in your life recently, perhaps some major changes or stresses you've had to deal with?"

Megan thought for a moment, hesitant to reveal too much of her personal life.

"I started a new job after an unpleasant experience with my last employer. My new job involves more pressure than I expected. I guess the strain has been the reason for some arguments with the other people around me."

"Our personal demons do not necessarily represent people. The shadowy attacker could represent some aspect of yourself that you struggle to overcome. The threat of seeing a knife could represent how serious it has become. Do you think that is possible?"

Megan hesitated. "I suppose that could be. I hadn't thought of it that way. So, what do I need to do?"

"Are you open to trying a visualization exercise to help you release your tension and fears?"

She nodded. "I'm ready to try anything. Even when I'm not dreaming, I keep seeing that dark figure lurking behind every shadow. I only want it to go away."

"Let's begin, then. I want you to close your eyes, take a few deep breaths, and allow your body to relax. Imagine yourself sinking deeper into the couch. Then, I want you to bring back the image of the shadowy figure, but this time, I want you to visualize yourself turning to face it, meeting its gaze without fear, knowing the danger is no longer real. Can you see it?"

"Yes," Megan said. "In my mind, I can see a light turning on, and the shadow is gone. The scary person is not there anymore."

"Do you feel more confident now?"

"Yes, I think so," she said as she opened her eyes and took in a deep breath. "Yes. I feel better now."

"Now that you feel you have regained your sense of control, there's something else to try. Perhaps you have heard the term 'lucid dreams'?"

"No, I'm not sure I have. What is that?" Megan asked.

"You might say it's a technique for becoming the director of your own movie. It's known as the Mnemonic Induction of Lucid Dreams. I think you should try it. We have a video on our website that explains it all."

"I'm glad I came. I feel lighter somehow, and in control. I don't have to fear change or pressure. Yes, I think I'm ready to face down the man in the shadows."

Dr. Miller smiled. "And I'll be here to support you every step of the way."

Megan wanted to try the doctor's suggestions for creating her beautiful dream.

On the doctor's website, the video explained how to prepare for a peaceful sleep. She made sure not to have any coffee or sodas after noon to prevent caffeine from affecting her sleep. When getting ready to sleep, she lowered the thermostat and closed the bedroom curtains. She deliberately stayed away from the blue light and distractions of television, her cell phone, and her computer. Instead, she took it easy in a lounge chair, enjoying a book until bedtime.

As she drifted off to sleep, a lucid dream appeared, a dream of her own creation.

She found herself under the canopy of a lush forest. The air was alive with the sounds of birds. Gazing ahead, she saw a winding path. She took control of the dream and began walking along the path, breathing in the scent of flowers and experiencing all the sights and sounds around her.

Ahead, she heard water cascading down a waterfall, generating a mist that rose to the clouds above. She turned to watch as colorful birds darted about, chasing the wind in the mist over her head. A tiny bird fluttered to the ground at her feet, looking up to greet her with a soft chirp before flying off to tend a nest on the branch of a nearby tree.

As the dream faded, Megan felt a strange sense of belonging, peace, and beauty within the magical forest. As the morning light crept through the edges of the window shades, she awoke feeling relaxed and peaceful. At last, the shadowy figure was nowhere to be seen.

This dream was not only an escape but a glimpse of the beauty and joy that could come from breaking free of limitations and facing down the demons of inner fears and doubts.

Back at work, the tension of her job was no longer a burden. The people around her reflected her new positive attitude. Her relationship with her fellow workers was much better, and she didn't feel threatened by competition. She felt equal to the challenge and began enjoying her life.

Megan thought, "Perhaps I should sell the wonderful new dream of my peaceful walk in the forest to the man in the brown coat at the Dream Catcher store?"

***

Chapter Eighteen

The Man in the Mirror

G eorge was in a state of depression.

This time it was more than his normal depression, but still not the kind that pushes people toward alcoholism or suicide. No, this depression was subtle, more like a *'shoulda-woulda-coulda'* depression that refused to leave.

Today had been one of those times when thoughts felt like a dull pain.

It happened as George was having lunch at an all-you-can-eat buffet restaurant. He enjoyed eating at a buffet because it didn't force him to make choices like a regular restaurant. He could select whatever food item appealed to him at the moment.

This particular depression had been triggered by the music in the restaurant; a collection of "oldies." The song stayed on his mind all day.

Well, it wasn't so much the old music that he found depressing. No one song stood out, hailing from decades ago, when George had the opportunity to alter his path and make different decisions.

He had heard the song many times, maybe hundreds of times, before. Maybe not hundreds, but enough that he could follow along. But this time he felt like Peggy Lee was communicating with him.

"..is that all there is?"
Copyright 1969, Embassy Music Corporation

George repeated the lyric to himself: *Is this all there is?*

But his life wasn't that bad, all considered. He had been successful enough to have retired early. His house wasn't exciting, but it was paid for. He was comfortable. His only discomfort was that nagging feeling he kept having about what might have been, what could have been different.

If only ...

If only he had held onto that Amazon stock for a few more years. Sure, he had made his investment way back in 1994. It had paid off, too. When it split in 2021, he cashed it in, along with most of his other investments. The next January, the stock he sold shot up 14%, raising Amazon's value by $100 billion in a single day.

Why hadn't he held on a little longer? That's when he decided on early retirement.

That wasn't the only regret nagging him. Retirement life was not the dream he expected.

If only he had found the courage to marry that girl he fell in love with back in college, but was unwilling or unable to make a commitment. What if he had chosen a different career, something more lucrative or challenging than retail management? He could have been a banker, even a stockbroker, or invested in real estate. Those years in the late 1990s had been perfect for real estate investment.

As George sat gazing out the window in his easy chair, a sound interrupted his thoughts. It sounded like someone calling his name: "George."

There it was again. "George," the voice called to him. The voice was coming from the bedroom. That was not possible! He was alone. He was ALWAYS alone.

There was no one else in the house. He hesitated before getting up to investigate.

As he entered the bedroom, he listened. Nothing. But as he turned to leave, he heard it again:

"George" the strangely familiar voice repeated slowly, now much closer and clearer.

The mirror! The voice was coming from the mirror hung inside the bedroom closet door! As he approached, he saw his reflection. But the reflection was his younger self, and that younger George appeared angry.

"What's wrong with you?" the reflection demanded.

The sound startled George. He leaned forward and looked deeper into the mirror. The reflection matched his motion as if to mock him.

"What's wrong with you?" the reflection repeated. "You have achieved everything you wanted: a successful career and money in the bank. You don't owe anybody anything. What more do you need?"

George convinced himself that his imagination had gotten the better of him. After all, it was all in his mind, he grumbled. He closed the door, trapping the apparition inside the closet. At least for the moment.

Rick was a long-time friend, about his same age. From George's perspective, Rick "had his act together." Rick had a wife and two grown sons. Rick invited George over for dinner. George assumed it was to celebrate his retirement and was happy to accept the invitation, if mostly for Rick's wife's cooking. George was such a familiar guest that the guard at the gated community waved him through.

As he walked up the circular drive to Rick's impressive home, the door opened.

"Adelante!" Rick's wife Maria said in Spanish as she gestured for George to enter.

The warm fragrance of the meal she was preparing greeted him as he entered. Rick waved George in from his lounge chair by the pool. As George passed through the elegant living room with tall ceilings and modern decor, he could hear the pleasant gurgling of the swimming pool outside.

George took his usual place in the chair across from Rick's as Maria busied herself delivering various dishes to the outdoor dining area.

Looking around as if to be taking it all in for the first time, he confided, "You certainly have it great."

Rick might have considered it an insult, but they had been friends too long for him to take it that way. Rick turned his head to study his friend. "What's wrong, George?"

George tried to shrug it off. "I'm sorry. I'm just a little down lately. I thought I had it all figured out. But, well, things haven't turned out like I might have wanted. I guess I'm a little disappointed in myself. I didn't make the kind of decisions you made."

Rick was thoughtful. "Are you OK? I mean, you don't have any problem with your health, do you?" That's always a concern for those of us who reach a certain age. There's always something."

"No," George quickly answered, "Nothing like that. I wish sometimes I might have been more like you. You know, quit the 9 to 5: take charge!"

"Let me explain something, Rick said. "When you go to work for yourself or own a company, you trade that nice, reliable 9 to 5 for the stress of 5 to 9."

He continued, "Things are not always what they appear to be. For example, you mentioned you have paid off your house, right?"

"Yes, such as it is," George agreed. "I don't owe anything to anyone."

"You envy *me*? I envy *you*! Since the kids moved out, this house makes no sense at all. I still have a sizeable mortgage, the HOA fees go up each year, and the taxes are ridiculous," Rick answered. "But Maria loves this house. She always has, from the day we moved in. I have no alternative."

"But that's just it," George replied, recalling his earlier thoughts about that girl in college. "You've got such a wonderful marriage."

Rick looked to see that Maria was busy in the kitchen as he lowered his voice. "You realize Maria's not my first wife, right? I mean, we have a wonderful marriage, but it's never the same the second time around."

George furrowed his brow but said nothing.

Rick continued, "My first wife was Janice. Janice wanted the good things and saw me as the way to get them. The nice house, the great neighborhood, the pool, even a live-in maid. That was what she was after, and I was too dumb to see it. After two kids came and went, she grew bored with her life, and I was preoccupied with achieving success."

"But Maria ... " George stopped as he heard Maria bringing out the last of the food.

"Listo? Empecemos!" she said.

Rick whispered to George, "Oh, Maria's the best thing that ever happened to me besides my two kids, I guess."

The outdoor table had a bowl of Mexican long-grain rice, tomatoes, onion, garlic, and chicken broth. Another bowl held the traditional refried beans. Maria's recipe began with pinto beans, cooked until soft, then fried with oil, garlic, spices, and more onions. A basket of tortilla chips completed the picture, with small salsa dipping dishes at each table setting. As George and Rick sat down to eat, Maria brought out the featured attraction, her own Chiles Rellenos recipe of poblano peppers with popcorn shrimp swimming in a queso blanco sauce. Once all the food was on the table, Maria asked George if he cared for a margarita. George nodded approval, and she prepared drinks for the men while she opened a *Modelo Especial* for herself. She placed the drinks on a tray and served the men before she sat at the table.

Dinner with Rick and Maria usually featured one or two of Maria's specialties, but she went all out this time.

"Is this a special occasion?" George asked Maria.

Before she could answer, Rick explained. "It is, but it needs some explanation. Maria came to this country as a child. The problem came when she applied to renew her driver's license. She had her license for years, but they required her Mexican birth certificate. She didn't have it. They turned her down. We've been going back and forth with the authorities for almost two years. When they finally gave in, we invited you to share in our victory celebration."

George nodded in understanding. He was about to ask another question, but he let it wait until after they enjoyed their meal. Instead, the conversation revolved around grocery prices and local gossip.

After dinner, Rick went inside to the living room while Maria began clearing the table. George offered to help, but Maria smiled and gestured for him to join Rick.

As he selected a comfortable armchair in the living room, George wanted to piece together a puzzle in his mind.

"So, how did you meet Maria? It looks like you have known each other forever," George cautiously queried.

"I said Janice had to have a live-in housekeeper," Rick answered as he tilted his head toward the kitchen.

George nodded with a knowing smile.

"Like I said," Rick continued, "Maria's the best. After Janice packed up, Maria would have been out of a job, and I realized I really didn't want to see her leave. She had been an important part of the family while the kids were growing up. With the kids gone to college, she was my family. So we got married."

"You see, George, things are not always what they appear to be. There's no divorce in your past, no debts weighing you down, and nothing holding you back. With your pension in hand, you're free to enjoy life. And you got out before the retail economy came apart. So, be careful what you wish for. And I need to mention one more thing I've learned: never look back."

The wisdom in Rick's advice swept over George like the cool evening breeze coming through the open door to the pool deck. George thanked Rick and Maria for the invitation and the meal and headed home.

As George got ready to turn in, he heard that voice again. The man in the mirror wanted to talk with him, but this time, the reflection was no longer his younger self.

"Did you learn anything tonight?" the mirror asked.

George was still trying to adjust to this strange relationship with his reflection.

"What do you miss the most?" it asked.

George thought for a moment. He had once wanted to learn music, to be a real musician, creating melodies that would bring him the joy of accomplishment. He had secretly hoped to learn to play an instrument.

Reading his thoughts, the mirror asked, "So what's stopping you now?"

George had no suitable answer, so he gently closed the closet door and went to bed.

The next morning, his OCD kicked in, and George busied himself with arranging things around the house. That same OCD had provided him with the attention to detail that propelled his retail success. It had fueled his rise to chain management, supervising, and training store managers.

With nothing left to tidy up, George again headed to his favorite buffet for lunch. While making his selection and sitting alone in the comfort of the soft seat of the restaurant booth, George's attention was again drawn to the music coming from the round speaker in the ceiling.

Cyndi Lauper was the artist. The song was familiar to George, but this time, the words had a different meaning for him:

> "Money changes everything."
> (Copyright 1983) by Cyndi Lauper, published by BMG
> Rights Management

George remembered Lauper had ruined her voice in 1977. They told her she would never sing again. Success had brought her lots of money, but it had cost her the high notes. Her determination and the help of her vocal coach, Katie Agresta, returned to resume her career a year later. She hadn't let the money change her. The song brought home the message from the man in the mirror: what was stopping him from pursuing his dreams now?

His thoughts were interrupted when a woman approached his table.

"Do you recognize me?" the woman asked, carrying a tray of food from the buffet.

She looked familiar. He studied her momentarily as he realized she had been one of the store managers he had trained.

"Of course, you're ... " George stumbled for a name.

"Alice," she informed him. "You *do* remember!" She seemed pleased as George nodded recognition.

He pointed to the empty seat across the table. "Won't you join me?"

Alice accepted the invitation and caught the attention of a passing server to explain her change of tables.

The two shared "war stories" from the department store world, and Alice explained she left her position right after George's retirement.

"So, what are you doing now?" George asked with sincere curiosity.

"I'm teaching music. I realized it was what I always wanted to do. I remember you once told me you wanted to get into music someday?"

George answered, "Funny you should ask."

And let's just say the rest is history.

***

Chapter Nineteen

The Meeting

Location: The Pentagon, Arlington, Virginia, Sensitive Compartmented Information Facility (SCIF)
Event: Special Briefing
Attending: UN Ambassador, Space Force Intelligence Chief
Presenter: Colonel Richard "Cipher" Anderson, DIA Chief Information Officer (CIO)

In a Sensitive Compartmented Information Facility meeting room at the core of the Pentagon, the DIA CIO greeted his arriving guests.

U.N. Ambassador Elara Sinclair had a commanding presence as she walked to the table.

"Thank you for joining us." The colonel welcomed her as she moved toward a long table in the center of the room.

The Ambassador had once served as a New York Representative in Congress. She had received top secret clearance as a requirement for her position. At the direction of the DIA, she had completed *Above Top Secret* clearance from the Defense Security Cooperation Agency. Conducted by the CIA, the process involved various steps, including an in-depth foreign disclosure review and intense interrogation. Throughout the process, Sinclair questioned the necessity for extra high-level security beyond that required for her role at the United Nations. She would soon learn the reason.

"You didn't explain what this meeting is about," Elara asked, as she took a seat at the table.

"All in good time," the Colonel assured her, as he walked to the front of the room, where a large video screen displayed the logo of the Defense Intelligence Agency.

General Stratos was last to join the Ambassador at the table. The president appointed Dominic Stratos, callsign "Phoenix", Chief Intelligence Office of the United States Space Force. Before the appointment, he had been assigned to Edwards Air Force Base at Groom Lake in Nevada. He also held a security clearance "Above Top Secret."

His appearance was very military in his Space Force uniform, clean shaven, and buzz-cut hair..

The colonel began by saying, "On the table in front of you is a briefing binder. Before I begin, I would call your attention to the security notice. Much of this material is top secret and is for your review, but it is not to leave this room. You will not make any notes." He looked at each of the attendants for a nod of acknowledgement. "However, if anyone should ask, this meeting never happened. By the end of the presentation, you will understand the reason."

The top of the binder read "CLASSIFIED MATERIAL". Below that was a line that read "TOP SECRET/SCI", with the date, a Change Management Control Number and the Point of Contact. Also included was a sheet labeled *UNIFIED EXTRATERRESTRIAL INCIDENT LOG*. Another document was the 2021-06-25: US Government UAP Report Release. There were several other documents in the package, many stamped "TOP SECRET – EYES ONLY."

Anderson pressed the button to display the first screen of the presentation, showing a bullet list of dates. The first bullet point was 1948-01-23: Project Sign.

"While there were significant events prior to this date, this will be our starting point," the Colonel began. "Roswell triggered a UFO fever. Air bases and police stations were flooded with flying saucer reports. To calm public fears, Truman decided something needed to be done. The Air Force director of research and development, Major General L.C. Craige, stood up, or established, *Project Sign*, initially named *Project Saucer*, later to be known as *Project Grudge* and then replaced by the better known *Project BlueBook*. The public was told the purpose was to *investigate* the rising number of reports. That wasn't really the case."

The second bullet appeared on the screen. 1953-01-10: The Robertson Panel. A photo of President Truman appeared on the right side of the screen.

"Next, 1953, and the creation of the Robertson Panel tasked with investigating UFO reports in response to public concerns over sightings of what were being called *flying saucers*. In its report, the panel recommended an education campaign to reduce the public's interest in UFOs and to debunk UFO sightings. The goal of the panel was to prevent public hysteria. The idea was to downplay UFO reports following the incident at Roswell, New Mexico. Certain extraterrestrials requested a meeting with Harry Truman, but Truman refused."

Anderson continued by clicking the control for the next item on the bullet list: 1954-02-20: First Meeting, with a picture of Dwight Eisenhower fading in, replacing the Truman photo.

"Our first high-level contact took place on this date," he said, pointing at the screen. "Shortly after taking office, Dwight Eisenhower arranged for a sudden vacation to Palm Springs, California. It was unusual, in that he had only just concluded a golf vacation in Georgia."

Ambassador Sinclair interrupted, "Why are you telling us all this? As far as we know, these are all rumors and conjectures."

The colonel raised a single finger before continuing. "One night, Eisenhower secretly slipped away, took off in his Constellation, 'Connie', landed at Edwards and walked over from Connie to an alien ship parked on the main runway. Although there are no records from that meeting, and nobody debriefed Ike, we're pretty sure it did not go well. After a short time, maybe 20 minutes aboard the spaceship, Ike walked back to his plane. He was not in a pleasant mood when he left. The word was the aliens demanded total nuclear disarmament and Eisenhower refused. Military brass at the base described the aliens as what we now know as Tall Whites, often referred to as Nordics."

The colonel paused and turned to face his guests.

"I believe I can see where this is going," General Stratos interrupted. To the Colonel he said, "Please continue."

The next date was February 20-21, 1954.

"This is the date of an unofficial agreement when President Eisenhower again met with alien representatives, this time at Holloman Air Force Base. From what we can surmise, under the terms, the aliens were allowed free access to move about and conduct research while we asked for access to their anti-gravity technology. They agreed to keep a low profile as far as the public was concerned. We did not agree to stop nuclear research as the aliens had demanded at the first meeting."

Clara Sinclair objected. "I don't recall any treaty like that being ratified by the Senate."

"You are correct, it was not. Whatever agreement came out of that meeting was never presented to Congress for approval. Under the Constitution, the President is allowed to negotiate treaties and sign them after Advice and Consent of Congress, but that process did not occur. There are no official records of the treaty, and the President never submitted it for ratification.

The expression on the ambassador's face expressed her discomfort with the answer.

With a click of the presentation remote, the next bullet point appeared: 1967-03-16: Malmstrom Air Force Base.

"This is where it got serious," he continued. "Ten of our nuclear missile silos went off-line almost all at once. At that same time, base security reported seeing a UFO hovering overhead. When the UFO disappeared, the missiles went back online. We don't know if it was a test or a demonstration, but it got the military's attention."

Another bullet point: 1974-11-07: Loring Air Force Base.

"This event involved several unidentified craft, hovering over the base's weapons area, observed both visually and on radar, by air and ground crews."

The next bullet point on the screen was 2023-02-10

"It gets worse. Ground radar picked up an object at 40,000 feet over northeastern Alaska. An F-35 was scrambled to investigate and confirmed the contact. Over concerns of the potential threat to civilian air traffic, an F-22 from Joint Base Elmendorf-Richardson launched an AIM-9X Sidewinder missile and shot it down inside U.S. territorial waters near the Canadian border."

"I heard about the Chinese balloon, but not that one. Is that why we're here?" the General wanted to know.

"The purpose of this briefing is to prepare you for a special meeting next week at the UN. This will be a different kind of meeting in that you will not be addressing the General Assembly, nor will you be meeting with any of the delegates," Colonel Anderson continued.

"Then who are we meeting? Space aliens?" General Stratos asked with a chuckle, glancing at Sinclair.

The colonel responded to the General's remark with a stern look.

"I need to direct your attention to the U.N. document in your folder. You'll find the report from the United Nations Office for Outer Space Affairs workshop on *The Search for Extraterrestrial Intelligence, or SETI, in the Context of the United Nations.*"

"Quoting the document: The United Nations takes a cautious and proactive approach to the issue of extraterrestrial life. They recognize the potential for both peaceful and harmful contact with extraterrestrial civilizations and have prepared for both possibilities."

DOCID: 3052333
~~FOR OFFICIAL USE ONLY~~

Lambros D. Callimahos

Communication with Extraterrestrial Intelligence

We are not alone in the universe. A few years ago, this notion seemed farfetched; today, the existence of extraterrestrial intelligence is taken for granted by most scientists. Even the staid National Academy of Sciences has gone on record that contact with other civilizations "is no longer something beyond our dreams but a natural event in the history of mankind that will perhaps occur in the lifetime of many of us." Sir Bernard Lovell, one of the world's leading radio astronomers, has calculated that, even allowing for a margin of error of 5000%, there must be in our galaxy about 100 million stars which have planets of the right chemistry, dimensions, and temperature to support organic evolution. If we consider that our own galaxy, the Milky Way, is but one of at least a billion other galaxies similar to ours in the observable universe, the number of stars that could support some form of life is, to reach for a word, astronomical. As to advanced forms of life—advanced by our own miserable earth standards—Dr. Frank D. Drake of the National Radio Astronomy Observatory at Green Bank, West Virginia, has stated that, putting all our knowledge together, the number of civilizations which could have arisen by now is about one billion. The next question is, "Where is everybody?"

The nearest neighbor to our solar system is Alpha Centauri, only 4.3 light years away, but, according to Dr. Su-Shu Huang of the National Aeronautics and Space Administration, its planetary system is probably too young for the emergence of life. Two other heavenly friends, Epsilon Eridani and Tau Ceti, about 11 light years away, are stronger contenders for harboring life. Nevertheless, if superior civilizations are abundant, the nearest would probably be at least 100 light years away; therefore it would take 200 years for a reply to be forthcoming, a small matter of seven generations. This should, however, make little difference to us, in view of the enormous potential gain from our contact with a superior civilization. Unless we are terribly conceited (a very unscientific demeanor), we must assume that the "others" are far more advanced than we are. Even a 50-year gap would be tremendous; a 500-year gap staggers the imagination, and as for a 5000-year gap ... (By the way, if they are as much as 50 years *behind* us, forget it!) It is quite possible that "others" have satellite probes in space, retransmitting to "them" anything that sounds nonrandom to the probe. But they have probably called us several thousand years ago, and are waiting for an answer; or worse yet, they have given up; or, more probably, they have reached such impressive technological advances that they have destroyed themselves. In this connection, Professor Iosif Shklovsky, Russia's greatest radio astronomer, has cited the profound crises which lie in wait for a developing civilization, any one of which may well prove fatal:

(1) Self-destruction as a result of a thermonuclear catastrophe or some other discovery which may have unpredictable and uncontrollable consequences;
(2) Genetic danger;
(3) Overproduction of information;
(4) Restricted capacity of the individual's brain, which can lead to excessive specialization, with consequent dangers of degeneration; and
(5) A crisis precipitated by the creation of artificial intelligent beings.

Epsilon Eridani and Tau Ceti were the targets on which Dr. Drake focused his attention in the spring of

The article was given as a lecture at the Cosmos Club in Washington earlier this year

4   ~~FOR OFFICIAL USE ONLY~~

"Document number 3052333, from the National Security Agency, titled Communication with Extraterrestrial Intelligence[1] in your folders. The first line reads, *'We are not alone in the universe'*. The NSA declassified it, but if you search their website today, it's not there. However, it's easy to find with a Google search."

The Colonel continued: "One-to-one-meetings in the distant past were attended by delegates from some of the alien races. For example, in the first meeting, Eisenhower met with what were described as Tall White aliens. To you and me, they look very much like albino humans, only they stand about 8 feet tall. The second meeting was with representatives of the Grays. They might look familiar to you. They are the short, gray creatures with three fingers and big slanted almond-shaped eyes, perhaps most often featured in popular depictions of aliens."

"The last group, known as the Reptilians, resemble creatures you may have seen in science fiction horror movies. At this meeting, you can expect to see representatives of all three."

Ambassador Sinclair interrupted, "From rumors I've heard, they only communicate through telepathy, by thought. Just how are we expected to communicate with them? "

"I'm glad you asked. We have developed a solution. Our researchers in Nevada created a computer which uses artificial intelligence to translate brainwaves into sound and back the other way. Let's just say, their experiments with test subjects have been successful."

The General nodded in agreement. "Just exactly what is our goal for these negotiations? What do we want to achieve? Do we know what they

---

1. https://www.nsa.gov/portals/75/documents/news-features/declassified-documents/cryptologic-spectrum/communications_with_extraterrestrial.pdf(Real)

want? This country is not going to give up nukes, considering the ongoing turmoil everywhere. I can guarantee the military won't go for it, and you can count on total rejection from Congress and the President."

"We've made it clear that is not on the table," Anderson assured them. "It is fairly certain there have been crashes in other countries, and it's possible that Russia and China may have recovered some wrecks. We can only hope they haven't learned more secrets than we have."

The General objected. "What do we hope to accomplish at this meeting, especially if we are going at it alone, without other countries involved? You said this meeting will be at the United Nations building, for heaven's sake. How the hell do we keep a lid on it?"

"The specific meeting location is under maximum security. The aliens will arrive by a secret underground passageway from an undisclosed location. What we hope for is an assurance these beings will stop interfering in our military activities. They want to operate in the open, but we know how that will turn out. Panic. Revolt. Attacks. Pandemonium and chaos. We learned that lesson from the Orson Wells radio broadcast in 1938. Maintaining continued confidentiality is essential until we have devised a solid strategy. In the meantime, putting an end to interference with our nuclear defense is a priority."

"Have they done that? I mean, have they interfered with our defense?" The Ambassador was clearly alarmed.

"There have been several times when systems went offline for no apparent reason, and, yes, we have reason to believe aliens were behind it."

The General was sure of his words. He looked for a reaction.

"Are there any other questions?"

"Has the president been read into this situation?" the General asked.

"I can't say," replied the Colonel.

"With all respect, sir, you don't know, or you just can't say?"

"I can't, of my personal knowledge, give you the answer to that question, but I can assure you will have the full authority and responsibility to represent the government in this matter."

Both the Ambassador and the General were silent in thought.

"Then we can conclude this meeting. Review the items in your folders, but remember, nothing leaves this room, and that includes everything you have heard today. Lives, and a lot more depend on it," he stressed.

Location: The United Nations Secure Basement Meeting Room
Event: (Classified - Above Top Secret)
Presenters: UN Ambassador, Elara Sinclair, and Space Force Intelligence Chief, General Dominic Stratos. Also in the room, DIA Chief Information Officer, Colonel Richard Anderson.
Attending: Representatives of the extraterrestrials: Grays, Tall Whites, and Reptilians.

Two armed guards stood outside large, heavy doors in the basement of the United Nations in New York, as the United States Ambassador and another man wearing the uniform of an officer in the United States Space Force approached. A guard held the door open, revealing another set of double doors just beyond. The pair entered the space between the doors and waited for the guard to close the outside doors before opening the second set of doors to the secure meeting room inside. In the center of the room, there was a long table with three executive chairs on each side. Another set of double doors was visible at the far side of the secure meeting room.

Colonel Richard Anderson, already standing by the table, motioned for the ambassador and the Space Force officer to take seats beside him. In a few moments, they all sensed a presence and heard a commotion behind the big double doors on the other side of the room. As one of those doors opened, the figure of a Tall White alien timidly looked inside. The creature seemed concerned at seeing a military uniform, but appeared relaxed after recognizing Colonel Anderson.

Close behind, the smaller figure of a gray alien emerged from the shadows and followed the other alien. A few moments later, the last to enter was clearly an alien  of the Reptilian species. The first two, finding chairs inappropriate or unsatisfactory, stood while the Reptilian sat awkwardly in the last chair.

Colonel Anderson reached to switch on the Artificial Intelligence Translating device on the meeting table. As it cycled on, there was a brief humming sound followed by a low chirp and then the words, "We greet you". Anderson then took the last seat across from the aliens.

Ambassador Sinclair responded. "We greet you as well," she replied. To the General she whispered, "This is awkward!"

"Be careful," he cautioned. "Don't forget, they are reading our minds."

Elara Sinclair eyed the alien guests with unease. "How do we begin?" she thought to herself.

"Let us start by informing you of our concerns," the translator machine barked, startling all the humans. It appeared this message had come from the Tall White alien.

The General nodded and glanced at the Ambassador for confirmation. Colonel Anderson remained silent.

The Gray alien leaned forward as the translator sounded. "We are concerned about attacks on our craft and our pilots. If this continues, it will require a response."

The general answered. "While I understand the danger in the situation, it is difficult to tell our forces not to respond, while our government is not prepared to acknowledge your presence."

The Reptilian faced the humans. "We have been with you for centuries of your time."

The Ambassador held up her hand toward the General as he was about to speak. The General relaxed and paused before he replied.

"If we were to acknowledge your presence, I feel it would put your forces in greater peril. There are too many who would not be ready to accept you into our society. We still can't accept many of our own kind," he admitted.

"You must find a solution," was the response from the translator, although it was not clear who was speaking. "You are aware of our capabilities," the voice warned.

The general nodded in understanding, although he was uncertain the aliens would recognize the meaning of that motion. He looked to Anderson for signs of support, but Anderson remained motionless.

Turning back to the alien group, he replied. "We would ask your patience until we can safely reveal your existence to our population."

"They are now aware," it appeared the Gray alien was saying, though there was no movement to confirm that impression.

"I believe this contact has been a positive step," the Ambassador proposed, not wishing to respond to the challenge.

The aliens looked at one another as if to consider the statement.

"Before we can make an agreement, we must receive approval," said General Stratos.

"Then it will be," was the translated response. "We will have another meeting."

As the Gray alien moved away, the general made a gesture to shake hands. The alien stared at the outstretched hand and met the General's eyes for a moment before turning to leave. The Reptilian alien also ignored the gesture while the Nordic merely smiled. General Stratos did not sense any hostility, but made a mental note to forego hand shakes with aliens in the future.

The General and the Ambassador turned to Colonel Anderson, who appeared to be satisfied with the conference. Anderson thanked them for attending. The meeting ended and everyone left the room without further discussion.

Ambassador Sinclair received a letter in the mail from the Office of Legislative Affairs. Inside was an invitation to appear at a Congressional hearing in two weeks. Noted in the invitation were the names of others invited to testify. The list included Colonel Anderson, Space Force, and Agent Mitchel Harlan with the Central Intelligence Agency.

A Congressional committee issued "invitations" to several key people in government to appear at a closed-door hearing.

Location: Congress of the United States, secure chambers, closed-door meeting, no reporters.
Committee: The House Subcommittee on National Security, International Development, and Monetary Policy (Closed hearing)
Subject: Contact with extraterrestrial beings.

Members of Congress:
Representative Sarah Mitchell, chair, (Texas),
Congressman William "Bill" Reynolds (Ohio),
Congresswoman Olivia Chang (California),
Representative James "Jim" Anderson (Virginia),
Congresswoman Rachel Rodriguez (Florida),
Congressman Brian McCarthy (New York),
Representative Michelle Thompson (Illinois),
Congressman Robert "Bob" Harris (Arizona),
Congresswoman Natalie Walker (Colorado),
Representative Samuel "Sam" Carter (Georgia)

Committee Clerk: Ralph Johnson
Witnesses: Colonel Richard Anderson, Chief Information Officer, (Defense Intelligence Agency), General Dominic Stratos, (U.S. Space Force Public Information Officer), Deputy Director of Intelligence, (Central Intelligence Agency), Ambassador Elara Sinclair, (United Nations Ambassador).

The rumble of discussion in the hearing room quieted with the bang of the gavel by Chairperson Sarah Mitchel.

"Good afternoon, everyone. I call this secret house hearing to order. The purpose of today's session is to discuss the proposed markup on the bill requiring government disclosure of what it knows about alien beings. Mr. Johnson, please call the roll."

The clerk called the roll, a quorum was present, and the chairperson thanked the clerk.

"Ladies and gentlemen, esteemed members of the committee, and special guests, I thank you for joining this hearing on an issue of utmost importance and sensitivity. This session of the House Committee has been called to address certain matters pertaining to government disclosure regarding the potential existence of extraterrestrial beings operating within the United States and elsewhere."

"As we convene behind closed doors, it is essential to recognize the gravity of the subject before us. The purpose of today's hearing is to explore and deliberate on information that may have significant implications for our understanding of the world, and the role of the United States government in managing the impact of such information."

"We have gathered here with a shared commitment to ensure the safety and well-being of our citizens. As we delve into matters concerning potential extraterrestrial activities within our borders, it is crucial that we approach this discussion with the utmost responsibility, discretion, and respect for the classified nature of the information at hand."

"Before we proceed, I must remind all present that we are sharing classified information in this closed session and it must not be disclosed to the public. Our duty is to engage in a thoughtful and rigorous examination of the evidence presented while upholding the principles of national security."

Congresswoman Mitchel next moved to introducing the witnesses.

"Now that we have set the stage for this hearing, it is my privilege to introduce our distinguished panel of witnesses, individuals whose expertise and insights are invaluable in shedding light on the matters before us. Each witness has been called to provide testimony on their respective areas of knowledge and responsibility.

"First, we have Colonel Richard Anderson, representing the Defense Intelligence Agency. Colonel Anderson brings a wealth of experience in intelligence and defense matters, and we are eager to hear his perspective on the information related to potential extraterrestrial activities within the United States."

"Next, we welcome General Dominic Stratos, a distinguished representative from the U.S. Space Force. General Stratos, whose career has been dedicated to the defense and security of our nation, is uniquely positioned to offer his perspective into space-related implications associated with today's subject. Joining us from the Central Intelligence Agency is Agent Mitchel Harlan. Agent Harlan's role within the CIA involves intelligence gathering and analysis, and we look forward to hearing any pertinent information he can provide regarding the agency's understanding of the matters at hand.

"Last but certainly not least, we are honored to welcome Ambassador Elara Sinclair. As the United Nations Ambassador, she brings an international perspective to our discussion. Her presence underscores the potential global implications of the information we are about to explore. I ask our witnesses to approach their testimony with the utmost clarity and honesty. The committee is eager to benefit from your collective expertise, and we appreciate your willingness to contribute to this important dialogue.

"As we are aware, there have been several efforts to include a provision in the National Defense Authorization Act, directing the government to disclose what it knows about extraterrestrials operating within the United States. We are here to further discuss the merits or drawbacks of such disclosure.

"The chair first recognizes Representative Sam Carter of Georgia. "

"Thank you, Representative Mitchel. My question is directed to Agent Mitchel Harlan. Mr. Harlan. The CIA continues to resist full disclosure of interaction, if any, with extraterrestrials. Can you tell us why the CIA has taken that position?"

Agent Harlan leaned toward the microphone on the desk. "Certainly, Representative. The answer should be obvious. It's about national security. If we were to disclose interactions with extraterrestrial beings, it could inadvertently reveal classified technical capabilities to our enemies. It would certainly create public panic and unrest. The existence of space aliens might involve diplomatic considerations. Premature disclosure could lead to misinformation and confusion. When and if we come in contact with extraterrestrial entities. we need to evaluate the full scope of what that might mean."

Sam Carter looked at his notes as he said, "That's all I have. I may have other questions at a later time."

"Thank you, Sam," said the chairperson. "The chair recognizes Congressman Reynolds. Bill?"

Congressman Bill Reynolds surveyed the witness table, and his attention came to focus on the Defense Intelligence Officer.

"Colonel Anderson, does your agency agree with the CIA's position?"

"No, Representative Reynolds, we do not. My agency sees contact with alien civilizations as an opportunity to foster global collaboration in addressing the potential for both threats and advantages. Withholding information from the public is both ill-advised and futile. In recent months, we have seen a steady flow of leaks and revelations. The public feels it has a right to know about discoveries that may impact humanity's future. Concealing such information erodes public trust in government institutions. Congressman, to be blunt, people are figuring out these things have been going on for a long time; decades, maybe centuries."

"Madam Chair?"

"The chair recognizes Congresswoman Olivia Chang, of California."

"Thank you." Olivia Chang addressed the representative of the Defense Intelligence Agency, "Colonel, you don't share Agent Harlan's concern about national security?"

"Of course," the Colonel replied. "But keep in mind, transparency can help us rebuild the public's trust. Doing that would allow us to develop contingency plans to minimize panic in case of unexpected events."

"I see Brian McCarthy would like to speak next," said Representative Mitchel, gesturing with an open hand toward the Congressman from New York. "It's your turn."

"Thank you," he replied. "My concern is where this puts us regarding foreign countries. I see we are graced by our United Nations Ambassador. Ambassador Sinclair, what is the position of the United Nations in all this? Have they developed any plans?"

"Yes, Congressman," Elara Sinclair responded. "In 2018, the U.N. Office for Outer Space Affairs held a workshop on the implications of research on Extra Terrestrial Intelligence. The U.N., as a body, recognizes the potential for both peaceful and harmful contact with extraterrestrial civilizations and has prepared for either possibility."

"If I may," Congressman Bob Harris of Arizona spoke up.

"The chair recognizes the gentleman from Arizona."

"What I want to know is how far is this going to go? I mean, are we going to accept little green men adding to the problems we already have?"

The panel members could be heard commenting to each other as the chairwoman rapped the gavel.

"Come to order please," she said, "To whom are you directing that question?"

"I don't know, but somebody needs to answer it. That's all I want to say."

"All right, the chair recognizes the Congresswoman from Florida, Rachael Rodriguez. You have a question for our panel?"

"Yes, I do, thank you. We have not yet heard from General Stratos. General, where does the Space Force stand in all this?"

"I'm certainly glad you asked. Thank you, Representative Rodriguez. It is common knowledge that the United States Space Force was created to address our nation's interests in the space environment. We stand ready to work collaboratively with relevant agencies to plan a responsible disclosure strategy, balanced by the need for stability and national security. If ET is out there, we can easily assume they have far superior technology. It would be unwise to provoke a response with hostile action on our part. We need to stress that all airborne military forces have to work with the Space Force in avoiding unfortunate circumstances. "

"If I may," said Ambassador Sinclair.

"Yes, Ambassador," replied Congresswoman Rodrigues.

"I would like to ask if the Congress might be open to forming an agreement with the aliens, if we should be in a position to propose one?"

Again there was the buzz of hushed discussion.

Agent Harlan raised his hand.

"Does the CIA have a suggestion?" asked the chairwoman.

"Yes. I would suggest that we not get ahead of ourselves here. We don't officially know if any of this is real. I am concerned about the negative implications for national security."

Committee chair Mitchel asked, "Is there any further discussion?" She paused. " Hearing none, Is there a motion to proceed with the markup?"

Congresswoman Olivia Chang responded. "Madam Chair, I move we proceed with the markup on the bill."

"We have a motion to proceed with the markup. Is there a second?" asked the Chair.

Representative Michelle Thompson raised her hand and was recognized.

The chair proceeded with the vote. "The motion has been made and seconded. All those in favor, please say, aye."

A few committee members were heard to say "Aye"

Mitchel then said, "All those opposed, please say no."

The response from the members was a much stronger "No".

"The noes have it." Mitchel confirmed, "The motion is not carried. The markup on the bill requiring government transparency about alien beings is not approved. With that, we conclude our business for today and we thank you all for your time."

And the meeting ended.

Elara Sinclair turned to Colonel Anderson and asked, "What was that all about?"

Colonel Anderson stood and faced the Ambassador. "What's it always about? Power and money."

With that, he smirked at General Stratos, and they left the room.

Following the Congressional hearing, Ambassador Sinclair took the three and a half hour Acela Express train home to New York. During the trip, she replied to email messages, clicked through several YouTube channels, and checked news websites. She also arranged for an Uber ride home from the station.

It was late when she rode the elevator to her apartment on the fourth floor. She was about to get ready for bed when there was a tap on the balcony glass door. Who could be knocking from outside this high up? As she opened the drapes, she was taken aback by a Tall White alien, perhaps the Nordic from the meeting, standing outside on the balcony.

Once she recovered from the shock, she considered what to do. Against her better instincts, she unlocked the glass balcony door, allowing the alien to enter. The alien reached out to her with what appeared to be a common pair of sunglasses.

"What's this?" she asked.

She sensed the telepathic answer: "This will allow you to see what is real," it said.

"I don't understand," Elara protested.

"Things are not always what they seem," it replied. "Wear them to see through disguises."

Ambassador Sinclair was about to ask for an explanation when the alien returned to the balcony and vanished into the night. Still curious, she put the glasses in her purse, closed and locked the balcony door, and prepared to go to sleep.

She had requested a meeting with the head of the CIA to get a better understanding of why that agency adamantly opposed the call for transparency. The next morning, the Ambassador's phone buzzed with a text message granting approval of her request. The appointment was for 2 pm with the Deputy CIA chief.

"Another three-hour train ride," she thought. Except the trains don't go to Virginia, so it was back to D.C.

Back in Washington, Elara took a taxi for the 15-minute ride to CIA headquarters at the George Bush Center for Intelligence in McLean, Virginia.

At the security check, she reached in her purse for her I.D. badge and felt the special glasses, and wondered if they would pass the scanning device. On a whim, she put the special glasses on top of her head as she walked through the scanner. Her purse passed through, and the security agent directed her to a hallway to the left.

On entering the Director's office, she checked in with the secretary and took a seat in the outer office as people came and went. She looked up to see Mitch Harlan, the agent she met at the Congressional hearing, leaving the Director's office. They both smiled. As he passed by, she thought to pull the special glasses over her eyes.

She held her breath to stop from gasping at what she saw. The glasses showed something completely different. Through the glasses, the agent took on the appearance of a large chameleon, with segmented ridges along a bald head. Green scales that resembled the hide of an alligator covered the exposed backs of his arms. She tried to tie all the pieces together in her mind until the secretary motioned it was time for her to meet with the Director.

As she entered the Deputy Director's office, she briefly lowered the special glasses to her eyes to be sure she was meeting with a human and not another alien. In the meeting, the Deputy Director's response was little more than a rehash of Agent Harlan's testimony before Congress. But now, that testimony and the CIA's position took on a new meaning.

After meeting with the Deputy Director, Ambassador Sinclair made a call to Colonel Anderson. After a few moments, the switchboard connected her call to his office.

"Anderson," he answered.

"Good afternoon, Colonel. I have some new information I would like to share with you."

"Okay, go ahead," he replied.

"No, I need to meet with you in person," Elara Sinclair answered. "Can we meet where we did before?" She was referring to the SCIF location.

"Certainly." checking his schedule, he continued, "Are you in town?"

"Yes, I'm in town," she answered.

"If it's urgent, I can meet you this afternoon. How about 16:30? Does that work for you?"

"I'll be there," Elara replied.

Upon arriving, someone guided her to the secure area in the Pentagon where the Colonel was waiting.

"There's a problem," she began, even before taking a seat at the round mahogany table, but not before she briefly looked through the sunglasses and put them back in her purse.

"The CIA will never budge on the disclosure issue."

"How can you be that sure about it?"

"Let's say there's a factor we didn't count on. I'm not sure how wide-spread it is, but let's say there's an alien factor at the CIA," she said. "My source is absolute and first hand. There's at least one alien reptilian under cover in the CIA and who knows where else. That's probably why they like things just as they are; no transparency."

"I can see that you are serious about the accusation, but that's not enough for me to go on," replied the Colonel.

She pulled the special glasses from her purse and handed them to Anderson, who looked them over with curiosity and handed them back.

"This is how I know, " she said. "I got these glasses from the Nordic alien. When I put them on over at the CIA, I saw a Reptilian posing as one of the agents we saw at the hearing. He was just coming out of the Director's office. In my meeting with the director, he stood firmly against any disclosure, no matter what, come Hell or Congressional subpoena. Keep in mind who he met with before I talked to him. Add it up."

"Where does that leave us?"

"It probably leaves us with no agreement," she answered.

"So, we've got one less card on the table, but we still know what the aliens hold in their deck. I would really like to know how much Stratos has been holding back. I think he knows more than he's letting on," Sinclair stated.

"I agree we need to bring Stratos in on this, but let's not let him know you just told me. Let's see if he's in his office," Colonel Anderson said. He stepped out of the SCIF to send a message to the Space Force headquarters office. The response was almost instant.

"Great! he can be here in a few minutes," he said as he closed the door behind him.

The Pentagon building has sections of rings and corridors, and the headquarters for the Space Force were in a neighboring ring. There was a knock on the door and Anderson pressed a button on his desk that released the lock for Stratos to join them.

"Good afternoon, General. I'm glad you could meet with us again." He continued, "Congress seems to have closed the door on transparency, at least for the current session. I wonder if there is something more about the presence of aliens that you would care to share with the Ambassador and myself."

The General paused to consider how to begin his reply.

"As you know, I've only been in my position for a short time, but I have long had an interest in the subject of aliens before the Space Force was created. There is more I could tell you. I'm just not sure you are prepared for it."

Colonel Anderson stared down at his desk as he collected his thoughts. "If you can provide us with a bigger picture, that's what we need. Everybody's under increasing pressure and I'm not sure how long we have before things start to get.... out of hand."

The General sat back in his chair before he continued.

"Okay, here goes. The aliens we met in New York represented the Grays, the Tall Whites, and the Reptilians. Let's consider each variety. The Grays seem to be prevalent, or at least more common in encounters with people. The so-called flying saucer that crashed at Roswell was one of theirs. They seem to be intent on biological research. We suspect they may be responsible for the animal mutilations as well. For the most part, they are friendly enough, if you can overlook the human abductions. For all we know, they could be breeding hybrids to repopulate their own planet."

"What about the others?" Elara Sinclair asked.

"I'll start with the Tall Whites, or Nordics, as they've been called. They seem to be interested in more benevolent concerns, environmental and spiritual wisdom. It's possible they may have been the source of some of the guiding principles found in most, if not all, of the ancient religions. People have often seen their delta-shape spacecraft near nuclear facilities. Nordics appear to have the most advanced technology and they could be behind events occurring at those nuclear facilities. Namely, we suspect they may have developed the ability to disable nuclear weapons. If some country declares war and nothing happens when they push the red button, that's when we'll find out. I've often wondered if they are responsible for the crop circles, as an artistic expression."

"That leaves the Reptilians," Anderson commented.

"Oh, yes, the lizard people. That's where things get interesting. Frankly, I'm surprised they were even willing to meet with us. From all indications, they can change their appearance. It's called shapeshifting. They could be anywhere and we have no way of knowing. Reptilians could be in this building, for all we know."

Sinclair glanced at Anderson, and back to the General as the general continued.

"Their motives are not at all friendly. They show no signs of empathy and our people describe them as manipulative and aggressive. Reptilians have been suspected of involvement in genetic experimentation. They have certainly proven untrustworthy, so any agreement or treaty with that species is a pointless waste of time.

"Do we know which species is aboard the 'Tic Tacs' the Navy has been reporting?" Anderson asked.

"We don't have any information on that. Now if you were to ask about the small orbs, the translucent spheres with black cubes inside, those could be some kind of remote-control drones gathering data."

Sinclair wanted to know, "So, how do some of them skip around like a ping-pong ball, making ninety-degree turns and popping in and out of sight?"

"Interestingly, that appears to be one effect of anti-gravity propulsion. Within the anti-gravity field, the rules of physics and inertia don't apply. It's like they can jump in and out of a different dimension. It's possible that's how they can travel galactic distances."

"How are we getting away with shooting at flying saucers and other alien spacecraft?" the colonel wanted to know.

"That's the thing I can't understand. They have such incredible technology, and yet it appears the Air Force has managed to make a collection of alien spacecraft and wrecks, we assume from all over the globe. Of course, they can't admit it. They refuse to discuss it with my department because we transferred space matters to the Space Force when it was formed. Even NASA felt offended by that.

"Then where does that leave us?" asked the colonel

"It leaves us in a box. We can't make any promises, especially since none of the presidents after Nixon have been briefed about any of this. Congress has been sniffing around, and I think some in Congress may think they know more than they do. We can't tell the military not to shoot at them because they will want to know why not. If we admit any of this to the general public, it will be total chaos. Social media will cause people to go more insane than they already are. The Orson Wells radio program in the 40s was nothing compared to what this could cause. Beyond that, we don't know how much the Russians or Chinese or even India know, or what they might do if they were to find out how much we know. As far as negotiating any kind of agreement with the aliens, we have nothing to offer."

"Then what?" said the Colonel.

"It means we all sit tight and hope the aliens don't shoot back. Who knows? Maybe they have some kind of agreement among themselves that prevents them from destroying us. But if they start shooting back, everything we have will look like toys. That will be revelation day, no more hiding the truth. It will mean the start of a war measured in minutes. Let's just hope things stay just as they are."

"Is the commander of the Space Force aware of all this?" the Colonel asked.

"Of course not," replied the General.

"So, what is our strategy? Do we call another meeting with the aliens?" Sinclair asked. "How do we go about it?"

The Colonel thought for a moment. "I have a special channel of communications for that. I'll have to arrange for the secure room at the UN again without drawing attention. I'll let you know when. See you back in New York."

Two days later, they scheduled the new meeting. Anderson again reminded Sinclair to guard her thoughts.

Colonel Anderson removed the translator box from his briefcase and turned it on. As before, the aliens were the last to arrive.

As the aliens assembled on their side of the table, the translator box emitted an artificial voice.

"Greetings to you."

The Ambassador spoke first. "We know you would like for us to provide an answer, but I'm afraid that will not be possible, at least not at present."

She made direct eye contact with the Gray alien. "We will continue to work in that direction," she said. "However, at this moment, I must report we are not ready to propose an agreement."

"We were under the impression this is the organization representing all the nations," the voice from the translator replied.

"The UN is an organization of a large number of nations, but we are not yet ready to bring other countries into this discussion. Our intelligence agencies have precluded that."

"Then, you will have our response," was the strange reply from the aliens.

With that, the meeting ended.

On a sunny afternoon, a large triangular shape emerged from the clouds above the NASA Kennedy Space Center Visitor Complex in Florida. At first, only a few tourists took notice, until it cast a shadow over the Gateway building. The alien spaceship hovered silently less than 1,000 feet above. Visitors pointed eagerly, perhaps assuming it to be part of the NASA demonstration. The spaceship was perhaps two hundred feet wide, with glowing lights at each point. Visitors could see a bluish glow at the center of what was clearly an alien spaceship. Then, off to the east was another spaceship, the smaller round shape of the typical flying saucer. Both spaceships hovered in silence for perhaps fifteen or twenty minutes before silently and slowly ascending into the clouds and fading from view.

Surprisingly, there was little or none of the panic that might have been expected.

Photos and videos flooded social media. Sirens blared as space center security vehicles started arriving from all directions and established a command center in the bus parking area to the east of the NASA complex. Soon, visitors were being interviewed by security personnel as military officers from the Space Force arrived. Not long after, television news crews joined them.

In his Washington office, Colonel Anderson was on the phone with General Stratos while watching television news reports.

"Well, I guess we have our answer from the aliens," the Colonel told Stratos.

"I was afraid this would happen," Stratos confided, "But I'm not surprised. We can't avoid transparency now, and there's no way the military can excuse shooting at them. The aliens just forced their hand. I don't know how the wizard can hide behind the curtain now. What amazes me is that so far, there's none of the predicted public panic. In fact, in the television news interviews I've seen, people are saying they knew it all along."

"But why NASA? Why now?" Colonel Anderson asked.

"Do you really think NASA wasn't aware of the aliens?" Stratos countered.

"NASA had to know, "Anderson replied. "By the way, did you notice today's date?"

"July eighth. So what?"

"Think back to 1947. This is the anniversary of the crash at Roswell."

General Stratos paused, the significance of the date sinking in. "Well, I'll be damned," he muttered. "They certainly have a flair for
the dramatic."

***

Chapter Twenty

The Last Martian

Alone in his spacecraft, the pilot probed the conditions of the planet Phaeton, capturing data and images to plan for future exploration. After transmitting the data back to Galaxy Control, the pilot was concerned there was no confirmation. Concluding the exploration mission, the pilot configured the controls for a return to Mars.

At long last, the hyper-drive disengaged on approach to the fourth planet. The pilot listened for communications before making the call for landing instructions. The repeated calls to Galaxy Control went unanswered, and all the communication channels stayed ominously quiet.

The pilot gazed through the view port only to see an enormous red cloud engulfing everything below. The ship's sensors detected a massive neutron irradiation event devastating the entire planet, as they recorded a strong reading of Xenon 129 in the escaping atmosphere. In a horror scene, the pilot watched as a tremendous red cloud rose from the surface, pushing the tiny spaceship through an invisible vortex of space and time with a powerful neutrino force.

When the spaceship emerged from the vortex, the pilot was amazed to find all the ship's systems functioning normally, except for the chronograph, which had advanced by three hundred million years. The navigation instruments showed the tiny ship had somehow traveled more than a hundred million miles toward the next planet. That planet was Earth.

Though only a small exploration vessel, the spaceship's Zero-Point Energy system could continue to provide unlimited power for the ship and its anti-gravity propulsion system. However, survival on another planet would be another matter. The home planet, now centuries in the past and likely uninhabitable, severely limited the pilot's options.

As the small spacecraft approached the blue planet, instruments detected satellites and other items and objects in orbit. The pilot maneuvered the spaceship into position.

The spaceship maintained the orbit as the pilot turned his attention to selecting a landing point, its sensors scanning. The location would need to provide access to resources while still maintaining the secrecy of his presence in the hostile environment. Once the ship's computer identified a suitable location, the pilot set a course for a secluded and uninhabited section of the Great Smokey Mountains in North Carolina.

Anyone observing the small spaceship's rapid descent could mistake it for a shooting star or meteor.

The pilot knew he would need to learn about this planet's inhabitants at some point. With the spacecraft safely hidden in the dense forest, he turned his attention to intercepting communications signals. With no further use for its original purpose, the pilot reconfigured space communicator to receive local signals and transmissions. The repurposed communicator screen produced a jumble of sounds and images. The spaceship's computer assimilated the communications and generated language training for the pilot generated from television news and movie broadcasts.

The edible fungi on the spaceship would last a long time, but the exploration mission had depleted the ship's water supply. Fortunately, a small stream flowed through the bottom of the valley, providing the pilot with water to drink, to wash himself and his clothing. The pilot sat under a tree, absorbed in thoughts about his precarious existence. At one point, confronted by a bear, the pilot used a pocket-size laser beam to distract the bear, providing the pilot with time to escape inside his spaceship.

Over time, the pilot gained a rudimentary knowledge of the English language. He also decided on a common name, assembled from the various entertainment shows he received on the repurposed spaceship communicator.

Ryan Mitchel felt a powerful attraction to nature. He'd hiked countless trails, but the Appalachian Trail held a special attraction for the young college student. Spring Break was a perfect time for a hike on the Trail.

That day, he walked among the towering trees with cool breezes and the strong scent of pine in the air. The trail followed a ridge overlooking a deep valley. Looking over the edge of a precipice, he saw the glint of sunlight reflecting from something in the deep vegetation in the valley below. Concerned that it might be the undiscovered wreckage of a downed aircraft, he marked his location on the GPS application on his phone and ventured down the slope to find the source of the reflected sunlight.

Pushing his way through the vines and branches into a clearing, it surprised him to find an old gentleman, or perhaps a hobo, sitting on a rock outcropping. The man appeared to be deep in thought until the crack of branches and leaves drew his attention to Ryan's presence. The man wore what appeared to be coveralls with military-style boots, a strange attire not suitable for hiking on trails.

"Hello," Ryan called out.

At first, the man appeared flustered, unable to decide how to respond.

"Hello," Ryan called out again as he came to stand in the clearing just below where the man was sitting.

The man simply nodded, as if Ryan were merely a passerby.

"I'm Ryan," he said finally, looking up and hoping for a response. "How did you end up this far in the wilderness? Who are you? "

The pilot mumbled something.

Ryan repeated his question. "What is your name?"

"I am," he hesitated. "John," the man finally replied. "John Martin," he said with what appeared, for a moment, to be a sly grin. The pilot (John Martin), although he could be more than a hundred years old by Earth's measure, showed few signs of aging other than his thick silvery hair. His skin bore no visible lines or wrinkles but appeared almost plastic in texture. He wore loose dark coveralls and boots, bearing no markings of any kind other than a strange insignia on one sleeve.

As John fixed his gaze on the approaching hiker, he revealed human-like eyes, but with a decidedly orange tint.

"Are you lost?" Ryan asked.

"No, not lost. I am living here," John replied. "Please to not stay."

As the man spoke, his deep, steady voice did not match his hobo-like appearance. His words were almost robotic and devoid of intonation, in a strangely stilted accent Ryan did not recognize.

Ryan's anthropology education made him aware of subtle nuances in behavior and language, which only increased his curiosity as he pursued the conversation.

He paused for a moment, taking in the dimensions of the situation.

"It can be pretty lonely out here," he began.

With difficulty and some hesitation, John replied, "I ... prefer alone."

"People can be a bit ... perplexing," Ryan continued. "They can react with hostility toward those outside of their culture or don't fit in. I guess it's always been in our nature. People who are different have difficulty fitting in and being accepted."

Ryan sounded like an anthropology textbook.

John turned to Ryan, studying him for a moment. "What you say is true," he said. "I have seen it ... in the news and movies. That is why I stay here."

Judging from news and movies, I can see why you have that perspective, but it doesn't accurately represent everyone. I am fascinated by cultures and perspectives that defy convention. There are many who recognize and value the differences that make each culture unique.

"This world is ... complex," John replied succinctly.

Ryan thought he had gained John's trust. "Where did you say you are from?" he asked.

"I did not," was John's quick response. The reply came with such finality Ryan decided not to press the matter further.

John realized he could trust no one on this planet, knowing just how different it was from his own culture.

"Must go now," he said, but made no motion to leave.

Ryan took it to be an invitation for him to go.

Climbing back up the hill, Ryan turned to look back at the old man, but he had vanished into the forest. Curious to know how the man could survive out in the open, he crept back to see where he had gone. Careful to move so as not to make a sound, Ryan glimpsed the man just ahead. As he stopped to watch, he discovered the source of the glint of light that had sparked his curiosity. It was a small spaceship, secluded under the thick canopy of tall pines.

Ryan paused a moment in shock. Not seeking to confront the strange man, Ryan turned and climbed back uphill until his phone had a signal. Using the GPS, he returned to the trail on the ridge above. Darkness was falling in the forest, so he found a campsite along the trail.

He sat on a log by a campfire, enjoying the night in the forest and thinking about his encounter with the strange man, this spaceman, and his secret. In his anthropology studies, Ryan had observed the pattern of hostility prevalent throughout human history. If this spaceman had immersed himself in our media long enough to gain a working knowledge of the most common languages, he would have also developed a perspective of human nature. That picture should have provided a clear warning.

Ryan thought about the public outcry were the government to reveal what it knows about the existence of extraterrestrial beings on this planet. The bigger question was, what would happen if they were to realize the existence of such beings? How would the population respond?

We know how they would respond!

If history has taught us anything, it has taught us the predictable response from the population would be a combination of hostility and greed toward the alien technology and its inherently destructive capabilities.

Where did the spaceman come from? He looked nothing like the typical alien in science fiction or movies. Clearly, by his appearance, whatever the species, the common ancestral roots with humans were obvious. Only at close range were the differences visible: the odd skin texture and the orange eye color.

Ryan then remembered the old man's odd smile as he gave his name: Martin. Was he revealing a secret? Some scientists proposed Mars had once been like Earth until millions of years ago when some atmospheric nuclear event wiped away the planet's vegetation and atmosphere. But the Mars Rover's explorations of the red planet revealed nothing but dust and destruction, a planet showing no sign of habitation.

Unless...

Through time travel or some other means, was it possible that "John" could be the last survivor of a civilization that once existed on the planet Mars in the far distant past?

On reflection, Ryan now understood the old man's reluctance to make contact. Any objective observation of our planet would reveal an abundance of hostility to outside cultures, even among our own population, let alone that of another planet. Human hostility can surface even within cultural groups. All over this world, tribes fight among themselves, nations resist immigration and wars erupt over territory, power, and religion. We humans can't get along among ourselves, let alone with beings from other worlds. There have even been reports of our military trying to shoot down UFOs. In the scenario of beings from other planets, how could they expect a friendly reception?

Ryan also realized any alien technology aboard the spacecraft could create problems. It would be silly to expect otherwise. If alien technology could provide a source of clean and abundant power from a Zero Point energy system, for example, it would destabilize the fossil fuel industry and lead to economic turmoil in energy-producing regions, collapsing the local economy of those regions. Corporations and countries reliant on energy exports would resist any change, leading to conflicts and trade disputes. There would be international fights over the control of alien technology, leading to tensions and even military conflict.

Political upheaval from the sudden revelation of alien presence could undermine the credibility of political leaders who had withheld secrets for decades. Populations would express outrage that their governments had been hiding information, resulting in protests, distrust, or even the downfall of those governments.

The upending of entire industries, including aerospace and defense, would cause job losses and economic disruption, as well as unforeseen environmental consequences.

The world's religions would face a challenge to their power structure and could be expected to fight to keep that power. Extremist groups could be expected to exploit the chaos, fueling anti-government sentiments and violence.

The most predictable outcome would be fear and distrust of extraterrestrial beings and those who interact with them, which would cause further increases in social divisions.

It's the age-old question that is all too often overlooked: *then what?*

Ryan finally understood why world governments had spent decades denying the existence of extraterrestrial life—and, perhaps, why they were right to do so. Humanity wasn't ready. Not yet.

A soft glow flickered on the horizon, drawing Ryan's eye. As he sat in the quiet dusk, he watched the small spacecraft rise silently into the darkening sky. He recognized its shape instantly.

That's when the truth settled in: he could never tell anyone what had happened. The world wasn't ready for "John Martin," the last Martian. Not now. Maybe not ever.

Somewhere out there, the last of an alien race was searching for a place to hide—on a planet more dangerous than he had imagined.

***

Chapter Twenty-One

The Alien Abduction of Susan

Susan lived with her college roommate in a small two-story off-campus cottage. Her roommate, Cathy, was a bit of a party-girl, and was out for the night when Susan curled up with the TV remote for an evening of movies.

It was a little after 10 pm as she idly clicked through the TV selections. A light flashed through the French doors leading from her room to the second-floor deck. The doors were partway open, and a gentle night breeze tossed the curtains. At first, she thought it might be Cathy's headlights.

"Hmm. Must have been a lousy party," she thought. Listening more closely, though, she didn't hear a car. In fact, she heard nothing at all. Curious, Susan set the TV remote aside, opened the double doors and stepped out on the deck. The light came again, this time brighter, gliding over the treetops. As her eyes became adjusted to the darkness, she could make out what appeared to be something large, maybe a blimp.

Without warning, an invisible force lifted her up from the deck. She wanted to scream, but she couldn't make a sound. She felt herself being pulled higher and higher toward a giant craft overhead. As Susan was pulled inside, strange beings surrounded her. They fastened her to a long white table with rounded edges. One creature clutched several glowing crystals with three long insect-like fingers and waved them back and forth over Susan's body. Susan strained her arms against whatever was holding her down. As the creature brought the crystals closer to Susan's trembling body, they pulsed with light. That's when she lost consciousness.

Susan's housemate, Cathy, returned a little after midnight. As she passed by Susan's room, she saw the door was open, which was unusual. She also noticed Susan was not in her room. She called Susan's name, with no answer. With a wry expression on her face, she walked down the hall to her own room. Pulling her phone out of her back pocket, she dialed Susan's number. She stopped as she heard a phone ringing behind her. Cathy returned to Susan's room. Susan's phone was there on the bed with the TV remote. She noticed the doors to the deck were open, so she poked her head outside to check. No Susan. She closed the doors and came back inside.

Her curiosity was turning to worry as she continued to her room. That was when she thought about calling Susan's boyfriend.

Kyle answered, "Hi, Cathy. What's up?"

Without an explanation, she asked, "Is Susan with you?"

"No," Kyle answered, "I had to work tonight. I just got home. Why?"

"I don't know, I just wondered," Cathy replied, trying not to reveal her concern. "Her car is still here, but she's not in her room. And she left her phone. The doors were all locked, so I thought she might be with you. I'm sure she's out with her friends and just forgot her phone. Sorry to bother you!"

Cathy had just ended the call when she heard the shower running.

"Susan? That you?" she called out from her room.

"Yeah." came Susan's answer.

By then, it was almost one in the morning. Relieved, Cathy went on to bed.

Despite the late hours the night before, Cathy was up early, fixing something to eat in the kitchen. A few minutes later, as she was biting down on a warm toast, Susan joined her, glancing at her phone as she walked.

"Did you call me last night?".

"Yeah," Cathy answered. "I didn't see you when I got home, and I thought you were out. I got concerned, so I called your number."

Susan's face revealed bewilderment. "No, I was here all night."

Cathy returned her bewildered look. She was about to explain about her call to Kyle, but didn't.

"I had the weirdest dream," Susan remarked casually as she poured the last of the coffee into a cup rescued from the sink and plumped down at the table.

"Yeah?" Then, swallowing her toast, Cathy continued, "What kind of dream?"

"I dreamed I saw a bright light coming in from the deck, so I went out to see what it was. Then some giant thing in the sky flashed a beam on me. I wanted to run back in the house, but I couldn't move. I felt like I was paralyzed."

"That was some dream." Cathy said, about to finish the last bite of her toast. "Do go on!" she replied, now bemused.

Susan continued. "Well, as I was being lifted into the air, I looked down at the trees in front of the house. When I looked up, this ... thing, pulled me inside."

"So, what did you see in there?" Cathy asked, wanting to hear more.

"I saw strange creatures. They put me on a table and started waving these glowing crystals over me."

"Did they say anything to you?" Cathy asked, clearly amused and not convinced.

"I don't remember them saying anything." She paused, and then continued. "I wanted to ask them what they were doing to me, but I couldn't talk," Susan continued. "Somehow, they fastened me to the table," Susan said. "The one waving the crystals over me dropped one, and I felt it fall into my hand. I closed my fist and grabbed it, but the creature didn't see me do it."

"Then what happened?" Cathy asked.

"That was it. I woke up in my bed. I felt kind of weird, so I got up and took a shower."

Later, Susan recalled other details about her strange experience, which she shared with Cathy. She remembered strange creatures with big, dark, slanted eyes. Recalling the fear she felt while under their control, she noticed the creature's hands had three long, insect-like fingers and they all wore some kind of glossy dark uniform.

Cathy remained unconvinced, while Susan's curiosity grew.

Susan went online with an Artificial Intelligence app on her phone. She typed in a prompt, asking about alien abductions. The AI program explained how memories can be influenced by a variety of factors, including television and movies. The response continued, relating that certain psychological conditions can produce perceived experiences that are sometimes interpreted as alien abductions. Things like sleep paralysis and lucid dreaming.

"It sure was lucid to me," Susan told Cathy, as she shared what she had learned.

Eventually, Susan agreed with Cathy that her "experience" was only a dream, likely triggered by something she saw on TV. That still didn't explain why Cathy couldn't find her that night.

Later in the afternoon, the two girls worked together cleaning the house. They moved from room to room, dusting, tidying and vacuuming. When they got to Susan's room, Cathy was vacuuming the carpet under the bed when she heard a clinking sound. Concerned she might have sucked up a lost earring, she opened the deck doors and took the vacuum canister outside. She flipped over the outdoor rug and snapped open the dust canister. As she carefully shook the vacuum contents onto the back of the rug, she stared at what she saw.

"Susan," she called. "You want to see this."

"What?" Susan asked, as she came over from making the bed.

"This," Cathy replied, pointing at the dusty pile. "I thought the vacuum might have sucked up one of your earrings, but ... Look."

There, among the dust bunnies and sand, was a very shiny object, but it wasn't jewelry. Susan took one look and the two girls turned to stare at each other in disbelief. What they saw was not a lost earring, but the glowing crystal the strange being had dropped into Susan's hand aboard the spaceship ... in her "dream."

***

Chapter Twenty-Two

The Alien Abduction of Ralph

Now for a very short story about the abduction of Ralph, the plumber.

Actually, that should be *assistant* plumber. You see, there was this test, and ... Well, that's not important to our story.

As Ralph's eyes opened, he found himself staring into the creepy face of a space alien! The creature came closer and closer... and then just faded away.

To a commercial for *Ozempic*[1].

Ralph had fallen asleep on the couch watching the Late, Late, Late Movie. As he got up, he heard a metallic crunching sound. He'd been stepping on his empty beer cans.

He made his way to the bedroom, where he found the door ... locked. That was when he remembered *why* he was sleeping on the couch. Now fully awake, he decided to take a walk. Still in his bathrobe, He

---

1. (NovoFine® and Ozempic® are registered trademarks of Novo Nordisk A/S.)

slipped on his flip-flops. Out the front door, he
walked to the bus stop in front of the Last Resort trailer park.

As he sat on the bus stop bench, he heard a loud humming sound and looked up to see a beam of light. Well, the sound was more like a moped, but that's not important either.

He thought, *It's the space aliens!* Ralph jumped into the beam of light ... and it just kept moving. So, he ran and jumped into the light beam again. This time a strange force took hold of him, and he felt himself being pulled upward, on his back, into an opening in the bottom of a giant spaceship. Bang! His head bumped against the spaceship. Slowly, he felt himself being lowered and rotated to a vertical position as he slipped through a hole into the spaceship.

Actually, it wasn't really that giant. The ceiling was only about five feet, but it was the right size for the four-foot tall aliens inside.

The aliens levitated him onto a long, flat table, just like at the doctor's office, but without the paper. Unable to move, the little alien beings poked and probed at him. They pulled up his shirt.

And then they put it back.

The next thing Ralph knew, he was back on the bus bench in front of the trailer park when again he saw a beam of light ... back and forth. It went from side to side of the street.

He heard a loud noise coming toward him ....

A street sweeper.

He decided maybe it was time to go home. As he approached the door, he saw his wife carrying a basket of laundry.

"The Aliens abducted me!" he announced.

"So, what are you doing here?" she asked.

"They brought me back," Ralph replied.

His wife mumbled under her breath, "Hmmm. Just my luck. *They* didn't want you either."

"What was that?" he asked.

"I said," as she spoke louder, "I'M GOING TO THE LAUNDROMAT. Fix your own damn breakfast."

And that's the story of the space alien abduction of Ralph, the plumber's helper.

Err, assistant.

***

Chapter Twenty-Three

My Dog is my Doctor

William ("Will") Anderson was a busy corporate executive. His life was an endless series of high-pressure meetings, deadlines, and the endless pursuit of success. As a result, he never found time for any meaningful relationships.

There came a point in his life when he dreamed of more. Not more wealth or anything like that. No, he was at a place where he was comfortable, at least financially. The dream that kept nagging at him was for a more meaningful life.

Photography had always been Will's favorite hobby. In fact, he had become quite good at it, and his work was winning awards and becoming popular. It reached the point where his hobby occupied more and more of his free time. Photography offered him a welcome relief from the pressures of the corporate world.

The fast pace of urban life and the relentless demands were wearing him down. All at once, it came to a head. Some particular incident or other had brought William to his decision to leave and take a new direction in his life, no matter what.

His departure was not overly dramatic. He informed his employer he was leaving for a better opportunity. To his dismay, his boss warned it might be a mistake. No matter. For several weeks, Will had been laying the groundwork for his new venture in freelance photography. He moved from his expensive apartment in a large city to a cottage in a nearby small town. He made a list of contacts and mailed out an introduction letter, enclosing several business cards. A friend helped him create an attractive website displaying his best photographic work. The work soon followed, which is why this day found him walking home from a meeting with a new customer.

His path took him by the local dog rescue shelter. Each day, the shelter would select a dog to be displayed in the front window of the storefront. This day, they had selected a full-grown Golden Retriever. As Will walked by, glancing at the dog in the window, it stood up and began barking and wagging his tail with excitement, as if greeting an old friend. Will stopped, standing with one hand on his hip, intrigued by the dog's antics. A girl working inside noticed the dog's reaction. Her long auburn hair caught the sunlight as she opened the door. She brushed her hair aside to reveal the name badge that said "Jayden."

"I think he likes you," she said, her smile as warm as a spring day.

"What's his name?"

"His owner was a truck driver who had to give up driving when a disability forced him into a care facility, " she said. "The facility didn't allow dogs, and he had no relatives. He had to sell his truck and give up his traveling companion. So here he is. We started calling him Mack. You know, like the big trucks."

Jayden continued, "I've never seen him this happy. He must see something special in you. Have you had a dog before?"

Will had not even considered having a dog. In fact, there had been no pets in his life since he was a child when his sister had a thing for cats. His previous job kept him away for most of the day and sometimes into the night. His city apartment had a rule about no pets, but his new home had no such restrictions. It was a charming cottage with a fenced backyard, perfect for a dog to run and play when he was away. The hardwood floors provided a practical surface for dog ownership. His new freelance photography business allowed him the freedom to work from home much of the time, anyway. He also recalled noticing a dog park nearby.

"It just might work," he thought.

At Jayden's invitation, he followed her into the store. For all the abundance of animals, the facility still smelled fresh and clean.

Jayden produced a leash from a pocket in her apron and reached into the enclosure to attach it to Mack's collar. The dog bounded to the floor and instantly pressed a paw against Will's leg. As he looked up, Will reached to scratch behind the dog's ears. If a dog could smile, that's how Mack responded. Will glanced at Jayden.

Jayden smiled. "Well, he's made up *his* mind. How about you?"

Will looked around the pet store. At the rear of the shelter was a door to a room stacked with enclosures at different levels, with dogs of every size and description, from a tiny yapping chihuahua to a greyhound, along with an assortment of dogs of undetermined breed. On his left was a wall of shelves displaying a variety of collars, leashes, dog beds, and other pet products. On his right was a sales counter with a cash register.

What caught Will's eye was a large wooden sign on the wall, with engraved lettering spelling out a quotation credited to Anatole France:

"Until one has loved an animal, a part of the soul remains un-awakened."

Will gazed into the eyes of the eager dog and felt as if his soul really had been awakened.

"I hadn't planned on this."

Jayden looked at Mack and then back to Will as she said, "I think it was meant to be."

"What do you think?" he asked Mack. Mack responded with a short yelp and became calm as he sat comfortably at Will's feet, tail still wagging. Mack looked at Jayden as if to say, "Hey, let's get on with it!"

Will shrugged and nodded, and the trio moved to the sales desk to make it official, filled out the adoption papers, and paid the fees. Jayden went over the things Will would need as a new dog owner. She handed him a sample bag of dog food. He purchased a new collar and leash for the walk home.

"Oh, you'll also need this." Jayden opened a drawer on the desk, pulled out a yellow tennis ball, and handed it to Will.

And that was that. Mack was going home.

Mack quickly settled into his new home. He would lie at Will's feet as he edited photos on his computer and made calls to customers. When Will needed to go out for a photography job, Mack played with his tennis ball in the fenced backyard or curled up in the dog bed on the porch.

One Saturday afternoon, Will took Mack to explore the nearby dog park. At the park, the two played catch with the yellow tennis ball through the grassy areas until Will was exhausted. As he sat on a park bench, a girl of about seven years old with golden curls asked if she could pet Mack. Mack responded with a friendly lick that made the girl giggle.

It was their first of many outdoor adventures together.

A photography customer requested photos of a large rural property. Welcoming the opportunity, Will took Mack along.

It was a warm day, and since Will would be working alone, he wore shorts and a T-shirt. He set up his tripod at several places around the property. Mack appeared to enjoy the outing and the new surroundings. He darted in and out of the underbrush as they hiked along a picturesque pathway. Will stopped to rest, leaning against a giant oak tree as Mack continued to move about, playing with his trusty tennis ball.

On one of their trips to the dog park, Will was feeling more sluggish than usual. He found it difficult to keep up with Mack's seemingly boundless energy. When they reached the dog park, Will sought refuge on the park bench. Mack seemed to sense something was wrong and came to sit quietly beside the bench, unaffected by the sight of children and other dogs in the park. Beyond the unexplained fatigue, Will was experiencing muscle and joint pains. At times during the day, he experienced brief chills. Will wrote it off as a simple case of the flu.

But when the symptoms became more serious, Will made an appointment with a local doctor.

After what felt like forever, the day of Will's appointment finally arrived. The doctor's assistant called Will's name and directed him to an examination room. The nurse took Will's temperature and tapped some things into the computer terminal she had rolled into the room.

Sometime later, the door opened, and Dr. Miller introduced himself and asked Will to tell him the reason for the visit.

"It's like I filled out in the forms. I feel constantly drained," Will told the doctor.

"I'm sorry to hear that," Dr. Miller said. "The nurse said you are running a slight temperature. It could be a case of the flu. We'll run some blood tests to see what's going on."

With that, Will left the doctor's office and headed for home.

Later that day, the doctor's office called to say the doctor had prescribed some antibiotics that Will needed to pick up at the pharmacy. She also advised him to drink plenty of water and to get some rest (as if he had much choice at this point)

Will took the medicine, but his condition was not improving.

One evening, as Will lay resting on the couch, Mack came over and started pushing his nose against Will's leg.

Will pushed him away. "Sorry, pal. I'm not in the mood to play ball with you right now."

But Mack persisted, pressing his nose against Will's knee repeatedly.

"What's wrong with you?" Will asked, but Mack persisted, even to the point of gently gnawing at Will's knee. Will was studying Mack's expression when an image appeared in his mind. He saw the scene in the woods he had been photographing a few weeks before. Over and over, the image kept appearing in his mind as Mack made a soft growling sound, almost like talking. The closer Will moved toward Mack, the clearer the images appeared in his mind. Hard as it was to accept, it was like Mack was trying to communicate, perhaps through telepathy.

"What are you trying to tell me, Mack?" Will asked.

Mack responded by again nudging his nose at Will's knee.

Will rolled up his shorts to inspect the area of his leg that had attracted Mack's attention. Then, he noticed a rash, and a mark shaped like a bull's eye.

"Is this what you were trying to tell me about?" he asked Mack.

To his surprise, the dog responded with two barks.

Will immediately scheduled another appointment with his doctor.

At his next appointment, Will waited in the examination room until Dr. Miller arrived. Before the doctor could say anything, William spoke up.

"There's something I need to tell you. It's about my dog, Mack. A few days ago, as I was resting on the couch, he kept poking at my knee. I got this strange image in my mind of a forest where I was doing some photography, and I had taken Mack with me. Anyway, after he kept poking his nose at my knee, I looked to see what was there. That's when I found this rash."

Will rolled up his shorts to expose the inside of his knee joint.

"What do we have here?" the doctor said, adjusting his glasses. "That's a classic bull's eye rash."

"What does it mean?" Will asked.

"If I'm not mistaken, I think we may have a case of Lyme disease. If you've been in the woods recently, that probably explains where it happened." The doctor explained, "Lyme disease is often undetected because it exhibits many different symptoms. For example, your case looked very much like a typical case of the flu."

Dr. Miller continued, "Lyme disease is mostly transmitted through the bite of an infected tick. It comes from a bacterium. We'll need to run different blood tests to confirm it, but your dog may have helped us solve the mystery. I want to see you back here in a week to tell you what we find."

Will thanked the doctor, and once again headed home.

On his return visit, the doctor had news.

"I think we have our answer," Dr. Miller said as he greeted Will. "I have the results from your ELISA and Western blot tests. We confirmed the Lyme disease bacteria. I'm sending a prescription for *doxycycline* to your pharmacy. We should have you *out of the woods,* so to speak, in no time."

"Finally, a solution," Will replied with noticeable relief.

Dr. Miller continued, "The treatment takes about two weeks. Even if you feel better, I want you to complete the treatment. But the rash should disappear in a few days, and I think you will regain your strength in about a week."

"But how did Mack know?" Will asked.

"Dogs have incredible senses. I think you told me you got Mack from the shelter?"

"That's right. They said his previous owner was a truck driver, which is where he got his name."

"It's quite possible Mack had a previous owner who gave him some training." The doctor continued, "Some health-care facilities train dogs to detect diseases. Certain breeds are particularly well suited, including German Shepherds and Golden Retrievers."

"Or Mack may have come by it naturally," Mark replied. "Who's to say?"

"Well, however, it happened, your dog is certainly special. This one seems to have an extra ability. Anyway, you'll want to contact a veterinarian to have him checked for Lyme disease. You'll also need to check him for ticks and try to stay away from places where ticks might be hiding."

"Thanks, I will," he said. "And I promise not to tell anyone my other doctor is my dog!"

***

Chapter Twenty-Four

The Butterfly Effect

In life, there are no *do-overs*. That's just the way things are. Yet, people often wish they could change the past. However, they overlook a vital question: what happens when someone alters history's course?

History, it seems, is fragile.

A case in point: Li Tao[1]. After graduating from the University of Washington with a major in medical technology, Tao applied to several local companies for a job. When he received an offer from MediTech Solutions, a healthcare technology firm just outside of Seattle, he applied for an H-1B work visa. The authorities granted approval, and MediTech Solutions scheduled his job to begin on Monday. That meant he had the entire weekend free.

As he settled into the couch in his small apartment Friday evening, Tao's phone buzzed with a notification on WeChat, the multifunctional "super app" with well over a billion users in China and Asia.

A glance at the screen revealed a message from his family group-chat. As the evening began in Washington State, it was already 5 am the next morning in his hometown in China. His heart raced as he opened the urgent message from his father.

It was bad news.

Tao's father, Li Wei Tao, reported the family was at a local hospital. Mei, Tao's eighteen-year-old sister, had potentially fatal injuries from an acci-

---

1. Chinese names are reversed from non-Asian names in that the last name precedes the given name.

dent on her motorcycle and was hospitalized. The news was devastating to Tao. At that moment, he wished he could have somehow prevented the accident from happening.

Tao couldn't sleep, so he gathered up his laundry. The laundry room was in the basement of the old apartment building. He reasoned it was likely there would be no competition for the machines at that late hour.

As Tao placed the laundry basket on a table, he heard a strange sound. He turned to see a flash of light beneath the doorway at the far end of the room. His curiosity piqued, Tao approached the door and tried the handle. The door, to his surprise, yielded to his touch. He cautiously pushed it open and found himself staring at an odd contraption ten feet wide and stretching from floor to ceiling. There were wires and dials and a complex mechanism of gears and levers.

An older gentleman was adjusting some part of the mechanism when he noticed Tao standing in the doorway.

"How did you get in here?" he snapped.

Tao stammered an apology for intruding, but he couldn't take his eyes off the strange contraption.

"What is that thing?" he asked.

"Uhhh ... nothing. It's just something I've been experimenting with. No need to worry. It won't blow up. It's just gears and wires," the old man answered. "Who are you, anyway?"

"I'm Li Tao. I live upstairs," Tao answered. "I just came down to do my laundry."

"I see," the man replied. "Well, run along and finish your laundry, then.".

"Now that you know who I am, who might you be?" he asked.

"Well, if you must know, I'm Luther Elliot. Actually, they call me Lou. I live on the second floor. After my retirement, I wanted to conduct some experiments. I convinced the landlord that no chemicals or explosives were involved, so he agreed to let me use this part of the basement."

Now Tao was even more curious. "What is the thing with all the gears?" he asked.

"You wouldn't understand." The old man sounded a bit irritated.

"Try me!" Tao retorted.

"You've probably never heard of the Antikythera Mechanism," the old man challenged.

"Wasn't that the contraption they found in an old ship off the Greek coast some time back? I saw a news report on that."

"Well, you've impressed me. I didn't think you would know about that. Nobody could explain how such a complex mechanism would be found on a ship from 200 BCE."

"And you think you know?" Tao asked.

Mr. Elliot stood straight and viewed his unexpected guest over his glasses, deciding whether to share his secret.

After a few moments, he spoke: "They thought it was a device to *tell* time. What if it was part of a device to *alter* time? What else would explain how it got there?"

Tao thought for a moment. "I can't think of any other logical answer, assuming that's logical. Did you replicate that mechanism? Is that what this is? A mechanism to travel through time?"

The old man shrugged. "Maybe it is, and maybe it isn't," he said with a chuckle. "I once put a stray cat inside, and it disappeared. Then that darn cat turned up on my doorstep."

"Then it DOES work." Tao immediately knew how he could save his sister. "Can we try it out? I mean, it's big enough for me to stand inside. What can it hurt? The worst thing that could happen is I could wind up on your doorstep, right?"

Luther had a flash of a dark thought. His secret would remain safe if he could make this kid disappear. He struggled for a time as his mind battled between keeping his secret and the chance to prove his invention.

At long last, he agreed to the experiment.

"Before we consider this idea seriously, I need to share something with you. Do you know about the Butterfly Effect?"

Tao thought for a moment. "I'm not sure..."

"Time travel sounds like a radical idea in science fiction, but it can be dangerous," the old man explained. "Time travel comes at a serious risk. History could be negatively changed through the creation of paradoxes. Even minor changes can lead to significant and unintended outcomes, with the potential for creating a chain reaction of events. That's the Butterfly Effect."

"So, why did you build it?" Tao demanded.

The man seemed indignant. "Because I could," he replied.

"How about a small experiment?" Tao asked. How about we set it to go back just a short time, let's say, a week? What can happen in that short time?"

The old man may have suspected Tao had something in mind, but at long last, he agreed.

He gestured for his new friend to enter the wire cage at the center of the elaborate machine as he adjusted the dials. There was a sound of moving gears.

"Ready?" he asked.

Tao peered out from inside the contraption before he nodded in agreement. "Let's go! What can it hurt in a few days, right?"

The mechanism made another eerie whirring sound, and Tao saw a flash of light as the world around him became a blur. Then... nothing. He was still in the dark basement. The time machine was a failure.

Tao emerged from the contraption and looked around. The old gentleman was gone!

He wandered through the big door to the laundry, surprised to find his basket no longer there. As he reached the top of the stairs, he opened the door to his apartment. At first, he was relieved to see the laundry basket in the bathroom where he usually kept it. He thought about it for a moment as he glanced at his phone. Eleven o'clock, about what he expected. Then he looked more closely at the date: January 3rd. That was last week! He checked the WeChat application. The urgent message from his father was no longer there.

Maybe the strange machine DID work after all!

Right away, Tao hatched a plan. He found some clean clothes and stuffed a suitcase. He fumbled around on his desk to find his passport. If he planned it right, he could book a round-trip flight to China and somehow prevent his sister from riding her motorcycle. He could then return in time to start the new job on Monday. He flipped open his laptop and pressed the power button. As soon as it sprung to life, he entered his PIN and clicked open a browser. He typed in "flights to China" in Search. The Delta Airlines website came up, and he checked for flights leaving from Sea-Tac Airport to WUH International Airport in China. The scheduled departure time for Flight DL4005 from Seattle was 2 am local time. He had plenty of time to get to the airport. The flight would arrive in China the next day. He booked a round-trip flight, returning on the following weekend.

His next call was for a taxi to the airport. Tao made his way through the TSA to the boarding gate. Before boarding his flight, he sent a WeChat text message, telling his family he would arrive at 5 am Sunday morning for a brief visit before starting his new job.

The flight was on time, and Tao boarded and settled into his seat for the twelve-and-a-half-hour flight.

His father, Li Wei Tao, was waiting for him as his son passed down the ramp to the main airport. A taxi took them across the bridge over the Yangtze River to the family home in Ezhou. As his sister came out to greet them, Tao hugged Mei until he was afraid he might hurt her. She was glad and surprised to see him. They talked all day until Tao couldn't stay awake anymore after his long flight.

That night, he tried to think of a way he could prevent his sister from riding her motorcycle on Thursday. A helpful neighbor could skillfully repair anything as trivial as removing the spark plug or deflating a tire. No, he would need to find a way to keep her off that motorcycle, perhaps by getting her to take another form of transportation or not taking the trip at all.

Thursday morning, Li Mei wanted to go into town to the market for some things their mother needed. Tao told her he wanted to go along. So, instead of riding her motorcycle, she waited with Tao at the roadside until the bus came rumbling to a stop. They climbed aboard for the half-hour ride over the Yangtze to the local market.

Tao had only been gone a few years, attending school at the University of Washington, but the market appeared to be bigger and busier than he remembered. The brother and sister went from booth to booth until Mei had everything she came for, and they climbed aboard the bus for home.

Tao's return flight, DL4002, was to arrive back in Seattle on Saturday morning. His mission to prevent his sister from riding her motorcycle on the fateful day had been a success. He had changed history, and the world did not come apart. He was feeling pretty good about that.

But Tao wasn't feeling well. Perhaps the jet lag had taken its toll. He took a nap before it was time to leave to catch his flight. Several hours later, Li Mei shook her brother awake. He needed to be at the airport in time for his flight.

Still feeling tired, Tao processed through the ticket counter and security and boarded the flight for Seattle. He would have plenty of time to rest and recover on the flight home.

As his plane landed, Tao passed through security and found his suitcase. He headed to the front of the airport to find a taxi. Tao had again dozed off by the time his taxi reached his apartment. He was suspicious that he might have come down with a case of influenza from his exposure on the flight home.

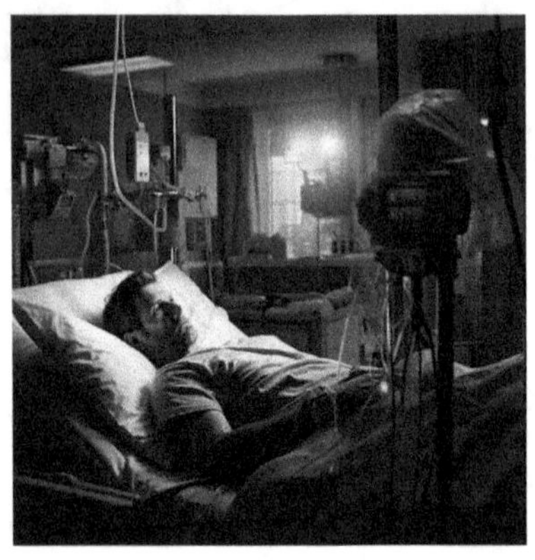

Sunday morning, Tao awoke feeling worse than before, bad enough that he checked himself into the Providence Regional Medical Center - Everett in Snohomish. Tao's temperature was over 100 degrees, so they admitted him.

On Monday morning, the day Tao was supposed to begin his new job, reports started circulating, attributing a death in China to what was known as the Wuhan pneumonia. Chinese media had reported a severe virus outbreak in December. A member of the Providence Hospital medical staff asked Tao if he had visited that part of China in the recent past. He confided he had. After a few tests, the doctors suspected Tao'sTao's illness was likely the result of Severe Acute Respiratory Syndrome Coronavirus 2, later to be named SARS-CoV-2. By Tuesday, the hospital recognized the outbreak of the virus in Snohomish and the surrounding area. On Wednesday, the fifteenth, the national office of the CDC reported Li Tao's case as the first confirmed case of COVID-19 in the United States.

After two weeks, the hospital determined that Li Tao's infection was no longer contagious, and he was allowed to go home. By then, rumors were spreading around the country about the new virus from China. Delta Airlines stopped offered flights from Seattle to Wuhan, China.

A week after he was supposed to start his new job, Tao went to MediTech Solutions' office. A note on the door explained the office had been closed and everyone was working from home because of the new virus pandemic. The pattern would repeat around the city and later the world as the battle against COVID-19 expanded.

The words of the old man in the basement came back to Tao's mind: the Butterfly Effect.

On returning to his apartment, Tao ventured into the basement to see if the old man was still working on his time machine project. As he pressed on the door handle this time, he realized the latch was locked. When he pushed, Tao found the door unlatched, and it opened. Inside, he saw the old man standing in the time machine cage, holding the gear mechanism. Tao's sudden appearance startled him, but with a whirring sound and a flash of light, Dr. Luther Elliot vanished. The remaining parts of the machine collapsed to the basement floor. The time machine was no more.

We already know from the news reports how the story ended.

What if this was how it all began?

***

Chapter Twenty-Five

Saving Mandella

In his living room in Philadelphia, Dr. Sipho Nkosi sat in a comfortable armchair in his living room, engrossed in a letter he just received. It arrived by airmail with South African postage. Inside, he found a newspaper clipping and a handwritten note from his brother-in-law. Thabo Mokoena lived in Cape Town, where their shared childhood had played out against the backdrop of apartheid-era South Africa.

The note read, "I'm sending you this clipping in case you didn't see the news on CNN."

The *Weekly Mail* newspaper headline, dated December 7th, 1988, said: *"Mandela Killed in Daring Highway Ambush."*

Cape Town, South Africa - Tragedy struck the South African nation today as anti-apartheid icon, Nelson Mandela, aged 69, suffered a fatal attack in a daring highway ambush while being transferred from the maximum-security Pollsmoor prison to Victor Verster Medium Security Prison. This incident sent shock waves through the country and raised questions about the safety of high-profile political prisoners.

South African Police (SAP) acknowledged receiving a tip that Mandela's life might be in danger, but they could not gather specific details of the plot in time to prevent the tragedy.

The ambush took place just after 3 pm local time on the N1 highway near the junction with M121.

While no arrests were made, the investigation is ongoing, according to SAP sources. Meanwhile, the Afrikaner Weerstands Beweging or AWB[1] is claiming responsibility for the attack.

Mandela was to be transferred as the government began secret talks with the African National Congress (ANC), hoping to negotiate transition plans before his eventual release. Rather than being held in a conventional cell, Mandela was to live in a private cottage at Victor Verster Medium Prison[2], in contrast to the more harsh conditions at Pollsmoor Prison.

They chose Victor Verster Prison, located 50 miles outside of Cape Town, as the location for Mandela's transfer due to its more accommodating conditions. The move was crucial as Mandela had been recovering from tuberculosis and required more suitable accommodations for his health during the negotiation process.

This shocking and tragic incident casts a long shadow over the ongoing negotiations between the apartheid government and the ANC, and it serves as a painful reminder of the deep-seated divisions within South Africa during this pivotal period in history.

---

1. [The Afrikaner Weerstands Beweging, or AWB, is the Afrikaner opposition movement. In English, the name translates to "Afrikaner Resistance Movement."

2. [Victor Verster Prison is now named the Groot Drakenstein Correctional Facility]

The news deeply affected Nkosi. With his connection to South Africa, he felt a personal loss. The death of Mandela represented a giant setback in the fight against the African National Party, or ANC.

The South African apartheid government restricted residency of black South Africans in certain remote territories designated as "Bantustans" or "homelands". The government forcibly moved millions of people to these rural, resource-poor homelands that were granted "independence" from South Africa but not recognized internationally. This policy was a pillar of the racist and oppressive apartheid system. The National Party was a white supremacist party that advocated for Apartheid, the system of racial segregation in South Africa.

The leading anti-apartheid party representing the black majority population was the African National Party, or ANC. Nelson Mandela was a leader in the movement.

Dr. Sipho Nkosi stood tall. His well-groomed beard and deep ebony complexion gave him a distinguished appearance. He had the appearance of a man who had seen much and learned even more.

Sipho Nkosi was born in South Africa in 1954, during the height of Apartheid. The oppressive policies of racial segregation and discrimination marked his early years. Sipho's academic excellence earned him a scholarship to study abroad, away from the limitations of South Africa's apartheid education system. After completing his physics undergraduate and postgraduate studies in Britain, he moved to the United States to continue his research and teaching. He joined the faculty of Jefferson University, replacing Professor Robert Andrews in that position.

At about that moment, in the physics department building on campus, Damien Mitchell, a 22-year-old sophomore, was completing lab work for a physics class with Dr. Nkosi. His athletic appearance disguised his inner science nerd.

His friend and fellow student, Elaine Reynolds, joined him in the lab. Elaine was a third-year Political Science and International Relations major. The two shared a common interest in world events.

"Hey! What are you up to?" Elaine asked as she looked over Damian's shoulder to see what he was working on. She fussed with her wavy blond hair and pulled it into a ponytail.

"I'm just wrapping up an assignment for Dr. Nkosi's class," he answered. "The experiment involves recreating the Michelson-Morley experiment with light beams. I just finished keying my readings into the Lisa computer."

"That's.... interesting, I guess," she said. "Want to go somewhere for lunch?"

"Sure, but first I have to put some of this stuff back in the basement storage room,. Here, grab this case."

The two of them lugged the instrument cases down the stairway to the basement. Elaine spotted something covered in a large canvas in a back corner as they were about to leave.

"What do you suppose is under there?" she asked.

"I don't know. Judging from the dust, I would say it's been there a while. I hadn't noticed it before," Damian replied.

Elaine's curiosity got the best of her as she went to investigate. She pulled a corner of the cover to see what was hidden beneath. The cover fell to the floor in a cloud of dust, revealing a large mechanism suspended from the ceiling with a bundle of wires stretching down to a black box about the size of a picnic cooler at the base.

"What in the world is that contraption?" she asked.

"Guessing from where it is, I would suspect it could be somebody's experiment. It's got to be something electrical, but there's no cord to plug it in." Damian raised the cover of the heavy box, only to find nothing inside.

"That's strange," he said. "It feels like it's made of lead, but it's empty."

"Look, there's a notebook." Elaine reached for a crumpled notebook stuffed behind the machine. She pulled it out and handed it to Damian.

Flipping through the pages, he found a name. "It says Robert Andrews. I wonder if he was a student here. We'll have to ask Professor Nkosi about it."

Monday afternoon after class, Damian approached Dr. Nkosi and handed him the dusty notebook.

"What's this?" the professor asked.

"I was hoping you might know. I found it in the basement."

Flipping through the notebook, the professor noticed the name. "Andrews!" he said. "This looks like plans for one of Bob's crazy experiments."

"You know him?" Damian asked.

"Not really. I replaced him when the college let him go. This might explain where the department's money went."

"I found it next to a big machine in the basement when I was returning the test equipment for my experiment. My friend Elaine was with me. She tried to look under the tarp that was covering it and it fell off. This notebook was stuffed in behind it."

Dr. Nkosi flipped through the pages. "I can see why he didn't finish it. Judging by the diagram, it would have required an incredible amount of power."

"It had an RS232 computer connector, but I didn't see any power cable," Damian said. "All the power wires went into a big black box, but when I opened it, there was nothing inside."

"Worse than nothing," the professor replied. "Judging from the drawings, he planned on powering it with a negative-matter generator."

The professor flipped through a few more pages of the notebook. He stopped and adjusted his glasses and shook his head. "Bob actually thought he could build a time machine. It says here, he expected to use 'exotic matter' as a power source to create a warp in space time. He postulated the exotic matter would create negative energy density, which we know is pure theoretical nonsense."

"Of course," Damian answered, only half understanding what the professor had just said.

Dr. Nkosi appeared lost in thought before speaking. "The concept seems to be based on *Closed Timeline Curves*. Interesting. I'll look this over a bit more and let you know."

Damian left the notebook with the professor and headed off to his next class.

Later that day, Damian met with Elaine at the library.

"What did you find out about that machine in the basement?" Elaine asked.

"The prof thinks it might be a time machine," Damien replied. "It turns out Robert Andrews used to be head of the physics department before Dr. Nkosi replaced him. Rumor has it that Andrews was relieved of his position for using physics department funds for unorthodox experiments."

"No wonder he gave up on it."

"Yeah, no way anything like that would work. Besides, professor Sipho said it would need an incredible amount of power," Damian said.

A few days later, Professor Nkosi called Damian into his office after class.

"Would you like to work on a special experiment?" the professor asked.

"Sure," Damian said. "What do you have in mind?"

"I've been reading through Bob's notes, and I think I have an idea how we can solve his power problem." The professor then outlined the experiment to Damian involving lasers and the common radioactive element, thorium[3]."

"It just might be the missing piece to the puzzle."

It turned out the college still had a sample of the element left over from an earlier project. For the next two days, Damian worked with the professor evenings after the last classes had left the building. They set up an experiment testing the quantum properties of thorium compounds under an intense laser beam.

At last, they had an answer. Under laser bombardment, at just the right oscillation frequency, the Thorium sample would charge up a high voltage direct current, just like a solid state battery. Now the challenge was to connect it to the machine in the basement. Using Professor Andrew's

---

3. Because the experiment involved working with radioactive material, Damian, and the professor, would need to pass a course on safety and handling of elements like Thorium. In 1988, the internet was still in its early stages and while it was not yet widely used by the public; it was available to colleges and universities. And even in those early days of the Internet, the Office of Environmental Health and Safety offered an online training module called "*Radiation Safety Training for Users of Uranium and Thorium.*"

notes, they calculated the power requirements of the machine's various parts and measured to confirm the load properties.

"It just might work," the professor concluded.

"A time machine? Really?"

"Yes, but a device like this could be very dangerous. There's always the risk of creating a paradox. But it also has great potential for good."

"You really want to turn it on, don't you?" Damian asked.

"I do have something in mind, yes. Something really important," he said. "I just learned that someone assassinated Dr. Mandela. I want to see if we can use this machine to rewrite that part of history."

"Can you do that?" Damian asked?

"We'll see," he said. "I grew up there. Besides, I have an advantage. My brother-in-law in Cape Town sent me a newspaper clipping. That clipping tells me when it happened, how it happened, and where. I just need a plan to stop it."

"You can't stop a murder by yourself."

"I won't need to. Thabo, my sister's husband, is a part of the African National Congress. I'm sure he could help me find the right resources."

"I want to help. I think I know somebody else who might be good to have along."

The professor was adamant. "I appreciate your willingness, but traveling back in time, especially to a dangerous place like South Africa, is no small matter. There are tremendous responsibilities and risks. They put people in jail just for being in the wrong place without the right papers."

"If we can fix history, I want to be part of it. I'm pretty sure we can get Elaine Reynolds to go along. She has her own special skills that could come in handy."

"You want to do what!?" Elaine responded.

"You're majoring in Political Science and International Relations. This could be a unique opportunity to make a positive impact on the world. This is as political and international as it gets," Damian countered.

With minimal hesitation, she declared, "I'm in."

Damian felt shocked. "What? Just like that? Are you aware of the challenges, the risks, the dangers?"

"That's precisely why," she replied.

Damian noticed the unwavering determination in Elaine's eyes. He admired her commitment, knowing that once she set her mind to something, there would be no changing it.

Later, the three of them met in the professor's office. He showed them the newspaper clipping, describing what had happened.

"We need a plan," Elaine said. "We have an enormous advantage because we can predict the future. We know what they plan to do, where and when they plan to do it. We just need to figure out how we can save Mandela."

"It says they had guns," Damian said. "That's about as risky as it gets."

"These are dangerous times in South Africa, even worse than when I left, but we won't need to work alone," the professor answered. "My sister's husband has a position in the ANC. When we tell them what could happen, I'm sure they will come up with the resources we need. We just can't give them any hint of how we know it."

Professor Nkosi added, "There's another complication. People in South Africa can't travel freely. They have to carry a *dompas* or passbook. The government calls them reference books or *kaffers*. The travel document includes a person's name and identification number, residence address, a picture, and the locations where that person may go."

"Well, we can just make up fake ones," Damian injected.

"That would be hard to do," the professor interrupted. "Not only that, but passbook forgery is a criminal offense. The consequences can include imprisonment and physical violence. We'll need to carry our passports and identification in case the police patrols stop us."

"I have mine," Elaine responded. "Besides, I'm sure they're more concerned about the movement of South African citizens than foreigners."

Dr. Nkosi cautioned, "It's more than a matter of black and white. There are a variety of power groups." Turning to Elaine, he asked, "Let's see how much they've taught you. Tell me what you know about South Africa."

"I've learned about the political structure," Elaine said. "The National Party has been in control since 1948. They established apartheid, enforced with over a hundred laws. The strongest opposition is the African National Congress, representing the black majority."

"I can see you've done your homework," the professor responded. "But that's not the complete picture. There are several more political groups. Our biggest problem, though, is the Afrikaner Weerstands Beweging, or

AWB. They completely oppose reforms. They want to continue maintaining apartheid and white minority rule."

"Support for apartheid has recently been weakening," Elaine added, "but that means they will be even more determined."

Turning to Damian, Dr. Nkosi asked, "The next question is, how do we make it work?"

Damian replied, "The notebook had a computer program typed out that looked like they wrote it in Apple BASIC. I've been playing with BASIC on my Apple IIc since high school. The college's computer department just got an Apple Macintosh. If they let us borrow it, I can key in the code and save it on a floppy drive. That way, we can tell the machine where we need to go in the four dimensions of longitude, latitude, elevation, and time."

"Do we even know the program worked, since the power supply was not finished?" Elaine asked. "I mean, we don't want to be turned into little sparkles like the transporter on Star Trek."

"We'll have to make a trial run to make sure it's safe," Damian replied. "We'll tell the computer to send something into the recent past. Then we just go see if it shows up there."

"There's just one complication," the professor cautioned. "I've determined the thorium power box can only hold enough charge to run 75 hours. We need to be ready for our return trip before the time runs out, with a margin for safety, say 72 hours total. If we're not where we need to be, we'll be stuck in a paradox, meaning we will find ourselves in two places at the same time."

"Is that possible?" Elaine asked.

"I assure you, we don't want to find out!" the professor replied.

"We'll need a target location. Where do we go?" Damian asked.

"We can begin from my sister's house. It's not too far from where the attack will take place. We can work out the details of a plan with my brother-in-law. As I said, he has a lot of connections and resources in the ANC."

Elaine's face was stern. "Can we risk going there without a plan?"

"Saving Mandela is our mission," the professor reminded them. "We do that, and we come back. That's the plan. With the time we have, we can get there a day ahead and work it out from there," the professor answered. "If we can't come up with a workable plan, we wait for the machine to bring us back and maybe try again. We just need to make sure we don't create any ripples in time along the way."

He continued, "They attacked and killed Mandela at 15:00 in Cape Town. Accounting for Daylight Saving Time, our time is seven hours different, so that means it was 9:00 am here in Pennsylvania. Subtracting 72 hours from that brings us to 8 am, December 4th, 1988, as our starting point. That should give us the time we need to complete our task and get back. Damian, make absolutely sure you get that right. We don't need any unfortunate surprises. I'll review your math, just to be sure."

"We're not too far from Northeast Philadelphia Airport," Damian said. "I'll pick up a pilot navigation chart for South Africa so we'll have the latitude, longitude, and elevation we'll need to program the computer for an open space near your sister's home."

The next afternoon, Damian and Elaine hung the tarp from the ceiling and moved some of the shelving in the basement to hide their project from view. They placed the Apple computer on a folding table and Damian went to work typing in the program from Dr. Andrew's notebook.

The professor brought the heavy, lead-shielded box with the updated power unit from the physics lab and hooked it up.

Damian put a small cage with a mouse inside, borrowed from the biology lab, inside the machine's time generator unit, and set it for the courtyard of his dorm, but an hour in the past. He sent Elaine up to the courtyard to wait. A few moments after he pressed the button on the computer screen, the cage with the mouse faded from sight. Moments later, Elaine returned with the mouse scampering around in the cage. They took it to show the professor.

"This is our test," Damian said as he and Elaine entered and plopped a mouse cage on the professor's desk.

The professor looked at the mouse. The professor picked it up and examined it for a moment.

"So, it looks like the computer program works," he said. "I guess we're ready for our trip back in time to save Nelson Mandela!"

Computer settings:
Departure: 11 am, December 4th, 1988, local time, Philadel-
phia.
Return: 6 pm, December 7th, 1988.
Total run time: 72 hours.
Location: Latitude -33.995381, Longitude 18.584906.
Elevation: 52 meters (171 ft.) above sea level.

They hung a sign reading, *"Do Not Touch Under Any Circumstances For Any Reason!"* over the computer.

The scene glowed with the flicker of the computer monitor. Professor Nkosi and Elaine stood huddled under the big mechanism suspended from above. Damian had programmed a delay into the start function of the time travel software. Transporting three people would stretch the power limits of the machine. He pressed the "run" command and joined the others. After ten seconds, the machine hummed under the strain, and a moment later, the trio vanished.

They materialized in South Africa at 5 pm on Sunday, December 4th, in Nyanga township. The newspaper clipping tucked inside one pocket for reference, the professor pulled out a section of a Cape Town city map from the other pocket. He looked around for his bearings before he determined the correct route to his sister's home, just a block away. Walls two meters high surrounded most homes, with many having an iron gate.

When they reached the address, the professor knocked on the door. They heard footsteps inside before Thabo, his sister's husband, greeted them with a surprised voice as he opened the door.

"What in the world? You didn't tell me you were coming! And who are your friends?" Thabo asked. He leaned to look behind the group and turned to ask, "No luggage?"

"I can explain," the professor said, turning to look behind him, "but first we need to come in."

Thabo Mokoena, the professor's brother-in-law, had cropped hair peppered with hints of gray. His eyes revealed signs of a man who has seen a life of both hardship and triumph.

Thabo swung the door open wider and stood to the side as the trio entered his modest home.

"I can't give you too many details, but we need your help."

The professor's sister, Ayanda, brushed past her husband to greet her brother with a hug. "How did you get here?" she asked.

"That's not important," Sipho Nkosi replied. Turning to her husband, he said, "You might say we're on a mission of life and death."

Ayanda directed the guests to the living room of the house. She apologized for the lack of seating as she carried in chairs from the kitchen table. Two small children peered around the corner from a hallway.

As soon as everyone was seated, the professor began, "We cannot disclose how we obtained this information or its source, but it is absolutely accurate. We need to prevent harm from coming to Rolihlahla Mandela[4]. We know the date and time of an attack on his life, and we know the location. We need to protect Mandela from harm, but we can't do it alone."

Thabo took in the gravity of the information. He didn't understand it all, but he trusted the professor's sincerity.

"I know some people who can help," Thabo responded. He went to a phone on a small desk in the hallway, shooing the children off to their rooms as he called a list of numbers which he produced from somewhere unseen.

After a few minutes, he rejoined the group. "I called Dumisani Khumalo and Muzi Mabaso. I don't know if you knew them before you left for America. They're with our local ANC organization. They should be here soon, and they'll be most interested in what you have to say."

---

4. [Nelson Mandela's actual birth name was "Rolihlahla Mandela." In the Xhosa language, "Rolihlahla" means "pulling the branch of a tree" or metaphorically, "troublemaker." He was given the forename "Nelson" by a
teacher at a Methodist school when he was a child, and this name is the one by which he is most commonly known.]

About twenty minutes passed before they heard a knock. Thabo looked through the peephole before unlocking the chains and opening the door. Two middle-aged gentlemen entered. They were uneasy and paused at first when they saw Elaine, but they then smiled and shook hands with all three of the American guests.

Thabo introduced his brother-in-law and explained that the three had arrived at his door on a secret mission.

The professor stood and addressed the group.

"Mandela is being transported to the Victor Verster Medium Security Prison this week. Our sources tell us there will be an attack on his life by the AWB, along the route. We know the time and the location. We will need people and we will need weapons to prevent any harm from coming to Rolihlahla."

Professor Nkosi then produced a map from his pocket and placed in on a coffee table. A red circle marked a location along the N1 highway near the intersection with M121.

"They will transport Rolihlahla Mandela on a prison bus. Our information is there will be an attack with automatic weapons that will block the bus and kill everyone on board."

"Then we will need weapons," said Dumisani.

"I know who can help with that," Thabo replied. "How do we get our people there?"

Muzi had an answer. "What about a bus? We could use a bus to move our people and weapons."

The rest of the plans could be completed later. For now, it was time to get some rest. Thabo and his wife laid blankets on the floor for her brother and Damian, and set up the living room couch for Elaine to sleep.

They spent much of that Monday putting the plan together. Thabo rounded up the most dedicated members of the ANC he could find for the mission without explaining the details. That way, they could maintain total secrecy.

Thabo, Dumisani, and Muzi scouted the location of the expected attack, noting access and exit routes along with potential trouble areas.

"There's road construction at that part of the National Highway," Muzi explained to the professor on their return. "Here's how it can work. We will have some of our people replace the construction workers. I know where we can get hard hats and safety vests."

"They might have someone trailing the prison bus as a lookout. What can we do about that?" asked Dumisani.

"What if we have someone right behind the bus to block the road as it comes into the construction zone?" suggested Thabo.

"That should work," Muzi responded. "The construction zone is being limited to one lane at a time, so that will help us contain the traffic."

"We will be going through some restricted zones, so we need to make sure everyone has their passbooks in case a police patrol stops us," Thabo added.

By morning, the route was planned, a dozen people volunteered, weapons were gathered, and the plans were ready. A nondescript bus was "acquired", along with several Fabrique National rifles. The French made automatic weapons were concealed by tarpaulins under the rear bus seats.

Just after 2 pm Wednesday afternoon, Thabo, Muzi, Dumisani, and all the volunteers, dressed as construction workers, climbed aboard the bus. The darkened windows prevented easy detection from outside.

In South Africa in the late 1980s, the N1 "National" highway was a simple four-lane route, not like the Interstate system in the United States.

Sometime later, the bus had worked its way through the traffic and stopped at the side of the road, just past the construction zone at the exact location where the attack would take place. Elaine emerged from the bus playing the part of a "damsel in distress," drawing the attention of the construction workers. As the distracted workers approached the bus, gun barrels appeared from the windows. The workers were told to go on break while Muzi's men took their places.

Dumisani Kumalo and another ANC volunteer, wearing construction vests and safety helmets, approached the flagmen manning the barricades at the start of the construction zone and took possession of their radios.

By 2:55, Muzi's people were in control of the traffic flow and two dump trucks.

And they waited.

The prison bus approached the construction zone and Muzi's man, with a caution flag, waved the driver through, only to be blocked by a truck a short distance further. As planned, the car behind the bus came to a stop, blocking other vehicles from following the bus into the construction zone. The driver signaled to the others that he could see Mandela through the window of the prison bus.

The bus with Mandela and the prison guards aboard was both contained and protected.

At the predicted time, two pickup trucks, or "bakkies" came into view from the other direction, twenty meters beyond the construction zone, as the two dump trucks moved into position, blocking their path.

Muzi's men appeared from behind the trucks, displaying automatic weapons. Muzi gave strict orders not to panic. The ANC was a non-violent movement.

The would-be attackers were both surprised and outnumbered.

After a tense but brief confrontation, the assailants dropped their weapons. Two of Thabo's people gathered up the weapons while two more moved the *bakkies* off the roadway, but they kept the keys. They left the white AWB attackers tied up in the bed of one of the small trucks.

Meanwhile, someone moved the equipment blocking the roadway and waved the prison bus through to complete its journey to the low-security prison near Paarl.

After the prison bus was out of view, the defenders climbed back aboard their bus for the return trip and soon melded into the flow of traffic. The construction workers emerged from their hiding places and returned to their work as if nothing had happened.

As their bus headed back, the professor kept looking at his watch. They had completed the mission in less than twenty minutes' time. It would be close.

He had reason to be concerned.

A celebration erupted at Thabo Mokoena's home when the bus returned. In the excitement, the crowd all but ignored the Americans.

Dr. Nkosi urged Elaine and Damian to hurry to the spot where they needed to be for the return through time.

They waited at the departure point as the time ticked away, with only minutes to spare, when a police van approached.

The officers were not expecting to see a white woman in the company of two black men in this township.

"We need to see your reference books, your travel IDs," one officer demanded.

Damian and Dr. Nkosi produced their passports and handed them to the first officer. The other officer confronted Elaine with suspicion as she retrieved her passport from a belt pouch.

The professor explained, "We're American tourists. We've been here visiting friends."

The officers reviewed each of the documents. After a time, they seemed satisfied. Soon, the police van drove away and, once again, the trio stood alone.

Just in time. With a flash of light, the world turned dark. They were back in the basement of the physics building.

The professor retrieved the newspaper clipping, still in his pocket. To his amazement, the headline now read: *"Gorbachev Announces Drastic Cuts in Soviet Military."* The news story about the attack in South Africa was gone. They had accomplished their mission and changed history. They had saved Mandela.

Damian hugged Elaine, and the professor hugged both of them.

The professor appeared reflective as he said, "If we could use the machine to change history for the good, someone else with different motives could us it to go back in history and kill George Washington or Albert Einstein. The danger is too great. We must prevent that."

Elaine and Damian agreed. Dr. Nkosi then said he was going to dismantle the power unit and directed Damian to use a powerful magnet to erase the program data on the floppy disk before returning the Apple Mac to the computer department. And so, the time machine was to be left as Elaine had found it, covered by a tarp in the basement.

***

Research note[5].

Epilogue:

Nelson Mandela was released on February 11th, 1990, after spending 27 years in prison. On his release, Mandela continued to work toward ending apartheid and promoting democracy in South Africa. Mandela's release from prison marked a turning point in South African history and paved the way for a more democratic and equal society.

In 1993, the Nobel Peace Prize committee jointly awarded Nelson Mandela and Frederik Willem de Klerk the Nobel Peace Prize for their work in peacefully ending the apartheid regime and laying the foundations for a new democratic South Africa.

During his presidency, Mandela worked to promote reconciliation between black and white South Africans and to address the country's social and economic problems.

After leaving office in 1999, Mandela continued to work on behalf of various causes, including HIV/AIDS awareness and education.

Nelson Mandela died of a respiratory infection on December 5th, 2013, in Johannesburg at 95. After his death, several Memorial services took place, including one organized by the South African government on December 10th, 2013. On December 15th, he was laid to rest at Qunu, in South Africa's Eastern Cape province.

---

5. *My thanks to Peiter Smuts for his personal insight and perspective on South Africa.*

Notation:

Named by paranormal researcher Fiona Broome, *the Mandela Effect* is defined as an instance when you remember something that doesn't match historical records. The phrase was coined after Nelson Mandela's death in 2013. Countless people swore he had died while being held prisoner in the 1980s and they clearly remember news coverage of the funeral.

Maybe those were just false memories. Or maybe a college professor, two students and a time machine changed that part of history.

***

Please review!

If you enjoyed these stories, please take a few moments to write a nice review where you purchased it and recommend it to your friends and social media followers!

You can also find a review form on my website at:
TimTrottWrites.com

About the Author

Tim Trott grew up in the tiny community of Clarcona, Florida, a single four-way stop intersection between Winter Garden and Apopka, just outside of Orlando. Tim began writing seriously after retirement from a blend of several careers, ranging from broadcasting to security systems and sound system contracting to website development and hosting to teaching for the FAA drone test. He grew up reading the Hardy Boys series, along with authors like Robert Heinlein or Isaac Asimov, and exploring the works of Aldous Huxley and Bertrand Russell.

Tim studied broadcasting and media at St. Petersburg College in the late 60s while working in local television and radio. After that, he began writing radio newscasts and commercials. Fast-forward past his time in broadcasting, security contracting, teaching drone courses, video production, web design and hosting, he published several non-fiction titles before being joining a local writer's group in Daytona, Florida. A member of that group, Veronica H. Hart (*Silent Autumn, The Knife, The Prince of Keegan Bay,* and many more), encouraged him to explore fiction writing. The future promises more science fiction short stories, perhaps even a novel, as well as non-fiction work.

Tim Trott invites you to visit his website at TimTrottWrites.com.

Please consider these other books by the author:

Science Fiction/Paranormal:

The Psychic Barista (The Brown Bean Coffee Shoppe)
  Short Stories
  More Short Stories

Biography:

Out of the Blue: The Life and Legend of Kirby "Sky King" Grant,
  First Through the Fire (the story of Talbert Gray)

Education:

Understanding WordPress 6.x for Beginners
  FAA UAG 107 Remote Pilot Study Guide
  Drone Operations

Online Security:

Guarding Against Online Identity Theft
  Proteccion de Identidad

Misc/LCB:

LOTTO TRAKR